Embrace of the Butcher

Embrace of the Butcher

ANTHONY BURTON

DODD, MEAD & COMPANY New York

Printed in the United States of America

1   2   3   4   5   6   7   8   9   10

Library of Congress Cataloging in Publication Data

Burton, Anthony.
    Embrace of the butcher.

    I. Title.
PR6052.U69E4 1982   823'.914   82-5068
ISBN 0-396-08059-6   AACR2

For Leonora

Among other evils being unarmed
brings you, it causes you to be despised.

——Niccolò Machiavelli
The Prince

Embrace of the Butcher

ONE

King came home as dawn was touching the dark clouds over Slieve Gullion. He rested his bicycle against the front wall of the cottage and looked back down the road. The cat that had started visiting him two weeks earlier was sitting on the grass verge watching him. A waking curlew called and across the field in front of the cottage he could see the angular outlines of a dozen bunched Holsteins; but no humans were about. Crossmaglen, where he bought his supplies, was three miles away.

He unlocked the front door and, grimacing at the smell of dampness, walked into the hallway. King never switched on the lights after a night in the hills and so he missed the brown envelope lying on the stone floor of the tiny hallway.

His hand on the automatic in his raincoat pocket, he moved swiftly through the cottage, checking the locks and catches he had fitted on the windows and back door. They were secure, as they always were. He went to the front downstairs room, which he used for sleeping. He was very tired, too tired to eat. He thought of making a pot of tea, for the whisky he had drunk from his flask during the night had left an evil taste in his mouth. He decided against it. All he wanted was sleep.

He sat slumped on the bed, his hands between his knees, staring dully at the pattern on the worn carpet. He was wasting his time. Not a smell of them. Nothing. For all the good he was doing he might as well be in Belfast. And yet London insisted he stay. He was a forward observer, London said. Well, he had observed nothing and now he was at the point of giving up hope that he ever would. If stuff was coming across the border, it wasn't here.

He straightened and, in the dim light filtering through the windows, looked at the photograph standing on the table at the side of the bed. Below her fringe of black hair, his wife gazed steadily back. She would be getting up now in the house in Blackheath. The two children were grinning self-consciously, obviously restless in the restraint of her arms. She said the boy was getting out of hand, needed the discipline of a father. There was no note of accusation in her letters. She was the daughter of a soldier and she knew how it was. Still, the problem remained. The boy should go away to school, but there was no money for that. Again King thought of asking his father for funds, but he knew that he feared the answer. He didn't fear rejection. He feared the old man would have to say that he didn't have it, that except for the house and his pension he had nothing. It was not a century that appreciated loyalty and service.

King took off his raincoat and tossed it on a chair. The rain, which had swept across the hills after midnight, had penetrated the fur lining. It had been an uncomfortable night. Even so, better than the Ardoyne, he had written her, and that was true enough. He wanted no more of the cities of death in the north. Except for the frustration and loneliness, this was a vacation. He picked up the Bible that lay alongside the photograph. King was not a religious man, but he had discovered that he enjoyed the dignified vigor of the King James version. He was reading Joshua and now his eyes fell on one passage.

And she said unto him, Get you to the mountains, lest the pursuers meet you; and hide yourself there three days, until the pursuers be returned; and afterward may ye go your own way.

Still wearing his sweater and trousers, he stretched out on the hard bed. No pursuers here. They left him alone as if he were a leper. In the town stores, in Crossmaglen, he was served, but no unnecessary words were exchanged. Not even a "good day." On the streets, people averted their eyes when he came near. He didn't doubt they knew who he was and where he came from. Probably had his rank and serial number. And the soldiers, the soldiers on patrol looked at him as they looked at all civilians in Crossmaglen, as if he were a bomb waiting to go off. It was ironic, he thought. His enemies knew who he was. His allies didn't.

He wondered how much longer he would have to camp in this damp and benighted corner of London's disputed domain. They had said a few days and he had been here nearly three weeks. In the crawl space above him, he could hear the mice running. Sounds as if they're holding the Olympics up there, he thought drowsily, complete with pole vault. But his last thoughts before he slept were of his wife and the children.

He saw the envelope when he awoke at noon and went to boil water for shaving and for the pot. It was cheap and grimy, bearing no name or address. It was sealed. It must have been hand-delivered, pushed under the front door while he had been out or while he slept.

He carried it into the kitchen. He was humming "The Men Behind the Wire." The rain was coming down again, the windows streaming with water so that he could hardly see across the field to the stone wall that marked the boundary of the cottage property. Sometimes he felt as if he were in a submarine resting on the ocean floor. The whole landscape was drowning.

He sat at the table, still littered with dirty dishes from the day before, and he took out the single sheet of lined paper such as might have been torn from a child's composition book. It was folded twice. He smoothed it out on the table and read the penciled words.

Go back where you came from.

He left it on the table, poured boiling water into the old brown teapot to warm it, swilled it out, and tossed in two spoons of tea.

Go back where you came from. Well, nothing subtle or complicated about that. He poured tea into a cup, added milk and sugar. The scrap of paper was the first overt gesture of hostility. He had noticed no increased tension, no indication that his presence in the district had grown more insupportable. He began to cook eggs and sausages.

The check call came as he was filling the sink with his food-stained dishes. He walked into the bedroom, waited until the telephone had rung the sixth time, lifted the receiver, and replaced it.

He could tell Loughton about the anonymous message, but it was unlikely that London would be impressed by a few words on a bit of paper. That's all it was and yet he felt a stir of uneasiness. For the first time he felt as if he were being watched.

By the time he had cleaned up the kitchen the rain had slowed to a drizzle and he opened the back door. The black cat was waiting. It was a wild creature that would only come to him when it was hungry. He brought it some milk and some pieces of meat he had saved the night before.

"Here you are, Blackie, you little scoundrel," he said. "You look as if you had a rough night."

The animal's fur was sodden and there was a dab of congealed blood matting the hair on its tail. Since he had started feeding the cat it had put on some flesh, but still the flattened fur showed the press of its ribs. He stood in the doorway and watched it eat the meat before turning to the milk. When it had finished, it made a brief pass against his legs, purring softly, then stalked off around the corner of the cottage.

"You're learning some manners, Blackie," he murmured. He had no wish to make a pet of the animal; he might have to leave any day. The cat needed its wildness, needed to retain its hunting skills to survive. Like me, he thought.

Four days later, there was another message. It was waiting for him on the hallway floor when he came back from another night in the hills. He wondered if they watched him pedal off before pushing the envelopes under the door. This time it was shorter.

Get out.

He put it with the other letter. He would report it to Loughton when they met that afternoon in Bessbrook.

One message could be ignored. Two was another matter, a campaign.

Loughton was the sort of man who looked natural only behind khaki and shiny buttons and a regimental badge. Now, out of uniform, he seemed uncomfortable and irritable, as if he had been forced to wear a costume for some vulgar masquerade.

Loughton didn't approve of King's high-wire act in Crossmaglen. Loughton had certain beliefs about the way things should be done. In particular, he disliked his compulsory supporting role. He was a messenger boy and he knew it. They talked as they sat in Loughton's old Rover in a car park in Bessbrook.

"They're sending in the John Waynes soon," Loughton said. "Then they'll pull you out." He didn't approve of the Special Air Service, either. The SAS was elitest, arrogant, mysterious. It was much hated by the Provos, for it played their own game on their own ground with equal ferociousness. As far as Loughton was concerned, it consisted of a bunch of thugs with an overly dramatic idea of themselves, as evidenced by the SAS motto: "Who Dares Wins."

"When?" King asked.

"No exact date set yet, old boy. But not long."

King suspected Loughton knew no more than he did. Loughton was just the contact man, sent to make sure he was following orders.

"Did you tell them I'm not getting anywhere?"

"I did. They said, keep on trying. They're convinced the bastards are bringing the explosives over in your area. Don't ask me why they're so sure, because I don't know."

King handed him the two scribbled messages. Loughton read them and puffed his cheeks, staring through the wind screen at a scrawny terrier rooting in a pile of rubbish. "When?" he said.

"The first one four days ago," King said. "The second, today."

Loughton looked at them again, then stuffed them in his pocket.

"I probably shouldn't tell you this," he said. "But we picked up some rumblings about you in the Ardoyne. Nothing definite, but it seems your name came up at a Provo meeting six days ago. If I were you I'd be careful."

King pulled out another envelope and gave it to Loughton.

"Send this off for me, will you?" he said. "It's to my family."

He left Loughton sitting in the car and went to retrieve his bicycle from the wire fence surrounding the car park. He looked back once and saw Loughton's white face peering at him through the driver's side window. It was raining again.

O'Hara came in through London. It gave him cold amusement that he was setting out on the job from London. Like a dangerous virus moving down the bloodstream from the heart to lodge in an extremity, he thought. And send tremors to the brain.

He was at London Airport only two hours. After passing through customs, he drank a cup of coffee in the cafeteria, then made his way to the Dublin flight. He carried only an overnight bag. The tools of his trade would be awaiting him at Dublin Airport.

As the Trident came down over the Irish coastline and banked for the approach to Dublin, he felt a sourness in the roots of his tongue, a distracting pressure in his temples. He was already short of sleep and there was no immediate prospect of any. And when he reached home he would have to go straight on duty. Unless he stayed the extra day . . .

His blood quickened and he knew he would do it. He could call Lenane in New York. Lenane would cover for him. His mind was filled with her now, with her abundant flesh and tumbling hair and the wildness in her eyes, and all thought of physical discomfort had fled. He had known all along he would go to her. The pondering was only a charade. He would see her. The job first and then . . .

At the airport, he found the locker. They had sent the key by mail. The brown grip was inside. He pulled it out and without opening it he carried it away. The weight told him all he needed to know. Connors was waiting for him in a car parked some distance from the airport building entrance. There had been bombings in the city and the airport could be approached only on foot for fear that a parked car might hold primed explosives. They drove toward the city.

"How are things over there?" Connors asked.

"Better than here," he said, looking at the rain-soaked landscape, feeling the chill already sinking into his flesh. Did it never get warm in Ireland?

"Is it true the pubs stay open all day and all night?"

"You can always get a drink." Connors irritated him, pretending to be a country bumpkin. Connors had spent five years on oceangoing freighters. He had been everywhere.

"Where's the job?" he said. He already knew but he asked anyway.

"Just over the border. Armagh. You'll be over and back in a flash."

O'Hara pulled the zip on the bag. The AK-47 was clean and oiled. The ammunition was in a brown paper bag. Two magazines. Generous, he thought sourly. They always provided him with the same type of weapon. Probably he had used this on earlier jobs. Probably it had always been the same one. He started to look for the number, keeping the gun in the grip, then shrugged. What the hell did it matter?

"Okay?" Connors said, looking at him sideways.

"Okay."

"And you get the nine o'clock flight out. Tonight."

"For Chrissake," O'Hara exploded. "When am I supposed to sleep?"

"Arranging your sleeping isn't my job. Meeting you, giving you the car, that's my job. Nothing else."

"I want to talk to Donovan."

"Donovan's up north."

"Tell him something from me. Tell him I'm not his hired hit man. Tell him this is the last time unless I talk to him."

"I will." Connors's voice was as equable as when they had first met. "I'll tell him gladly."

O'Hara stared ahead. The hell with Donovan and his orders. He would see her and be with her and feel her and she would smile at him with those eyes that knew everything about men and their needs. He would leave when he chose to leave.

"Where are you getting out?" he asked Connors.

"In the city. Then you can take the car on. It's a hired job. You'll find the papers in the locker. Just sign where it's marked. D'you have your driving license?" He had everything he needed, the green passport that shielded him, money, a credit card. And he had the gun.

"Who's the subject?"

"Fellow name of King. You know Crossmaglen? Of course you do. Well, they'll be waiting for you. That madman, McCarthy, is running things. Find him and he'll make the arrangements. You'll be back here before you know it. Straight to the airport and off you go."

"The car?"

"Leave it at the airport. Same spot where I picked you up."

They would know from that, O'Hara thought. When the car wasn't there in time for him to catch the nine o'clock flight, they would know. The hell with them.

"Just follow the instructions," Connors said, as if reading his rebellious thoughts, "and you'll have no problems. Look out for the SAS men, though. Those bastards'll lift you if you're the Duke of Edinburgh."

Connors drew in to the curb on Eccles Street in the northern part of the city. "You're on your own now," he said. "I'm off." Leaving the engine running, he slid out of the car and O'Hara moved across to take the wheel. It was a black Ford, dirty and battered with use, but the engine sounded strong. He sat there for a moment, watching Connors scuttle off down the street and around a corner.

He looked at his watch. She would be in now, with any luck. Half a mile further on, he stopped by a street telephone booth. He put his hand in his pocket and he swore. He hadn't changed his money at the airport. He rammed in the gear and drove toward the center of the city, looking for a bank.

When he came out of the foreign exchange on O'Connell Street, he thought he saw Connors watching him from across the street, but then a bus blocked his view and when it had gone there was no sign of the man. Imagination, he thought, and he strode toward a telephone booth. She answered on the first ring, as if she had been waiting for his call.

"It's John," he said.

"John who?"

"For God's sake, Mary, it's John O'Hara. How many Johns do you know?"

"Enough to be going on with." She was laughing now.

"Didn't you get my card?"

"I did."

"When can I see you?"

"Oh, the impatience of the man. All hustle and bustle and let's not waste time." She was laughing again, the warm, remembered laughter that brought a thickness to his throat.

"I've got something for you," he said.

"I'm sure you have."

"Tonight."

"I'll be working."

"Take the damn night off. It'll be worth it."

"Oh, will it?" Again the soft laughter that challenged and invited.

"I'll see you in that bar downstairs at the Gresham. Seven o'clock tonight. I'll buy you dinner. Be there, Mary."

"Well, I suppose I could take one night off."

"Seven o'clock."

"Perhaps." She would be there. She was drawn to him, as he was to her. He knew it. His mind was turbulent with her voice, the generosity of her body and spirit. She would be there. He moved back toward the car. First, though, the job. First, the duty and then the delight. In the glove compartment he found a map and the car-rental papers. He signed where there were penciled crosses. Then he opened the map and looked for the road north to Crossmaglen.

As he approached the cottage, King found himself automatically searching for the cat. The animal had become part of his day, welcoming him home with its negligent haughtiness, eating what he provided, vanishing on its own pursuits.

It wasn't on the verge in its usual position and there was no sign of its long back weaving through the grass toward breakfast. Perhaps it had enjoyed a successful night of hunting. Perhaps it didn't need his food. He heard the distant clattering of a helicopter and, turning, saw a Wessex heading northeast toward Newry or Bessbrook. He watched the lights on the machine blinking and he thought of the warmth and companionship of the mess in the abandoned linen mill at Bessbrook. He shivered in the dawn chill and wondered if there would be another message lying in the hallway. In the last few days, when he had gone into stores in the town, the clerks had ignored him, finally serving him with insulting reluctance, not speaking to him. He was in quarantine.

He put his bicycle against the cottage wall and went to the front door. There he found the cat. He stared and anger swept away the cold of the morning.

The animal's underside had been slit from clavicle to anus. The carcass, its bloody innards exposed as if for a biology lecture, had been nailed to the wooden door through its ears. Blood ran in streaks down the rough slats of the door. He touched the body. Still warm. He looked around, down the road and across the fields, but he knew he would see nothing. They were watching him, though, he was sure of it. A battalion could hide behind the stone walls out there.

He tried to pull the nail free, but it was hammered deep into the wood. Blood staining his hands, he went inside to look for a tool. There was a hammer in a box at the head of the cellar stairs. He slipped the claw under the nailhead, hearing the crack of the cat's skull, and pulled it free. The corpse fell to the ground. The open eyes were no longer lustrous and exotic. They were blank with death.

"Poor Blackie," he said, and now foreboding was nibbling at the edges of his anger.

He dug the grave in the back garden with a rusty trowel, his mind busy with possibilities. They wanted him out, away from there. He wondered how much time he had, how many more warnings they would allow him. He stamped the earth flat over the animal that had wandered into the middle of an argument born hundreds of years ago and he went inside.

In the bedroom, he looked at his watch. It was early, but Loughton would be out of bed by now. He put in the call. Loughton wasn't there; he had gone into Newry, his sergeant said.

"D'you want him to call you when he gets back, sir?"

"No," he said, suddenly feeling foolish. They knew about the messages. All he had to add was a tale about a dead cat. "Forget it, sergeant," he said, and he went to bed.

O'Hara crossed the border on a lane where the invisible boundary curved west of Crossmaglen. He had been worried that they might have set up a vehicle control post, but the way was clear. Now his concern was the possibility of being stopped by a roving patrol. Even with his passport and his accent, they might pull the car apart, might stumble across the weapon taped under the car's hood. The bastards knew all the tricks.

He turned onto a better, wider road, heading east. Not long now, and then back to Dublin and Mary. He accelerated.

The check call woke King. He listened to the six rings, tempted to pick up the receiver and speak. Ask for Loughton and tell him about the cat. He could imagine Loughton's bland voice, saying that he would pass on the word. At the sixth ring, he lifted the receiver, stared at it, and then replaced it.

King was in the kitchen, listening to the radio news from London, when somebody rapped on the front door. He went swiftly to the bedroom and looked through the window. A man, bare-headed, wearing a blue raincoat, was standing on the little path looking up at the second-floor windows. On the road outside the cottage stood a car. King could see nobody else.

He slipped the automatic into his pocket and went into the hallway.

"Who's there?" he called.

"I'm looking for help," the man replied. "I've got a flat and I can't fix it." The accent was American.

His hand on the automatic in his pocket, King opened the door. The man smiled at him. He had a thin, ascetic face, the face of a Jesuit, King thought. There was a coldness to the smile, so that it appeared as nothing more than a brief display of teeth, a meaningless social gesture.

"For a moment there, I thought nobody was in," the man said.

"What's the trouble?" Hidden by the half-open door, King's hand was still on his weapon. He looked over the man's shoulder, but there was nobody else.

"A flat. Happened down the road aways, but I managed to get this far. It's the second I've had this trip."

"Don't you have a spare?"

"Yeah. I got the other one fixed so I'm all right there. Trouble is they used air pressure on the nuts and I can't get them off."

"Just a minute," King said. He closed the door, locked it and ran upstairs. He went from room to room, looking out of the windows in the front and back. There was nobody else in sight. He looked at the car. The front near side tire was flat, the hub cap on the ground.

He went back to the front door. The man was still standing there, a puzzled expression lifting his dark eyebrows.

"Anything wrong?" he asked.

"Just something I had to do."

"If you have a hammer, or something heavy . . ."

The hammer. He had dropped it after freeing the cat from its crucifixion. He looked down. Still bloody, it lay just off the path. The man followed his eyes and gave a grunt of satisfaction.

"That should take care of it," he said and he picked it up. He didn't seem to notice the dry blood on the head. King followed him to the car, his eyes moving restlessly.

"You're American?" he said.

"Yeah. New York. I'm on a vacation trip, but I didn't expect all this rain. I'm heading for Dublin and then I'm going home."

He began to hammer at the wrench gripping one of the wheel nuts. It loosened and started to turn.

"Got you, you little bastard," the man said. He hammered at the other nuts until they were loose, then jacked up the car.

"Roll over the spare, would you, buddy?" King saw the spare was leaning against the rear bumper. He hesitated, reluctant to take his hand from his gun, but the man was struggling with the punctured wheel, no threat for the moment. King shrugged and rolled the spare forward. Five minutes later, the jack was removed, the hammer back in King's hand.

"Thanks a million," the man said. "I'm okay now. Thank God it didn't start to rain again."

King turned and walked toward the cottage. He heard the car door open and he heard the man say something. He looked back and now the man was standing braced against the car, his two hands holding something. That was all King saw.

The slugs drove him back against the front door where the cat had been nailed. His body twisted under the impact, his arms splaying out helplessly, and then he crumpled, the blood running out of him, soaking his clothes.

O'Hara walked up the short path. King, slumped against the bottom of the door, looked up at the advancing gunman.

"Please," he said. "Not any more. Don't." His voice was a tired whisper. O'Hara raised the AK-47, fired a short burst from four feet. One bullet went into King's right eye. Another took away part of his jaw.

O'Hara returned to the Ford and taped the gun back under the hood. The barrel was hot. He lifted the spare wheel into the trunk, slammed the trunk shut, and wiped his hands with a rag.

McCarthy in Crossmaglen would take care of the gun. He looked at his watch. Nearly three. He'd be back in Dublin by six easily. She'd be there. He knew she'd be there.

They had four men on him now in four cars. They had since he'd crossed the border back into Eire. At first they had leap-frogged him along the country roads, but now the men behind were content to follow far back, out of his sight. Telephone calls had been made. Other men would be at the city boundary waiting for him. On this road he could only be going to Dublin. They would pick him up again in the city. In the city it would be easy to follow him.

TWO

Peter King looked at the four-sided clock hanging above the city desk in the center of the newsroom. Ten minutes to go. He wouldn't do it until five o'clock.

In the slot, Burr glanced up from his terminal screen. "Nothing to do?" he said. "Try the Washington file." King pushed the key that brought the Washington bureau stories onto his screen. "The president today signed . . ." "The Senate today passed . . ." "The House today . . ." The bureau seemed to believe that hard-hitting journalism consisted of rewriting wire service copy and putting it on the wire to New York.

He protested without hope. "I handled their shit yesterday and the day before. They're driving me mad."

"Get on with it," Burr said.

King began to edit the stories. They wrote like retarded computers. He looked at the clock again. Another five minutes. To hell with it.

With his left hand, he opened his bottom drawer, took out the pint bottle, and uncapped it. He put it on the floor. He took a cup of coffee, almost empty, from the desk top and placed it alongside the bottle. Burr was shouting for a copyboy, waving a library slip.

King knocked a pencil off the desk and leaned down to recover it. In a series of swift movements, he poured a slug of liquor into the coffee, recapped the bottle, slipped it back into the drawer, closed the drawer and sat upright, the coffee cup securely in his hand.

Burr was watching him with a thin grin. "Coffee not strong enough for you?" he said.

"Bad throat. Purely medicinal."

"King, if you're not careful . . ." he began. His telephone rang. "Just get on with it," he said.

Like the racket in the engine room of a ship reaching the open sea, the noise in the newsroom was intensifying as the first deadline approached. A layer of thickening cigarette smoke hung over the bent heads of the deskmen, swirled occasionally by the passage of a copyboy. Terminals and telephones spilled out their tales of disaster, politics, crime, and human folly. King's head was aching as badly as it had when he awoke. He drank more coffee. He was in no shape to play poker.

At the head of the news desk, Anderson was pondering the front-page splash. Anderson, sprung from some manse on one of those bleak Nova Scotian islands, coming out of nowhere via the Chicago office to take over the tabloid. Anderson, with his pale eyelashes and the hair plastered close to his skull, looking like a farmer with nothing more than his crop yield on his mind, until you detected the calculation behind the braying laugh.

He had come to New York with his God-fearing manner and his blandness and his computers and he had thrown out the irreverent vulgarity that was the paper's soul and the reason for working there. He used phrases out of marketing handbooks and he dined with the governor and the mayor and the other men of power instead of pillorying them. Burr was a member of his coterie. Burr knew how to handle Anderson. With admiration. Burr always agreed with Anderson, guarded his backside, avoided decisions, turned away from new ideas. Unless they were Anderson's.

Midway through a turgid piece about the House Appropriations Subcommittee, King looked up and saw that Burr had left the slot to talk to Anderson. Burr accepted the editor's jovial condescension as a basic part of his job.

The two talked and once they turned to look at King. Anderson said something and Burr nodded. His nod conveyed not only agreement but deep appreciation of Anderson's wisdom. King guessed they were discussing the Runyon trial in New Orleans and who would go down to cover it.

He sipped his coffee and crossed the frontier into fantasyland. The iron balustrades in the French Quarter. Jazz in Preservation Hall. Weekends with no story to file, brunch at Brennan's. The writhing near-naked girls behind the bars on Bourbon Street. Boozing with all the other guys from papers across the country, all the guys who would be covering the big one.

Once, King's dreams would have included the splash of his stories on page one, the fat by-line. Now his pleasures lay outside the story. He didn't keep a scrapbook of his work anymore. New Orleans was part of the sixties, before the advent of Anderson, before his retreat to the cable desk.

Wallace in the school doorway with a speech in his hand; Medgar Evers in his carport with a bullet in his back.

Sitting there in the controlled chaos of the newsroom, King remembered the black kids in Jackson, holding tiny American flags as if for protection while they marched, and the state troopers snatching the flags and throwing them to the ground before herding the children into trucks waiting to take them into custody in the fairgrounds.

Years after, at a Manhattan party, he had met one of those kids, by then a young man studying law at N.Y.U. But after swapping stories of Jackson, there was nothing left to talk about. The black was working on his dream. He was on his way. King had lost his somewhere, in one of a hundred barrooms, and now he was becalmed in an antiseptic ocean ruled by the Andersons and the Burrs and their dust-free computers.

It was as if King and the black had changed places. Before they parted, he thought he caught a shadow of pity in the young black's eyes, as if he knew about King and what he had lost. It could have been imagination.

Anyway, it had been good while it lasted. There had been adrenaline as well as the smell of magnolias in the air of the dangerous Mississippi nights when they rode the back roads to meet and talk with rights leaders in sagging churches and lonely homes, while slack-mouthed, threatening whites watched from pickup trucks, shotguns racked across the rear windows.

Sitton and Fleming and Portis and Nelson and the rest of them, they were outside agitators, guerrillas behind enemy lines, some in greater jeopardy because they were southerners, traitors despised more bitterly than any Yankee. King wondered if they ever thought of him. Probably not. They had moved on.

He remembered one time coming out of Alabama with a photographer from New York, Johnny somebody, and a London correspondent, David Brodie, who maintained an air of perpetual astonishment at the things he had seen in the South. "But can they do that?" he kept asking.

King and Brodie and the cameraman were headed home to New York, but they didn't go there directly. They flew to New Orleans because they wanted to celebrate their safety, one more escape from the dark state and its heavy-browed little ruler. They were killing whites from the North at that time. On the plane out of Montgomery, they had ordered drinks even before takeoff and then, as the wheels left the ground, King had felt the fear and the tension draining out of him. No longer would he have to worry about every car that appeared in the rear-view mirror; no longer would he have to lock his motel room and sleep on the floor, away from the bed, for fear of intruders with guns.

New Orleans was the decompression chamber. They went to the Royal Orleans and took the best rooms available, two suites with connecting doors. They ordered bottles of champagne and showered and put on fresh clothes and drank the champagne before going out to dine high, wide, and handsome. Including the wine with dinner, they didn't stop drinking for eight hours. They were free men again, as free as if just released from high walls, and it was time to proclaim that freedom.

By midnight, high on alcohol and safety, they were touring the bars on Bourbon Street. They exchanged rude comments with the strippers who, bored with the slack weekday trade, seemed glad to tangle with this riotous trio. At one almost-empty bar, a girl was stripping out of an academic gown and mortarboard. They turned to leave. The photographer was barely conscious.

"Hey," she shouted. "I ain't finished yet."

"My dear girl," Brodie called back, "we've seen quite sufficient, thank you very much."

In perfect time with the music, she bent over and presented her buttocks to them, blowing them out of the place with a genuine, hearty fart. It was so expertly done that, out of respect for an artist, they turned and spent the rest of the tattered night in her bar.

But all that was before it happened, before Ginny's death. There's no great trick to controlling your thoughts, he told himself. You just don't think about some things, that's all.

Burr returned to his seat and smiled across at King. "Bad luck," he said, enjoying it. "We decided to send Masters. Very reliable man, Masters."

King hadn't really expected to be assigned to the New Orleans story. Not after the scene last week in Jimmy's, with a dozen witnesses eager to report every detail back to the office. New Orleans was ten years ago.

"This appropriations story," he said. "Not only does it make no sense, but even if it did it would still be a load of nonsense. How about a rewrite?"

"You know perfectly well we don't rewrite the bureau's work," Burr said without looking up. "Get on with it. Mark it up and send it through."

King transferred it to the working file. What the hell. Nobody read Washington stories anyway so Burr was probably right. What was the point of making them readable?

Across the newsroom, Masters was leaving his desk at a secretary's bidding and heading toward Anderson. The reporter was limping slightly, the result of twisting his foot while playing tennis. He played a lot of tennis and was always talking about "improving my game." Cynics, and there were plenty of those around the paper, noted that he had taken up the game after it became general knowledge that Anderson was a tennis enthusiast. Somebody had suggested that the truth was that Masters had twisted his foot in his eagerness to buy a drink for an editor.

King watched gloomily as, agleam with dedication and good health, Masters stood almost at attention to get his instructions for New Orleans. Through the turmoil of the newsroom, King heard him say, "Rely on me. I'll give it everything I've got."

He would, too. Masters wasn't a bad reporter if you liked the wire-service approach, with nothing original to disturb an editor's sense of order. Masters filed his copy on time. Masters never complained. Masters was competent. Masters didn't drink on the job.

King looked at the clock again. Another two hours and he could escape.

In Jimmy's, Freddy had his usual ready, even before he sat down. King touched the glass as if it were an old friend. Sometimes the anticipation was better than the alcohol.

Ransom came in on a visit to the boondocks from the center of the world, police headquarters downtown. Like most police reporters, he looked like a detective and talked like one. It was a useful camouflage. Working the phones, they always introduced themselves as detectives, browbeating patrolmen and witnesses alike to get what they wanted. King bought him a drink.

"Who's getting the Runyon case?" Ransom asked.

"Masters."

"Little prick. They should have expelled him from journalism school." Ransom had never been to college and scorned reporters who had.

King looked at himself in the mirror behind the bar. Even at that distance the frayed fold of his shirt collar was unmistakable. He looked away.

"It would have been your meat, King. You had the touch for that sort of case."

"Who needs it? New Orleans. Nothing but tourists and grits."

"Oh, sure."

Freddy said quietly, "You want to settle your tab, Mr. King? It's over a hundred dollars now and then there's another ten fifty for breakages the other night. I know it was only fun, but we have to charge you." It had started with arm wrestling on the bar and had ended with a free-for-all with an Australian on the floor.

"Friday. I'll settle the whole thing on Friday."

"If you don't mind me saying something, Mr. King. The trouble is that you buy too many drinks for other people who can afford to buy their own."

"Hell, nobody can afford your prices, Freddy." The bartender shrugged and moved away.

By the time King was ready to leave for the poker game the old warmth had settled in his belly, spreading until it blossomed into the familiar blur in his head. The bar had filled and Freddy was sweating as he labored and the sound of individual conversations had merged into a subdued roar. King looked around and saw nothing but friends, good fellows all. Even Burr, drinking a few elbows away with the visiting Paris correspondent, even Burr wasn't such a bad guy. Away from the office, anyway. He called for a last round.

"That'll be fourteen fifty," Freddy said.

"Put it on the tab."

It was five-card stud and King was fifty dollars down. Benson was riding his luck as if it were a Rolls Royce carrying him to a fortune. In swift succession he had pulled a straight, three of a kind, and then a full house.

Benson was the sports editor. Before coming to the States, King had thought the image of the cigar-chewing, cynical newspaperman in a green eyeshade was a cliché. But Benson was a cigar-chewing, cynical newspaperman who wore an eyeshade in the office and when he was playing poker. Perhaps his whole life was a cliché, an old mold into which he had carefully fitted himself.

King was moderately drunk on Scotch, but not so drunk that he didn't recognize the foolishness of playing poker under the influence.

The others were drinking beer and eating sandwiches filled with bologna. The air reeked of stale cigarette smoke.

Benson played like a parsimonious banker contemplating a loan request, hesitating and pondering and humming and finally making his call with excruciating irresolution. He usually won.

At eleven, when King was twenty-five dollars in the hole, the luck changed and King began to win. He took four hands and was forty dollars ahead. Benson took it out on Mahoney, one of his writers.

"Fucking Mahoney," he said. "You should have stayed in. Screw around like that and you don't go down for spring training."

"Screw you," Mahoney said cheerfully. He was Benson's best writer and he knew it.

King's chance came at eleven-thirty. With his fourth card, he was one diamond away from a king high flush. Benson was ace-high, with nothing else showing. The others dropped out. There was thirty-five dollars in the pot.

Benson chewed at his cigar, stared at his hand, looked at King. "Fucking Mahoney," he said. "He should have stood in."

The fourth man, Justice, dealt for the last time. Benson peeked at his hidden card, stared at King. "I bet you double the pot," he said. King's fifth card had been the wrong suit, but now he had a pair of kings.

"Okay," he said. "Double the pot."

Benson had a pair of aces.

"That's thirty-five you owe me, King," he said.

"Friday," King said. "I'll pay you Friday."

There was a party only a few blocks from Benson's apartment. King was at the stage where alcohol anesthetizes the body against minor irritations so that he could enjoy the forced intimacy of crushed bodies and the noise and the absurd things said at such parties.

He smelled burning pot and cast around until he found Logan, who always had a supply. There was a birthday cake, bare of candles, and somebody was sick down his trouser leg. King made a pass at a girl in a flowing blue dress who stared at him with eyes in which glinted a spark of craziness. He never learned her name.

It was another of King's big nights in Manhattan and somewhere in the midst of it all a sadness seized him, sadness at how it had all fallen apart after the bright beginnings of the sixties. It was the booze talking, of course, and those intrusive memories of the South. But, in the center of that smoky, noisy room he stood still for a moment and looked to the years ahead with something like dread.

He tried to tell the girl in the blue dress about it, but the words didn't come out right and she just stared at him with those mad eyes. When a few diehards transferred the party to the Bells on Thirteenth Street, he went with them.

The telephone woke him. Oh, God, he thought, it's Burr. I've overslept again. But then he looked at the clock and saw that it wasn't even noon.

He knew immediately from the sound in the earpiece that it was a long-distance call. It was his mother. Her voice was strained.

"Peter," she said. "Martin's dead. They killed Martin."

THREE

They left the Three-Two precinct in O'Hara's battered, muddy Rambler. Scoppetta, in the back, was complaining as usual about the way he was treated. He wore his black beret, he was unshaven, and his clothes stank of sweat and dirt.

"I want you guys no more than a block away," he was saying. "This mother's carrying a piece, I know it, and he's the douche bag who'll use it. So I want you close in. Not like that deal on Hundred Twenty-sixth Street."

"Don't worry," O'Hara said.

"Don't worry," Scoppetta mimicked. "It's my fucking neck on the block. And lissen, I'm pissed off with the way I have to sit back here. This seat's springs have sprung. They're giving me hardening of the arteries in my ass."

O'Hara hardly heard him. He was no longer thinking of Dublin and Mary and the flight back into Kennedy. He was thinking about Lenane. Where the hell had he gone? Downtown, they had said. What was that supposed to mean? Internal Affairs? Oh, shit. He looked sideways at the partner they'd given him in Lenane's place.

A kid, but he was supposed to have a hook in the chief inspector's office. He was dressed like he was on his way to the country club, with his white shoes and his check pants.

"I'm first grade," Scoppetta was saying, "and that means I should sit up front. I'm entitled."

"You can't sit up front," O'Hara said, "because you stink. Okay, you're supposed to stink, but you still don't sit up here with me." He opened his window wider.

"Fuck you," Scoppetta said.

"How long you got on the job?" O'Hara asked the new man.

"Five years." Christ, he even had a country-club accent.

"Five years!" Scoppetta was outraged. "I was eleven years in before they give me third grade. Hey, who's your rabbi?"

"No rabbi," the kid said. "Just a high degree of intelligence, dedication, grit, and superb deductive capabilities."

O'Hara looked at him. The kid, his name was Bryant, was staring ahead straight-faced.

"Hey," Scoppetta said. "You know what you're doing? You been on a back-up team before?"

The kid shook his head.

"But the sergeant told me what to do," he said. "The sergeant said I should arrest the perpetrator, secure the heroin, and keep my wits about me at all times. Then I read the perp his rights and bring him in. I should only use such force as is necessary."

Scoppetta stared at the back of his head. He couldn't decide whether the kid was putting him on. Finally he shrugged and turned to stare out of the window.

"Fucking department's gone to hell," he said morosely. "It's the Irish. They been running it too long. Hey, look, there's Youngblood. He's gotta be dealing."

They were on 135th Street. It was a wilderness, O'Hara thought, a wilderness of deserted tenements, their windows blocked by tin strips like eyes hidden behind glazed lenses. Ripped-off cars stood double- and triple-parked. Children, the marks of their hopeless future already on their faces, darted about like ferrets. Nothing like Bond Street in London, he thought, with the colonel sprawling in sudden death, or like the cottage outside Crossmaglen and the

English spy flung back against his front door. Or maybe it was. Violent death was no stranger here.

He thought of McCarthy and his idiot followers, writing anonymous notes, believing scraps of paper would scare away the Englishman.

Amateurs, all of them. Killing cats instead of the enemy. No wonder the English sneered at them. And now this senator and his pal, the cardinal, both Irish-Americans, had come out against the Provos. Well, they could be dealt with, too. Fucking traitors.

"Okay," Scoppetta said. "Drop me here. You sure you got the address?"

"I got it. You just make the buy. We'll be on tap. Don't worry."

"Don't worry," Scoppetta said. He was nervous now like he always was before leaving the team and going off on his own. Like a good actor waiting to go on stage, O'Hara thought. And Scoppetta, from Pleasant Avenue and 116th Street, by way of the Police Academy and the dirtiest precincts in town, was a helluva good actor. O'Hara watched him now wandering off down the street, hands in pockets, head lowered, weaving slightly as if he was coming down. In need. They let him get half a block ahead and then followed. They double-parked down the block as Scoppetta, without looking back, ducked into a tenement. A woman, covered from neck to foot in a yellow and red robe, was standing on the steps.

"Sheba," O'Hara said. "The lookout."

He took a pair of binoculars from the glove compartment and studied her through them. She was looking back through the door after Scoppetta. When she turned to survey the street, O'Hara saw that her expression was unruffled.

"How long's Scoppetta being doing this?" the kid wanted to know.

"Six, maybe seven, years," O'Hara said. "He's a maniac. He enjoys it. Likes to live like them."

Ten minutes later, Scoppetta reappeared. He was moving faster now as if he had somewhere to go, needed somewhere quiet to shoot up. The woman watched him scuffle down the street.

Scoppetta walked by the car, not giving it a glance. Now his beret was stuffed in his pocket.

"Okay, he's made the connection," O'Hara said. He started the car and drove to the steps where the woman still stood. He had to triple-park.

"Sheba," he called. "Look what we've got for you."

She stared at him and at the .38 in his hand, poking through the window at her.

"Freeze," he said. Bryant was getting out the other side, his handcuffs dangling.

"Come here, Sheba," O'Hara said. She was beautiful, ripe as a September plum. A torrent of obscenities poured from her sensual mouth. She took a step backward. O'Hara waggled the .38.

"I'll give it to you, Sheba," he said. "You know I'll do it." Then to Bryant, "Cuff her to the wheel."

Keeping out of the line of fire, Bryant, his white shoes twinkling, went to her. He got her arms up behind her and moved her forward. O'Hara stared at the thrust of her breasts through the thin material of the robe. Now she started to plead.

"He'll kill me," she screamed. "Let me go, O'Hara, let me go. Please. He'll kill me . . ." She could be heard a block away. The street had cleared except for a couple of dogs trotting, unconcerned, past the drawn gun.

"He can't hear you, Sheba," O'Hara said. "Be a lady."

The kid snapped the handcuffs on her right wrist and pushed the arm through the window. O'Hara clipped the other bracelet around the steering wheel, securing her. She began to kick the car, pounding on the roof. O'Hara slid over and out the other side.

They both went up the steps, guns in hand, heading for the fourth floor in back. The familiar smells of urine, stale cooking oil, and filth enveloped their nostrils.

On the fourth floor, they paused to get their breath back, then padded down the corridor, O'Hara in the lead. At the end door he motioned Bryant to stand back and raised his right foot. He stood balanced for a moment before smashing the foot forward against the lock. The door was made of tin. Probably reinforced. It gave a bit, but it didn't open.

"Police," O'Hara shouted, and he smashed his foot at the door again. This time it burst open and they went in. The room contained a bed with a stained mattress showing through gray sheets, a sagging chest of drawers, and a refrigerator. Somebody had drawn a smiling face on the refrigerator door and written the words "Have a happy day." The windows had been painted over black and the only light came from a bare bulb hanging from the middle of the speckled ceiling.

A heavily built black, his head shaved, was standing in the middle of the room, a knife in his hand.

"Drop it, Subway," O'Hara said, showing his .38.

The black shrugged and threw the knife onto the bed. Bryant circled him and pocketed it.

"Give it up," O'Hara said.

"Where's your warrant?" Subway said without hope.

"You kidding? Give it up."

Suddenly the black was angry. "What you mean, give it up?" he demanded. "I pay and I pay and still you come in here and say give it up. I'm a businessman. I buy and I sell and I pay my dues. I pay the stationhouse, okay. That's part of doing business. But still you come in and say give it up. Last time I give you twenty and now . . ."

He didn't finish. O'Hara was close to him now, moving swiftly. He lashed out, using the revolver like a club. The blow caught the man on his cheekbone and he staggered, blood staining his white shirt.

"Hey, man . . ." he began. O'Hara hit him again and this time the man went down. It wasn't O'Hara's game, this stuff, but he didn't know about Bryant, the new face with a hook in the chief inspector's office. What the hell was Lenane doing downtown? Did Internal Affairs have him? He touched the man with his shoe.

"We don't want talk," he said. "We want the shit. Now give it up." Bryant was watching impassively.

Wearily, the man got to his feet. He staggered, dazed, then pulled out a handkerchief and put it to his bleeding face. He went to the chest of drawers and opened it.

"Go down and see how Sheba's doing," O'Hara said to Bryant.

"I'll bring this scumbag down." He took the plastic bags from Subway and went to the door, listening to Bryant's retreating footsteps.

"You ever seen my partner before?" he said.

"No."

"You're sure?"

"I never seen the dude before."

"You see me with a stranger, somebody you don't know nothing about, and you open your fucking mouth in front of him. Right?"

"He a cop ain't he?"

"Yeah, and he could be a shoofly who'll fix me up with a ticket to Dannemora. Just because you gotta run off at the mouth, you stupid fuck. Come on."

They let Sheba go and took Subway to the Three-Two. O'Hara gave the arrest to Bryant, not because he thought it would placate the kid, but because he wanted to make some calls. Maybe Cahill could find out about Lenane, whether Internal Affairs had got him. Cahill had better. If O'Hara went, he wouldn't go alone.

In the squad room he saw Scoppetta. The undercover man was complaining bitterly about Bryant.

"Five years," he said. "He's got five years on the job, still needs his mommy to wipe his mouth, and they give him a gold badge. I tell you, justice sucks."

Cahill was waiting for him in Giambone's, behind the gray mass of the Criminal Courts Building. He was alone at a rear table eating veal parmagiana and drinking a cola. Cahill didn't touch alcohol and he didn't smoke. O'Hara ordered a Cutty Sark on the rocks and looked around. There was enough noise coming from the other tables for them to talk.

"How are you, John?" Cahill asked. Everybody else called him Johnny, but with Cahill it was always John. Ever since he'd been a kid.

"I guess I'm okay. What d'you hear? About Lenane?"

"Not here. When we've finished, we'll go for a walk. It's a nice night. Spring's really round the corner."

"I have to know what's going on."

"Of course you do, John," Cahill said, primly patting his mouth with his napkin. "But later."

O'Hara accepted it, like he had accepted everything from Cahill. It seemed as though there never had been a time when Cahill wasn't there to guide him, tell him what to do, praise him, reprimand him.

"How's Ellen?" Cahill asked.

"She's okay."

He supposed she was. He hadn't been home since coming back into Kennedy. He had telephoned, explained the endless stakeout was still on at the Hilton, and gone straight to the Three-Two. Straight to the Three-Two and Bryant instead of Lenane.

Cahill finished, paid the bill, and led the way out. As he passed one of the tables in front, three men arose to shake his hand, all young assistant district attorneys who knew Inspector Timothy Cahill even though he was no longer on the street but tucked away in a corner of the high rise on Police Plaza. Cahill exchanged a few words with them and then walked with O'Hara toward Chinatown.

"I'll miss all this, the respect of good men," Cahill said. In three months he would retire to his little house outside Phoenicia in the Catskills. He would tend his garden and grow vegetables.

"What about Lenane?"

"He spent six hours with Internal Affairs. Schmidt is handling the case. Very good man, Schmidt."

"What did he tell them?"

"I tried, John, but they wouldn't talk about it."

"The rat fink. Did he give me up?"

"I tell you, I don't know."

"I always knew he was a badass. They'll put a wire on him and he'll sit there talking, with those big innocent blue eyes, and he'll try to bury me."

"Yes, you'd better assume he's wired, John. But look at it this way. If he is, it means they've got nothing but his say-so. I'll keep my ears open."

Nobody in the department knew that Cahill was O'Hara's uncle. Cahill had said it was better that way because he could help his young nephew, free of the accusation of nepotism. Ever since O'Hara's father had run off twenty-five years earlier, Cahill had always been there to help. There had been a price, of course, but O'Hara had paid it willingly. Cahill had taught him to believe in a risen, united Ireland and they both had worked for it.

"I hear your latest task on the other side was concluded satisfactorily." Cahill paused to wait for a light. The sidewalk was busy with tourists buying Oriental knickknacks they would throw away when they got home.

"You have to talk to Donovan," O'Hara said. "They give me a schedule that's impossible. No sleep. I don't mind doing the jobs. I'm proud to do them. But when I come back I'm dead for a week."

"Yes," Cahill said. "I heard about that." They turned up Canal Street, away from the crowds. "I also heard that you managed to get some relaxation over there."

O'Hara shot a sideways look at him. "Less than twelve hours," he said. "They want the whole thing done in less than twelve hours."

"You took longer than that. You didn't catch the flight back that you were supposed to."

"I had to get some sleep. I was dropping."

"It wasn't sleep you were after."

"You don't know what it's like."

"It was a woman. You disobeyed your orders and you went to see a woman. Didn't you?"

"Yes." O'Hara felt a rush of resentment. He was an adult, a second-grade detective who could handle the worst ball breakers in town, and with a few words Cahill could transform him back into a snot-nosed kid. "Things aren't good at home," he said.

"I thought you had street smarts, John."

"I know what I'm doing."

"You know what you're doing, hell. You risk blowing away an important operation because you can't keep your cock under control. Who is this woman?"

"She's a barmaid. In Dublin."

"A barmaid. A slut. When did you meet this barmaid?"

"Two trips back. The job in London. I went in through Dublin because you wanted me to talk to Donovan. Remember? Well,

Donovan got called away and I had the night on my hands and I met her."

"You got in bed with the slut?"

"She's no slut. She's a widow who works hard to survive." They were facing each other now and O'Hara was angry, the skin tight on his thin face. "She loves me and I love her. She knows how to treat a man."

"Women like that always do."

"Fuck you." They stared at each other. It was the first time O'Hara had talked like that to his uncle. He felt a kind of triumph. He had asserted his independence and the heavens had not cracked asunder.

"I'll forget you said that, John."

"Don't call her a slut."

"All right. I don't know the woman." Cahill put his hands out and took O'Hara by the shoulders. "Listen, boy, just listen to me. I don't care if you bed a different woman every night. I'm sorry things are that way between you and Ellen. She's a good woman."

"She's an iceberg."

"Okay, you have your needs. But you don't satisfy them while you're on an operation for the organization. You're a soldier, John, a soldier in an unknown army, but you're just as much under orders as a rifleman in the front line. I've told you that many times before."

He had. Right back to his childhood. O'Hara knew them all, Patrick Pearse, Cathal Brugha, Michael Collins, Kevin Barry, those saints of the terrible beauty, the heroes and the martyrs who had fought in the underground army.

While other boys had dreamed of DiMaggio or Koufax, O'Hara had listened to his uncle telling of 1916 and the Dublin Post Office and the Black and Tans, and he had yearned to join the fight. His heroes had worn cloth caps and raincoats and their victories had been marked by gravestones.

More than once his uncle had told him, "For all the love I bear you, John, I'd sacrifice you if the organization demanded it. And I'd expect you to do the same with me." O'Hara had accepted that. And then, as a reward for his good work at Delehanty before joining the department, Cahill had paid for him to go to Northern Ireland and he had seen the truth of all he had been told, the oppression along the mean streets and in the projects, the idle men at street corners, idle because of their beliefs, and he had known the anger that had put the spur to all the old heroes and martyrs.

"I couldn't stay away from her," he said. "I've never known a woman like that before." He paused. "Who told you about it?"

"They know everything that goes on in Dublin, Donovan and the rest," his uncle said. "They were displeased."

"It did no harm. I just caught a later plane."

"You disobeyed."

"I did the job for them."

"Yes, and you doubled the chance of being picked up."

"For Chrissake, I was in Dublin."

"You think you're safe once you're across the border? D'you think the English take any notice of borders? They'll send their thugs after you whether you're in Derry, London, or Dublin. It was your job to get out as soon as possible. You understand?"

"I do."

"And you'll stay away from this woman?"

O'Hara was silent. He could refuse or he could lie, but he couldn't stay away from her. Even here, thousands of miles away in another republic, his body warmed at the memory of her sitting on the bar stool in the Gresham waiting for him as he knew she would. She had been facing the door with her long, fleshy legs crossed, doing nothing to hide the eagerness in her eyes. He remembered the way the silk of her dress had clung to her hips, the way the bodice had been cut to hint at the splendor it clothed. Too avid for each other to eat, they had gone straight to her room and the narrow bed and the liberation she offered.

"John?"

"I can't promise I won't see her. I'd be lying."

"The organization has the power to deal with that problem, John. It can break anybody who hinders its work."

"My seeing her doesn't hurt them."

"That's not for you to decide. Find a woman here. There are a million women in New York who'll open their legs for you. And nobody gets hurt. Think about it, will you, John?"

"I will. But what about Lenane?"

"Just keep your nose clean for a while. I'll find out more." He put out a hand for a cab heading uptown, climbed in, and was gone. O'Hara turned back toward his car and the joyless ride home to Forest Hills.

FOUR

The church had been built by Cotswold merchants when wool was king, but now only a handful of villagers, old men and women, attended and there was no money for fuel for its furnace. The cold was like a palpable embrace, enclosing the little group in the front pews. King sat and listened to the ancient ritual of loss, trying to remember his brother as he had last seen him. But somehow the face that came back was that of the eager boy, not the man.

He looked up at the blackened old beams high above the apse, remembering the squirrel. He must have been about sixteen, which would have made Martin about twelve. On vacation from their school in Dorset, they had been bird's-nesting in the woods in the valley west of the church where he now sat. They had found the squirrel under an oak tree, caught in a trap by its paw. They freed it and took it home. Martin wanted to tame it, make a pet of it. He had, King thought, the instinct for order. Perhaps it was that, as much as his father, that had made him join the army.

They put the paw in a little splint, which might have done no good but evidently did no harm, and they fed the creature with milk and bits of nuts until it recovered. It showed no gratitude. It would neither accept the boys as masters nor as friends. When they tried to touch it, it would bite them. The first time it happened, Martin cried, not from the pain, but because the animal had rebuffed his affection. They took the squirrel to an old countryman who sometimes worked in their garden. They asked how they could tame it.

The old man made a long leash, which he slipped over the squirrel's neck. He took it to the fence outside his cottage, perched it there, and began to bang the rail with a stick, making the animal scamper up and down, up and down, until it was weary. It became so tired that it could hardly find the energy to bite him when he put his hand near.

The old man reached behind the squirrel's head and began to stroke and massage the little neck. His gnarled hand was as gentle as a mother's. "Little bugger," he said softly. "He's just scared, ain't he? Sees a hand coming at him and he gets scared."

He motioned to Martin and the boy joined in the stroking. Like humans, the old man explained, animals enjoy the sensuous feeling engendered by gentle touching and this squirrel was no different. The next day, though, the squirrel tried to bite Martin again. The boys took it back to the old man who was shelling peas by his back door for his lonely supper. He told Martin what to do.

Every time the squirrel snapped at the boy's hand, Martin picked it up by the neck and put his teeth to the creature's hindquarters and bit, not enough to break the skin but enough to make the squirrel squeak.

"It'll learn," the old man said. "Every creature on God's earth is capable of learning."

Finally the squirrel understood. When it bit, it got bitten in return. It stopped biting Martin.

"Now we'll see," the old man said, holding the squirrel. "Martin you go over there." He put the animal on the ground, the leash still in his hand, and then he released his grip. The squirrel ran for Martin. It ran up his back and perched affectionately on his shoulder. The boys had never seen anything like it. Paul, roaring with laughter, clapped; Martin stood there, the creature on his shoulder. Martin's eyes were shining, full of wonder. He named his pet Tiger and took it everywhere. They were inseparable.

Once, while they were attending Evensong with their parents, Tiger slipped its leash and raced up to the old beams. It had taken Martin half an hour to persuade his pet to come down. The service had been disrupted and the church was barred to the squirrel.

When they went back to school, Martin took Tiger with him. Animals were forbidden there, but aided by a conspiracy by his classmates, Martin managed to keep it hidden from the authorities until November. Then King had come across his brother in a school corridor. Martin was crying and he was inconsolable. He had woken that morning to find Tiger was dead. He did not know what had caused it. "Perhaps it was old age," King had said. "Perhaps it was time for it to die."

They were carrying the coffin out now, six captains in formal blues staggering under the weight. A Union Jack hid most of the casket as if to lay a veneer of patriotism over the pain of death. It was much warmer outside, the pungent smell of spring in the soft air. Swifts swooped around the clock tower and a herd of heifers was being driven down the lane past the church. King's hangover began to lift. Down the path, past the yew trees, the undertaker's men waited. He could see the freshly turned earth. His mother was holding the general's arm, more to give support than to receive it. Joy, Martin's widow, her features hidden by a flop-brimmed black hat, was clasping the children's hands, pulling them close to her. The boy was more interested in the passing cows than in the strange procedures being carried out by these somber adults.

Inevitably, King remembered Ginny's funeral, the cool impersonality of the nondenominational church, the handful of mourners, all friends, no relatives. He remembered the horror of the telephone call to her parents, the flat, accusing voices coming down the wire. They had no doubt that he was responsible for her death. No, they wouldn't come to the funeral. She had gone outside the church and she was damned and it was his fault and he would burn with her.

After that, there was nothing he could say to them. There was nothing he could do but bury her and wonder if the mother and father, sitting in judgment in Pennsylvania, were right. That was the time it had started, the hollowness somewhere inside him. And the drinking.

It was curious, he thought, standing there to watch them bury his brother. He felt numb as if anesthetized against any sense of loss. He went through the motions of mourning, but he felt nothing. Afterward, after the twelve-man honor guard had fired its rifles, King went to the officers, who stood apart as if they feared their uniforms bore some responsibility for this sadness in a country churchyard.

"It was kind of you to come," he said. "The family appreciates it."

"He was a fine man," one of the captains said.

"A good officer and a good friend," another said.

"Were you with him? When he died?"

They looked embarrassed as if, somehow, they had failed King. "No," one said, "we're all at the regimental depot. He'd been detached for duty in Ulster in December."

"D'you know where he served?"

"First, he was in Belfast. Then he was assigned somewhere down in the south, close to the border. That's all we know."

"You don't know how he died?" The pale-faced undertaker's men were walking past toward the lych-gate, picking their way through the gravestones.

"Active duty. The micks. That's all we were told," one of the captains said. He was built like a rugby forward and he wore a paratrooper's flash. "Didn't the War Office give you the details?"

"I don't know. I only got home this morning. The general said he was shot. Somewhere down by the border."

"I'll see what I can find out," the paratrooper said.

"The family would appreciate it."

"I'll call you. How long are you staying?"

"A couple of days," King said. He needed a drink.

He used his father's car to drive Joy and the children to the station in Oxford. The children were fractious, barely understanding why they had had to make this tedious journey to the house in the Cotswolds.

"Will you be all right?" King asked her as they threaded their way slowly through the narrow streets of Charlbury. It was like entering a time warp coming back to this countryside from Manhattan, he thought. Nothing had changed.

"Peter, I'll never be all right again," she said.

"Financially, I mean."

"I suppose so. I'll probably go back to teaching physical therapy. But then I don't know who'll look after the children while I'm working. Oh, I don't know. . . . It's so damnably stupid, the whole thing over there. What's the point? They kill each other and nothing is solved."

"Did he tell you what he was doing?"

"You know Martin," she began. "Oh, God, he's dead, isn't he? And I can't accept it, Peter, I can't."

"Did he write much?"

"Yes, but he never said much about his duties. He talked mostly about the countryside, the hills over there. He loved the hills, he spent hours tramping through them."

"Did he say exactly where he was stationed?"

"No, it was strange. He said once that friends were mailing his letters for him. They used to be postmarked 'Bessbrook' and I wrote back to him, care of the officers' mess there. I looked it up. It's in a place called Armagh, close to the border. He was attached to the Fusiliers, who had some sort of outpost in the town. I suppose he was on a patrol and they shot him. I read somewhere they average one soldier a week. It was his turn." Her voice was bitter. "I hate them. They shoot our men in the back, you know. That's the way they fight for justice."

He didn't know what to say. She would spend the rest of her life hating the Irish and she'd pass it on to the children. He wondered about the men who had killed his brother. Had they relished it, glorying in the delivery of death? Or had it been to them a painful duty, an execution ordered by men who believed that only killing could clear their way to power?

"I'm going to find out," he said.

"What?" She spoke absently, staring out at the peaceful fields, ribbed by Cotswold stone.

"How he died. How they killed him. And why."

"I don't want to know, Peter. He's dead. That's all I need to know."

Now she put her gloved hands to her face and she began to weep, the tears streaming down her face. In the back seat, the children had been squabbling over the ownership of a toy racing car they had found in the garage. They fell silent, listening to their mother's distress.

In Oxford, he put them on the London train before going to a pub, a Victorian pile of red brick near the station. He ordered a Scotch.

"American, are you?" the barmaid said.

He shook his head, but she didn't notice.

"Thought so," she said. "We get a lot of American tourists in here." He doubted it. The place was like a tomb.

"D'you have an atlas?"

"A what, dear?"

"A map of the country, including Ireland."

"Goodness, no. What would we want with one of them?"

He finished his drink and went to Smith's in the Cornmarket where they sold him a map. Sitting in the parked car, the grief at last swept over him. He leaned forward, resting his head on the steering wheel. It was mourning such as he had not felt in the dimness of the church or at the graveside. After twenty minutes he raised his head and saw a chubby-cheeked woman staring in at him, her blue eyes concerned. He lowered the window.

"Are you all right, love?" she said.

"Yes, thanks," he said. "I'm all right."

"Thought you might be ill."

"Just tired," he said, and she went on her way. He opened the map and found Bessbrook, where Martin had mailed his letters home. It was five or ten miles north of the Irish border. A small town by the look of it.

He had thought that the killing grounds in Ulster lay in the larger cities, not out in the country. His knowledge of Ireland and its troubles was sketchy. He had a vague image of thatched cottages and Georgian squares in Dublin, of brawling pubs and gunmen in trench coats, of lonely cloud-dappled lakes and of children throwing stones at British soldiers in blackface.

On the way home, he stopped at the bank. The manager, a friend of his father's, had attended the funeral. He received King in his office overlooking the narrow village street. A gas fire popped uncertainly against the wall, throwing out a meager heat.

"Tragic," the manager said. He wore thick tweeds and cultivated the manner of a country squire. He was more at home riding with the local hunt than in the world of finance.

"I'm worried about the general. He didn't look well. That boy was everything to him. With you, of course. Thank God he has the grandchildren."

"He's an old man," King said. He had no great affection for the manager, who always struck him as a pompous social climber, fawning with the gentry, patronizing with the villagers.

"They should pull our boys out. Everybody says so. Let the bastards· kill each other off. See how they like that."

"That's what the Provos want."

"Who cares? I don't. All they're good for is boozing and digging ditches and moaning about injustice as if they discovered it. They're like the Jews. You know I was in Palestine after the war. Our hook-nosed brethren there were very good at shooting soldiers in the back. Even hung a couple of sergeants. Guerrilla warfare they called it. But when the Arabs start doing the same thing to them, they scream bloody murder. They don't mind a bit of torture, either."

"Human nature, I suppose," King said. He wanted to be gone.

"Yes, but some natures are more human than others. Now, what can we do for you?"

"I want to close out my account."

He had a little over five hundred pounds and he took it all. He would need it, for he already had decided to go to Ulster, even if the captain who had attended the funeral called up with a complete story. There was something unsettling about the vagueness that cloaked his brother's death, something that aroused his journalistic instincts. There was another aspect. Nothing had appeared in the newspapers and Fleet Street was not so jaded with news from Ireland that it would ignore the killing of any army captain, son of a general.

He had expected the familiar accusation in the general's eyes, but since he had been at home his father seemed to look on him more as a stranger than as a son who had failed him. Something vital, some spark, had gone from the fierce gray eyes under the ramparts of eyebrows and for the first time King noticed that a stoop had sapped the military posture that had dominated a hundred reviewing stands. He used a walking stick now and when he sat down his body seemed to crumple.

The arguments had been bitter. For a century and longer, the oldest son had gone off to serve the Crown. It was a duty and a privilege. They had gone out from the old Tudor house high on the wolds to the plains of India, the African veldt, the maelstrom of France. The general's father, King's grandfather, had been killed by a crossfire of machine guns on the ridge at Passchendaele. The general had been with Montgomery in the tent on Luneburg Heath in 1945. Perhaps, King thought, his father believed that it should have been his funeral that morning, not Martin's.

For King had refused the duty and the privilege and his brother had taken his place. King wanted to see something more of the world than parade grounds and officers' messes. The general was offended even more by King's preference. First, the squalor of Fleet Street and then the feral vulgarity of America.

But now, together with the strength, the anger was gone. The general was an old man, the fires out, the emotions deadened. The strength was in the woman who had marched with him for forty years. King's mother was a comfortable woman, comfortable in body and spirit. He had not seen her cry since his return; he suspected she would loose her tears when nobody, not even the general, was close. Women, he thought, so often had the steel demanded of men. But then he thought of Ginny and knew it was not always true. His mother was laying out the teacups.

"The poor vicar," she said. "He always seems to have a cold nowadays."

"I'm not surprised," the general said, staring into the fire. "That damned church. It's a penance to walk inside."

"Oh, it's not so bad, dear, if you wrap up well."

"I talked to old Pine at the War House," the general said. "He was extraordinarily equivocal. Said all he knew was that Martin was on special duties with the Fusiliers and got shot a few miles outside Crossmaglen."

"If Pine doesn't know, then nobody does," his wife said.

"That's the damnable part. I don't think he does know the full story. Don't think anybody there knows. Pine sounded quite embarrassed. Can't blame him."

King asked about letters home from his brother. "He didn't write much to us," his mother said. "He knew we'd get his news from Joy. The last time he wrote, he was in Belfast."

"Dirty business all around," the general said. "Where's the gallantry in fighting a bunch of street-corner loungers and farmers?" He sounded bewildered, hurt. Gallantry was his favorite word, King thought, always had been. You could be gallant in a cricket match, in your relations with others, on the battlefield. It was the mark of a gentleman.

"Martin did his duty," King's mother said. "That's all that matters."

King wondered if she believed the platitude. Perhaps it was the way to survive. He thought of telling them that he planned to go to Ulster to poke around, but he didn't. It wouldn't ease their pain and he couldn't be sure what he might find. Could it be discreditable? Had Martin been in some trouble? That would destroy the general. Yet, perhaps that was the explanation for the official vagueness. Protect the old man.

The parachute captain telephoned the next morning. He was in London.

"I put out some lines," he said, "but I'm afraid I can't help you much. It seems they sent him down to Crossmaglen as some sort of advance guard for the Special Air Service chappies. The cloak and dagger people."

"But why Martin?"

"Well, he'd had some training in counterterror. Went through a course or two, weapons, tactics, that sort of thing."

"And what happened?"

"Well, that's the trouble. Nobody over here seems to know." Did he sound odd, as if he knew more than he was saying, or was that imagination?

"That's insane. They must know."

"Awfully sorry. I know how you must feel. There's one thing, though. I put in a call to the Fusiliers in Ulster."

"Where? In Bessbrook?"

"That's right, down by the border, where he was based."

"What did they say?"

"Afraid I couldn't get much out of them, either. He was killed out in the country, near this place Crossmaglen, and they brought the body back by helicopter. It was a bit of a mess. Sorry to have to tell you this sort of thing, but you have the right to know if anybody does. Then they shipped it home through Belfast." Why would I want to know what sort of a mess they made of him, King thought. But then he realized he wanted to know everything.

"The fact is," the captain went on, "he seemed to have been operating as a loner. He didn't spend any time in the barracks at Bessbrook. He had a contact there, of course, to keep in touch with him, but he never appeared in the mess. Most of the fellows never even saw him."

"Who was his contact?"

"A chap called Loughton. Let me see, I've got it here somewhere. Here it is, Major Harry Loughton."

"Did you talk to him?"

"No, he wasn't there when I called. I can give you the number. Perhaps you'd like to try and reach him."

King wrote down the telephone number although he didn't plan to use it. He would go down to Bessbrook and look up this Major Loughton in person. First, though, he'd try Fleet Street. Perhaps Purgavie would know why the London papers hadn't bothered to carry anything about the killing of an English army captain on the Irish border.

*   *   *

King caught up with Purgavie in a Fetter Lane pub nicknamed "The Stab in the Back," where he was drinking with his secretary, Liz Withers. Purgavie had been born in a village outside Edinburgh but had grown up in London. As a result, his Celtic soul expressed itself in pure Battersea.

"Hullo, chum," he said, as if King had never been away. "Have a drink." Drinks were ordered, gossip exchanged. Minton, the motoring correspondent, arrived and called for champagne, an addiction he had formed on his annual visits to Monte Carlo. Purgavie launched into a rambling story about his direction of the pursuit of an errant viscount from one of the shires who had run off with a vicar's daughter. By nine o'clock, the voices in the bar had achieved a steady clamor and King's thoughts were beginning to blur. He pulled Purgavie away from his group of courtiers.

"Four days ago," he said, "maybe five. Did you hear anything about a shooting in Ulster? Down near the border?"

"Just a minute," Purgavie said. "Got to make a phone call. The wife. She doesn't understand the long hours a news editor has to work."

When he returned, he said, "Now, what's on your mind?"

"An army officer. Shot in Armagh within the last week."

Purgavie looked at King, a curious expression on his face.

"What's the game, then?" he said. "What's going on?"

"No game. An officer was shot and not a word appeared in any newspaper I can find."

"Now, look, King. You go off to New York, doubtless because of the well-known low morals of American women, and then, years later, you suddenly pop up again and start asking questions about the beautiful Emerald Isle and the goings-on over there. That sort of thing raises eyebrows, you know."

"All I'm asking is, d'you know anything about it? If you don't, fine, that's the end of it."

"And all I'm asking is, what's your interest?" A group of subeditors went by, heading back for the desk. They all had the pallid, sullen faces of night workers.

"The officer they killed," King said. "He was my brother." Purgavie stared at him, nodded, and went back to the bar for a refill. The drinks had made King feel light-headed, a little dizzy. He stared around the smoky barroom realizing he knew few of the newspapermen who filled it. How long had it been? Ten years? Jesus, more like fifteen.

"Sorry to hear about your brother," Purgavie said, back with a full glass. "We never got a name."

"You did hear something, then?"

"Oh, yes."

"But you didn't run a story. Nobody did."

"Nobody did because Whitehall issued a D-notice."

A D-notice. Now King understood. The government device known as a D-notice prohibited publication of stories that might threaten national security. National security, of course, was a flexible term. Armed with such a weapon, Nixon could have castrated the Watergate sleuths.

"What happened?" he said. "The army won't tell us, except that he was shot."

"Bastards," Purgavie said. "There's not much to tell. They put out the D-notice even before we got a whisper of the shooting. Somewhere down by Crossmaglen, wasn't it? Yes, I've been there. Did a tour among the smiling Irish eyes last year and wound up near the border."

He grimaced. "It's like the shootout at the O.K. Corral down there. Fucking bombs and guns going off all the time. I got out quick."

"It was near Crossmaglen."

"Well, I'll tell you, chum, if your brother was knocking around down there, he was asking for it. In Armagh, they think the war's over and they won."

"Did you get a story eventually?"

"Oh, yes, we got one. We've got a fellow in Belfast. Sent him over after he blew the Carmody story. Punishment post. A few hours after we get the D-notice, he files a piece saying an unnamed army captain has been picked off by the locals and the body recovered by helicopter."

"You didn't run it."

"Course we didn't run it. Think I want to end up in the Tower, watching the carpenters build gallows? We told our man to lay off it and that was the end of it. What was your brother in, then, Special Air Service? They've been mucking around down there."

"Infantry. He was detached for special duty down by the border."

"Well, it must have been cloak and dagger stuff. They don't put the gag on us any more than they can help. Every paper on the Street has a tame M.P. or two and the pisspot at Number Ten doesn't want too many questions asked in the House about indiscriminate use of the notices. They're too valuable. Christ, if I could publish everything I know . . ."

"Who's your man in Belfast?"

"Fairclough. Drinks too much. I'll give him a call if you like. See if he can find out anything more. Probably he's got something in his files. Didn't bother to send it after we told him to leave it alone."

"I'm going over," King said. "See what I can find. I'll look him up."

"Good luck," Purgavie said. "Sorry about your brother, chum." When they closed the pub, King went to the West End where they stayed open later.

FIVE

O'Hara telephoned the Three-Two precinct from home. They said that Lenane wasn't scheduled for duty for another three days. They said Bryant, "Twinkletoes" as O'Hara had sourly named the white-shoed detective, would be his partner again the next day.

O'Hara drove into the city, heading for Lenane's apartment around the corner from P. J. Clarke's. Maybe the fink would wear a wire on the street, with O'Hara, but he wouldn't be wearing it at home, and O'Hara had to talk to him. They had been giving him the treatment around the stationhouse, the looks, some sorrowful, some malicious, as if they all had a transcript of what Lenane had told Internal Affairs. Scoppetta, smelly, crazy Scoppetta, had asked for a different back-up team. He would deal with Scoppetta later, but right now he had to talk to Lenane, find out what the fuck was going on.

He flashed his badge at the doorman, said, "Police business—I'll find my own way up. And stay away from the intercom or I'll have your ass."

To make sure, he took the elevator to the sixteenth floor, then used the stairs to drop down to the fourteenth floor, where Lenane lived in his version of a swinger's paradise. O'Hara had been to some of his parties, populated by women with long hair and Queens Boulevard accents and hard eyes. The men were of a pattern— Cardin suits, no ties, and too much cologne, talking about football as if they were club directors, which for all O'Hara knew they might have been. High-class pimps and their women, he thought. Lenane took his money wherever he could get it. He knocked on the door, standing aside from the peeper.

For a moment, he thought Lenane might be out, but then he heard muffled movements inside the apartment and a click as somebody opened the peephole.

"Yeah?" It was Lenane.

"Maintenance," he mumbled. "Gotta fix the air conditioning."

The door opened and his partner stood there, staring at him. He was barefoot, wearing nothing but a pair of jeans. Lenane's chest was still tanned from the two weeks he had spent in San Juan in January. Nowhere to hide the wire.

"Johnny," he said. "What the fuck you doing here? Come on in." O'Hara went past him into the apartment. Deep, garish carpet, wall-to-wall. A TV console. Cushions all over, all the better to snuggle up in. A low, leather couch stretching along two walls. A bar, fully stocked. A view of the Manhattan skyline, with the Chrysler Building as a centerpiece. And a blonde. Half-naked. Detective second grade Michael Lenane knew how to live.

"This is Maxine," he said. "A friend of mine. Call her Maxi because that's what she is, the very maximum." It must have been an old line; she didn't try to smile at it. Lenane didn't bother to introduce O'Hara, who got the impression that Maxi was just part of the furniture, to be used like the refrigerator when needed. She was tying the sash of a black robe, which, however, remained parted enough to allow her bountiful chest full visibility.

"Got a moment?" O'Hara said. The two men were standing in the middle of the room, facing each other. Over Lenane's shoulder he could see into another room, which contained an enormous bed covered by rumpled black sheets.

"Sure," Lenane said. His eyes were watchful.

"Alone."

"Maxi," he said.

"Oh, neat," she said. "Very neat," and she padded into the bedroom, closing the door behind her. Lenane went to the bar. He had heavy fleshy shoulders, a narrow waist. He had the face of a corrupt altar boy.

"Drink?" he said.

"What's this with Internal Affairs?"

"I talked to them." He was busy with bottles and glasses.

"About what?"

"About nothing. They asked a lot of questions."

"What did you say?"

Lenane exploded. "What d'you mean, what did I say? You come finagling your way into my apartment, as if I'm some jungle bunny candy man, and you start interrogating me like some hungry fucking assistant D.A. trying to make a name. I'm telling you, Johnny, get off my back." He had turned from the bar and was standing with his hands on his hips. A gold medallion hung from his neck.

"They turn you?"

"No, they didn't fucking turn me. They got nothing. I'm telling you, they're fishing."

"I heard they turned you. Gave you a wire."

"Bullshit. They just tried to break my balls and they didn't do it. It's a bullshit case."

"What is? What's a bullshit case?"

"Now, listen, Johnny. Calm down. We owe each other. Two years, more than two years, I've watched your back and you've watched mine."

"What's this bullshit case?"

Lenane went over to the window and stared out. The sun was down behind the ramparts of midtown and the office lights were ablaze.

"They wanted to know how I lived like this. Where I got the money. I told them I'm single, no responsibilities. I can swing it."

"Don't pull my prick, Lenane." O'Hara was implacable. "What bullshit case?"

Lenane turned to face him, his body outlined against the brilliant, jagged towers. His face was in shadow and O'Hara couldn't see his expression.

"Okay," Lenane said. "Okay, Johnny. You remember that score on Fifth Avenue. In Brooklyn. Back in November, the end of November."

"Velez?"

"Right. Badass Velez." He moved to a wall switch and the apartment was filled with light. "Three kilos. A straight split, you remember, Johnny? No problem. We were Mr. Nice Guy and no problem."

O'Hara remembered. Nice score. The payoff was three hundred each. Lenane had bought his Porsche around that time.

"So?" he said.

"So, three weeks later, Velez steps on his prick again and this time it's another team picks him up, a couple of narcos out of Brooklyn South, Mannheim and Torres."

"And he gives us up?"

"Mannheim knows Schmidt, through that German club. You know, Johnny, they march around in German helmets every year at that PBA thing up in the Catskills. They take Velez straight into Internal Affairs and he starts opening his mouth to Schmidt. That's why they called me downtown."

"And that's when you gave me up."

"On my mother's grave, Johnny. I stand here and I swear to you."

"So why haven't they called me downtown?"

"I don't know. Maybe hoping the pressure gets to you. I don't know."

"Who was undercover on that job? Scoppetta?"

"Yeah. He made his second buy and he was long gone when we went in."

"Have they called Scoppetta down?"

"I tell you, I don't know. I don't know a thing more than I've told you."

"They fitted you up with a wire, didn't they?"

"They wanted to, Johnny. I told them to fuck off. I told them we're both clean. That Velez was full of shit."

"So why didn't you tell me you'd been downtown?"

"You were away, on one of your trips. Remember, you wanted me to cover for you and I did. Like I always have, Johnny. Remember that. I've never asked questions, I just covered for you."

The telephone rang. It was fire engine red, standing on the coffee table in front of the leather couch. Lenane looked at it, hesitated, then went to pick it up. When he talked, he didn't look at O'Hara.

"Lenane," he said.

"Uh-uh, right . . . not right now . . . no. Yeah. Okay, listen, I'll talk to you later." He put down the phone.

"A chick," he said, winking. "Works for Sassoon. You should meet her."

"Yeah?" O'Hara said. "What's her name? Schmidt?"

He turned for the door. His hand on the nob, he looked back. Lenane was refilling his glass at the bar. O'Hara went out without speaking.

SIX

There were three of them sitting in the fourth-floor office with its grime-glazed view of the admiral and Trafalgar Square and the tourists feeding the pigeons. The day was gloomy and the lights were switched on, searching out the details of the grainy carpet, the bank of dull gray filing cabinets, the walls of institution brown, bare of decorations except, inexplicably, a painting of H.M.S. *Repulse.* A vase of daffodils stood on the desk, as frivolous in that spare setting as dance music in a morgue.

They waited, settling themselves, rustling pieces of paper, preparing what they would say, while the girl poured tea from a tarnished silver pot into three cups and set out a plate of biscuits. When she had gone, closing the door behind her, the host, Redder, leaned forward on his desk, locking his fingers under his chin.

"Well, gentlemen," he said quietly, "let's hear from you. The minister has again expressed his displeasure and I have to give him an explanation tonight. He asked to see our appropriation and budget. Only a threat, perhaps, but our masters down the road are becoming nervous about Ulster and we could pay the penalty. Therefore, gentlemen, I need an explanation that will satisfy him and, perhaps more important to you, me."

He had heavy, almost brutal features, but his voice was low and cultivated. He gave the impression of a man who enjoyed his authority.

"LeGault?"

LeGault was prim-lipped, sad-eyed. He was suffering from a cold and he smelled of peppermints. He looked uncomfortable, and not just because of his ailment.

"There is no satisfactory explanation, I'm afraid, sir," he said finally. He shuffled the papers in the file on his lap and looked toward the third man, but there was no help there.

"It was, quite simply, a negative on our part."

"In the registry, or in the field?"

"The registry. There was no time for a field check prior to the selection and by the time we had recovered the ball it was too late. King was in place. The registry relied on army records for background."

"And those records didn't indicate the nature of his father's employment? Really, LeGault." Redder's voice was dangerously soft. He had a genuine horror of incompetence, for it could destroy him. Redder moved easily along the corridors of power, unaffected by the politics of the government whose representatives he served, yet he knew that a single blunder in his sensitive area could expel him into the world of ordinary men where there were no secrets, no hidden controls or influence. He would have said his motive was his country, but that would not have been true, any more than it was for the politicians he served. His real stimulus was power, the ordering of events.

"The records," LeGault said, "failed to develop the father's rank. They said merely that he was a retired army officer."

"Merely a retired brigadier general," Redder said. "With friends in every corner of the War Office."

"Unforgivable," the third man said. It was impossible to tell whether he was apologizing or condemning.

"There was something else," LeGault said. "Prior to the operation, the captain had been detached from his regiment for duty in

Belfast, chiefly because of his counterterror training. In Belfast, he was not known by his fellow officers. He didn't mention his father. Thus, when he was selected for Crossmaglen there was no warning signal from the Ulster command."

"Very well," Redder said. He swiveled his chair and stared across the square in the direction of Whitehall. "There are grenades and stink bombs going off down there," he said. "Embarrassment all around and there's nothing the red tabs hate more than embarrassment."

"The D-notice bled the worst out of it," the third man said. He was the youngest in the room. He had dark, watchful eyes that belied his languid, almost feline, manner. His name was Toby East and his rank was case officer, but his duties extended far beyond that. He sometimes made LeGault and others in the Department uneasy because they sensed a streak of anarchy in his makeup, a disdain for the rules that governed the lives of other men. There were those in the Department who called him the "First Murderer," without mirth, but when he heard about the nickname Toby East grinned, enjoying the classical allusion.

"Thank you for bringing up another aspect of the problem," Redder said. "We've just about used up our D-notice ration. You can't use them like lavatory paper, you know, Toby. Number Ten gets restive and Fleet Street howls."

LeGault allowed himself to relax a fraction. Redder's voice was slower now, more reflective. He had decided how to handle the minister, LeGault thought. Redder was an expert at bureaucratic infighting, had to be. LeGault admired him as a Saturday-night bridge player might admire Goren.

"We could bring in the general," LeGault said. "Give him the treatment, Official Secrets Act and all the rest."

LeGault knew about such things. As the administrator of the office, he was little more than a high-echelon clerk with no ambition to move upward. He was satisfied with the numbing minutiae that lay behind the Department's operations.

Yet because of the nature of the Department's mission, he was privy to plots and murder and the engineering of destruction half a world away. He accepted that as an official in the Ministry of Housing might accept the need to cut back construction.

"The Secrets Act would do it," he said.

"I think not," Redder said. "He made three calls to our chums down the road when he first got the news, but he's been quiet since. He's buried deep in the country—Gloucestershire, didn't you say, LeGault? If he stays there, we'll leave him alone. Let sleeping brass hats lie."

"As you say, sir." LeGault sneezed and apologized.

"Any more protests from the Street of Adventure?" Redder said.

"Only the *Mail*," LeGault said. "But the Wandsworth Common murder case goes to trial at the Bailey tomorrow. Give them another couple of days and they'll have forgotten the D-notice."

"Anyway," East said lazily, "none of them is that interested in Ulster nowadays. Another soldier shot? Oh, dear. Fleet Street thinks it's all become a terrible bore."

Redder nodded and leaned back in his chair. "All right," he said, dismissing the problem. "Brief me on the case."

"The bird is back in its nest," East said. "He left his car at the airport in Dublin. A rented job and we're checking, but we don't expect much from it. He took a morning flight out of Dublin into Kennedy. The Dublin team saw him on board and then the New York team picked him up over there. We've got a light surveillance going."

"Who's looking after him? Smollett?"

"Yes, sir. He's sent us a fairly complete dossier. John Sean O'Hara. Married, no children. He's thirty-five years old and he's a detective working on narcotics with the New York Police Department. Lives in Forest Hills . . ."

"Just a moment, East. Is Langley involved in this in any way?"

"No, sir. You remember you told us to steer clear of the spooks. Smollett's on his own on this one."

"Very well."

"O'Hara's been with the police for nearly fifteen years. One citation of any importance. He's a marksman. Served with the American army in Germany 1960–62."

"Nationality?"

"Oh, American, sir. That's the trouble, of course. Born in New York, then there was a certain amount of toing and froing across the Atlantic. His father ran off when he was a child and his mother took him back to Ireland for a while, then returned to New York. As we know, the trip seems to have become a habit."

Redder finished his tea and pushed away his cup. "Yes," he said. "And a very bad one. Motive?"

"Could be money or principle. I'd suggest principle. The Provos don't have enough money to hire assassins and fly them over for jobs. He's got enough Irish background to take Ulster very seriously. I think we should assume it's a matter of principle, which is bad. Nothing more dangerous than a man of principle who picks up a gun."

"Why do they use O'Hara, d'you think? He's been over at least four times that we know of. That councilor in Londonderry. Pancrass in Belfast. The colonel in London, and now our man."

"His nationality. As far as the Provos are concerned, it's a trump card. And for a number of reasons."

"Go ahead." Redder's eyes were half-closed. They had been through much of this before, except for the identification of O'Hara. Redder was thinking.

"First, there's the enormous advantage of using somebody based three thousand miles away. It reduces his time in hazard. He can come in, do the job, and be away before we know what's happened. He doesn't have to skulk around the back streets, risking a sweep and a visit to Long Kesh. It follows from that, that another danger is eliminated. He has hardly any contacts in the area of the killing ground, no family or friends to let something slip or even turn him in. There are probably only three or four people on this side of the Atlantic who know anything about him, who he is."

East was sprawled in his chair now, his long legs splayed. He spoke in a leisurely fashion, almost sleepily. He could have been describing the unsavory marketing methods of a rival firm.

"Then, of course, there's the matter of his American passport, as we know only too well. He has good cover, a vacationing New Yorker visiting the dear old sod. And if we should be lucky enough to catch him with a smoking gun, the embarrassment between Whitehall and Foggy Bottom would be too awful to contemplate.

"What would we do with him? Toss him behind the wire? A trial, with every civil-liberties lawyer in dear old Yankeeland screaming to high heaven? Oh, my goodness," East said sardonically.

LeGault stirred, reaching for his handkerchief.

"That's why we had to let him go through at Dublin airport," he said. "But we're further forward now. We know who he is and where he is." He blew his nose apologetically.

"Do we have any idea who his contact is in the States?" Redder said.

"Nothing so far, sir. Smollett has his lines out on that."

"All right. Now, do we have his movements in Ireland accounted for?"

"Going out, but not coming in. We first got a sniff of him in Crossmaglen after the job. Probably disposing of the weapon. Incidentally, the ballistics people say it was definitely an AK-47. Same as the other three killings."

"They had it waiting for him when he came in," Redder said. "He hands it back when he's finished."

"Exactly, sir. Again it cuts down the time he's in hazard. As you know, we had static surveillance on the border ever since King was slotted into place. O'Hara was logged over shortly before 2:00 P.M. on the day of the killing. Hired car, side road. Probably already carrying the AK-47. When he came back, he passed through a vehicle control post on the main Dundalk road. Routine search. Nothing. He must have dropped it off almost immediately after doing the job."

East studied his buckskin boots. He was almost lying in his chair now.

"That was the clincher," he said. "He was asked at the border how long he'd been in Ulster. He said two days, whereas we knew it was more like two hours. We got behind him, shepherded him into Dublin and all the way home."

"I wanted to ask you about that. It doesn't make sense, from what we know of the technique. He could have been gone that evening, been back in New York by midnight, their time. Yet he stayed overnight in Dublin."

"There's a woman, sir. He spent the night with a woman."

"Interesting. Who is she?" East had already pulled himself upright and was selecting a paper from a file at his feet.

"A barmaid. A Dublin barmaid. Her name's Mary Bannion, a widow with a twelve-year-old boy. Lives in the Saint Stephens Green area. They went to her place early in the evening and he went from there straight to the airport. Left his car parked at the airport and off he went."

"That *is* interesting," Redder said. His telephone rang.

"Redder," he said. "Yes . . . oh, what a shame . . . I see . . . well, I was looking forward to it, too . . . please give him my regards." He hung up.

"The minister," he said. "Called away to his constituency for the weekend so there'll be no meeting tonight. It sounds as if the pressure is off for the moment. Go on, Toby."

"This Bannion woman has no known connection with the Provos so far as we can find out."

"You think it was an unauthorized side trip?"

"Almost certainly. Very puritanical phase the Provos are going through at the moment. They've broken kneecaps for that sort of thing. They know O'Hara's a married man."

"And they'll know about his overnight stay."

"I'd be surprised if they didn't. Of course, he may be a special case, awarded dispensation because of his value."

"It would be worth probing around that one a bit, Toby. Could be useful."

"The Dublin team's on it now, sir."

"Very well, Keep me informed. Maybe his wife . . ."

"That had occurred to me."

"I'll want you over there, Toby."

"Smollett won't like that. Poaching." East didn't look particularly concerned at the prospect.

"It's your case. You stay with it. Washington's warming to the idea of the economic initiative, God knows why, and we'll have to act before they start signing sheets of paper. But I want it smooth and clean."

"You'll want O'Hara taken out?"

"Of course," Redder said. "But cleanly, Toby. Cleanly."

Peter King, bloodhound, he thought wearily. Well, his eyes were the appropriate color around the rims. He was suffering from the excess of the night before. Why did he do it? He looked out of the plane's port window. Through the drifting cirrus he could see the fields and woods of the Severn Valley. He had ended up in a gambling hell in Belgravia. No, that was earlier. He had ended up in a hotel room with a sulky girl named Charlotte who had talked incessantly about her mummy and what mummy would say if she didn't go home. Mummy, King thought, would be furious.

Unbidden, a memory of Ginny came into his mind. He had telephoned her after filing a story from Montgomery where the Confederate flag flew over the state capitol. That was before Anderson and his cronies, with their modern marketing approaches, took over the paper and benched him on the national desk.

"When are you coming home?" she had asked. It was what she always asked. He could imagine her sitting on the window seat of their apartment, chewing at her nails between puffs at her cigarette.

"Maybe the end of the week," he had said.

"And maybe later," she said. "Oh, Peter, just for once couldn't you take a human being into account?"

It was an old question and he didn't bother to answer it. She saw herself ranged against the paper in competition for him. She never understood it wasn't the paper that drew his loyalty; it was the story.

He wasn't sure what he had said, something about having to carry out the assignment, he supposed now, but he knew it wasn't just that. There had been a stimulation about the work in the South that no liquor, no sex, no drugs could conjure up. It was long gone now, but he could still remember it as if those few years were the height of his experience, watching the dreamer marching to his particular Calvary on a Memphis motel balcony, watching the hoses playing on the sprawled black bodies, watching it all as if it were some circus especially arranged for his entertainment.

Ginny never understood. Sure, she was sympathetic, she thought the blacks should get their rights, but she was too self-involved to understand what drove him in those days, or so he told himself. She had achieved her own liberation, turning her back on her family in a Pennsylvania coal town and on the Catholicism that was their core. She had come to New York because she wanted to be a dancer. She was free. Except that the blood and the faith never released her.

King lived with her because she was beautiful. At first the roller coaster of her highs and lows didn't matter. No relationship was perfect. During her highs, life with her was a party. During the lows, well, she had a credit card and sometimes Bloomingdale's was sufficient therapy.

After five months, though, she still didn't have work beyond the waitressing job where King first met her. She sometimes broke into bouts of weeping, and when he asked what was the matter, she would say she didn't know. That was the trouble.

He had suggested a psychiatrist and she had agreed, but she had never gone to one. She clung to him. When he left for out-of-town assignments she would beg him not to go. It was irrational, he used to think, but that didn't abate the turbulence of their stormy leave-takings.

When he was honest with himself, he knew that he would have broken with her within a month except for the relationship that bound them, which had everything to do with bed and nothing to do with love, or perhaps even liking.

During their seven months together, he had come to suspect that the heart of her problem was guilt at her rejection of her parents and their attitudes and, perhaps more important, the Church. She was God-haunted still, he had seen, only too aware that she was living in a state of mortal sin.

He had been in Alabama, watching an illiterate governor bar the way to a house of learning, when she telephoned him. She was in the midst of one of her crying fits. She begged him to come back to her. She talked of suicide, not for the first time. Yes, he said, he would be back the next day, and he meant it.

But then they had shot Medgar Evers in the carport of his home, shot him from the shadows, and King had been offered a seat on a chartered light plane leaving immediately and he hadn't hesitated, not on a story like this, and he hadn't telephoned Ginny to warn her because what could he say? It would have been absurd. She would have expected him to walk away from the biggest story of the day and he would have refused. He couldn't have abandoned the story just because she was suffering from one of her depressions. And so he had gone to Jackson with Sitton and Fleming and the rest of the carousel whirling around the circus.

By the time they reached Jackson the demonstrations had started and the blacks were being shipped off to the detention pens in the fairgrounds and a few days later there was the funeral, followed by rock throwing and fixed bayonets on National Guard rifles, and the town could have burned down except for that cool character from the Justice Department who managed, God knows how, to bring them all to their senses. King was on page one every day for a week.

When, finally, he returned to New York, he found her. She had hung herself from a hook on the door of their bedroom. She had left no note, but she must have been hanging there for days. You didn't need a pathologist to tell that.

It was after that return home that the dreams started. The feet bumping on the door, the head like a moon. And he began to drink because the alcohol acted as an anesthetic against the dreams, at least sometimes it did. Then came Anderson and his obsequious followers and King didn't go out of town anymore.

In the depression of his hangover, he began to wonder why he was going to Ulster. Perhaps Joy was right. His brother was dead and that was all that mattered. Would it make him, the family, any happier to know how Martin died? Was guilt spurring his pilgrimage to Ulster? He hadn't seen Martin in nearly five years. Hadn't written in a year. They had gone their own ways and weeks had passed without King giving his brother a thought. Martin used to send him a card or letter on his birthday, but that had ended, what, five or six years ago. King had never sent his brother even a card. Not lack of affection, he thought. Just laziness. He didn't like writing letters. It was a burden. He thought of Ginny and the old pain returned. She had been a burden, too.

Perhaps it was curiosity that drew him toward Ulster. It was a strong emotion. The thought of honor entered his mind. Honor? Honor bound? These days, that was a very old-fashioned concept. Probably the last time he had heard the word used seriously was in school and that was a long time ago. Had he believed in it, even then? He couldn't remember.

Martin did, he was sure of that. Fifty years ago, Martin would have been considered a very ordinary man, like his father. Today, though, it was different. He would be considered extraordinary because he believed in words like *duty* and *country* and in family strengths and sacrifice. King didn't know why he was different than his brother, but he was.

The Trident came into Aldergrove and King remembered the story of the London politician who had been put in charge of Ulster affairs. After his first tour of inspection, the politician had taken a seat in his London-bound plane and said, "What a bloody awful country. Bring me the biggest Scotch you've got." Well, here it was.

Hercules troop transports, helicopters, Saracen and Ferret armored cars were scattered around the tarmac, which was enclosed by a double wire fence like a concentration camp. Soldiers in flak jackets and carrying automatic rifles stood or leaned against the walls of the airport buildings watching the plane as it drew up, close to the terminal.

Security men were waiting. They stared with cold eyes at the arriving passengers, took two men and a woman away. King had reserved a rented car before leaving London and, while the baggage was being delivered to the carousel, he went to claim it. The girl told him it would be awaiting him at the end of the temporary walkway that kept nontravelers and ambitious Provo bombers away from the terminal building.

Sometimes, she said, the Provisionals brought up trucks, loaded with sand, which they used as launching pads for mortar assaults; but their aim wasn't good. She talked about the Provos as though they were an inescapable act of God, a fault running through the earth's crust.

King didn't go into Belfast. He turned his Hillman Avenger onto the motorway leading to Hillsborough and the south. He had decided to go directly to Crossmaglen. He would talk to the army later. The answer lay in Crossmaglen.

The army, however, talked to him first. Five miles south of Hillsborough, three Saracens were parked, two on one side of the highway, the third on the other, to form a narrow chicane. As King stopped, a paratroop sergeant, an Armalite strapped to his wrist, went to the driver's side. A paratrooper covered King with an automatic rifle from the right of the sergeant.

"Get out. Sir," the sergeant said. The term of respect was an epithet on his lips. He wore camouflage fatigues and a red beret, which ran to a peak over his left eye. He looked angry.

"What's the matter?" King said.

"Out. Now. Sir."

King shrugged and stepped out into a cold wind sweeping down from the north.

"Face the car, hands on the roof. Sir."

King turned to obey. He felt his feet being roughly kicked further apart; then a moment later hands went carefully up and down his body.

"Sorry, mate," a voice murmured. "Sergeant don't like this work. Wants to run around shooting off his gun. Thinks he's Gary Cooper." King realized it was the soldier, not the sergeant, who was searching him. The man had a Liverpool accent. Another paratrooper had appeared from behind one of the Saracens to inspect the car while the sergeant watched him. The third man opened the trunk and the hood, then opened King's suitcase and felt through his spare clothes. The soldier who had searched him was on his back on the ground, staring up at the underside of the car. The sergeant came back.

"Identification," he said. King showed him his passport and his New York press card.

"You work for an American paper?"

"Yes."

"Fucking Americans," the sergeant said. "Why do they do it? What's it to them?"

"Do what?"

"Send money over so the Paddies can get guns and shoot us in the back."

"I don't know." But the sergeant's question had an impact. It was the first time since his brother's death that King had thought that IRA fund raising in America might have bought the gun that killed Martin. There was a columnist on his paper, McEvoy, who was always ranting about the brutal British soldiers and the bravery of the gunmen who went out to fight them and the need for Irish-Americans to support the hard men with dollars.

"You don't know," the sergeant said. "Don't give a shit, either, I expect. What are you up to over here, writing stories for your paper?"

"Touring. I'm on vacation." The revelation that somebody would come to his war for a vacation silenced the sergeant. He stared at King for a moment, then abruptly turned away. His men had finished their examination of the Hillman and another two cars had pulled up, awaiting their turn. As King slid back behind the wheel, he could hear the sergeant shouting, "Out. Sir." He wondered how many Irishmen had signed up with the Provos after encountering British soldiers like the sergeant.

In Newry, a line of armored cars was drawn up outside the police barracks, which was swathed to the roof in barbed wire. Humps had been built into the roadway to slow vehicles carrying anybody tempted to toss a bomb at the barracks. A machine-gun post covered the main road. In Bessbrook, it was the same, the wire sweeping up the stone walls of the barracks. King saw burned-out bars and bomb-shattered old Georgian terraces.

There was a helicopter pad outside the barracks in a housing estate and there was continual noise from helicopter engines. People didn't look up. This was border country. It looked to King as though the army had to struggle constantly to prevent the border moving inexorably north, pushed by the force of republicanism from the south.

Ahead was Forkhill and Crossmaglen and the frontier, which leaked guns and explosives. As King approached bridges over culverts and streams, he saw tracks where armored vehicles had left the roadway and gone across the fields to traverse the waterways at a distance from the suspect bridges. He wondered if the arches were still mined. And so, past the white farmhouses and the stone walls and the fields with their outcroppings of rock and past the granite thrust of Slieve Gullion, King came to Crossmaglen, "the capital of the free state of South Armagh." Bloody Armagh.

It was a gray and melancholy place. The bitterness and the hatred it encompassed seemed to seep out of the pores of its bricks and mortar to muffle the noises that would be thrown up by an ordinary town. As King drove in, he saw a patrol of Fusiliers on the move. Only one man would stir at a time so that his buddies, watchful in doorways and against walls for snipers, could cover him. They wore shrapnel-proof jerkins and carried high-velocity rifles, the picture of men at war, and yet women pushing baby carriages walked by them with no more than a glance.

The center of the town was marked by a square surrounded by two-story buildings and dominated by a fire-gutted town hall. The Republican flag flew from the blackened tower. Every few minutes, it seemed the clatter of helicopters scythed through the quiet sadness of the place. He came to the barracks. The walls were spotted with bullet marks and darkened by the stain of petroleum bombs. Within the perimeter overlooking the walls stood a machine-gun nest on twenty-foot stilts. Piled sandbags left only a narrow slit for the marksman inside.

Scrawled on the metal surrounding the stilts by some disconsolate soldier were the words

> *We are the unwilling*
> *Sent by the unqualified*
> *To do the unacceptable*
> *For the ungrateful*

There were holes, made by rockets, in the metal. On ground level, a wall of sandbags formed a passage ten feet deep between the roadway and the walls of the barracks. The guard post, made from zinc sheeting reinforced with sandbags and barbed wire, stood to the right of the main gate. It was Beau Geste stuff, only this desert was dank and green.

King looked at it all and now he could understand better how his brother came to die. This was hostile territory, a battleground with not even a veneer of normalcy. If Martin had been on special duty here, where men with guns in their hands would not move without cover, then his last days must have been perilous indeed. He thought of the schoolboy crying because the squirrel he wanted as a pet had bitten him. He couldn't place his brother in this place. Even though Martin had become a soldier, King had always thought of him as a gentle man and there was no place for gentleness here.

Dusk was softening the gray outlines of Crossmaglen. He started to look for a bar. He needed a drink.

By nine o'clock, King was well on the way. He could feel the alcohol doing its work, driving the chill out of him and bringing the welcome blur to his head. The owner said his name was Pat. He was friendly enough, but at first he was too busy serving the old men in the snug to talk. It seemed that the older customers sat in the snug while the younger ones stood around in the lounge where King leaned against the bar. No soldiers entered the pub.

Finally, Pat came to where King stood.

"Cold weather, we're having," he said. His accent seemed to owe more to Dublin than to the north.

"It's cold," King agreed. He could tell the man was curious, was trying to catch his accent. "You still need a coat."

"They're talking about rain again tomorrow."

"You're used to that, I expect."

"Oh, we are that. You'd be just visiting, would you?"

"Just visiting," King said. "Somebody I know was living down here."

"Yes? Who would that be?"

King hesitated. He hadn't thought how to handle it. Plunge in and see what happened? Before he could answer the landlord was called away to the other end of the bar where a group of men in their twenties had gathered. After a moment he glanced toward them and saw that one of them was talking quietly to the landlord while the others stared openly at King. He guessed they were asking who he was. He nodded at them and they turned away. The landlord headed for the snug.

When he returned to his side of the bar, he immediately reopened the conversation.

"A bit quiet tonight," he said.

"Where are the soldiers?" King asked. "I'd have thought they'd have given you plenty of business."

"They don't come in here," Pat said. He was a gnomelike man with compressed lips that barely opened when he talked.

"Oh?"

"They're welcome, but they don't come in. You want another one?" King nodded.

"Not much for them to do around here," he said. "I'd have thought they'd be glad of a pint." Down the bar, the group was quiet, listening. There was a tension now, but King hardly noticed it. He felt the glow of the drink.

"Perhaps they have orders to stay away," Pat said. "They're busy men, the soldiers, keeping us under control."

"They've got their job to do, I suppose. They probably don't like all this."

"They're all volunteers now," Pat said. "They all joined the British army because they wanted to, not because they had to."

"Perhaps," King said. "But if they didn't have enough volunteers, the government would draft men so what's the difference?"

King could feel the hostility, from Pat and from the men down the bar, but he didn't care. He swallowed his Scotch and pushed the glass across for a refill. The landlord hesitated, then took the glass. King didn't care if they didn't like him because he didn't like them or their sad little town. Or their country, he thought, remembering again the comment of the London politician returning home. It suddenly came to him. My God, these were the sort of men who had killed his brother, these men or their friends in this town. Anger reached him through the veil of alcohol.

"Volunteers or not," he said, "the soldiers don't shoot men in the back and run away and hide." He didn't know whether Martin had been shot in the back, but by now he had an image of his brother walking alone down a street while a man in a raincoat appeared from the shadows behind him, a revolver in his hand. The man was raising his gun.

"The British army's shit." The voice came from the group down the bar. The group seemed closer now as if they all had side-stepped two paces toward him.

"Now, Mickey," the landlord said.

"I said it's shit." The speaker was moving closer, a burly youngster in blue jeans, a shirt open at the neck, and a leather jacket. A tumble of black curls fell over his forehead and at the side of his head merged into blue jowls. Black Irish, the blood of a Spanish sailor from the lost Armada in his veins and still fighting the English.

"Ah, one of the hard men," King said. "Shot anybody in the back lately, Paddy?"

It was ridiculous, he thought, like a hundred movie showdowns in a hundred Western barrooms. What was he supposed to do, go over and empty the man's glass on the floor of the bar? Then reach for his six-shooter?

But he could understand how it could be that way. The anger was solid in him now, and spreading. He wished his eyes would focus better. Was his speech slurring?

"Who are you, anyway?" the black-haired man demanded. "Another English spy, is that it? We know how to deal with them, boyo." Pat had vanished from behind the bar. King wondered if he was coming round to break it up, but there was no sign of him. A couple of men from the group turned away and went out of the lounge. He had the sense of things happening out of his sight.

He said the words, knowing they would precipitate the inevitable action.

"If you forgot your gun and can't shoot me in the back, Paddy, go home or I'll kick your bottom for you." Jesus, he thought, a barroom brawl. He hadn't meant this to happen. Behind them, he saw the door open and an old man start to enter. The newcomer swiftly took in the scene, muttered, "Holy hell," and retreated back through the door.

They came at him in a rush, the black-haired one at their head. There were four of them. He caught the words "fucking Englishman," and he managed to hit one of them in the throat, another in the belly, and then they had him, his arms behind his back, the smell of their beer and excitement in his nostrils. They started to hit him.

Trying to free his arms, he sank to the floor in the hope his weight would drag them down. But, grouped around him, they let him go. They started kicking him. "This is for the men behind the wire," one of them chanted. Every time he said the word *wire* King felt the thud of a boot.

When they had had enough, they pulled him to his feet. One of the boots had caught him on the forehead and something warm was trickling into his right eye, but the worst pain was in his gut and lower back.

He was gasping for breath and yet every breath shot pain into him. They searched him. The second time that day, and he remembered the angry sergeant south of Hillsborough. Why wasn't the sergeant here where he was needed with his Armalite and his random hostility? His mind was cloudy with alcohol and pain. He felt a hand reach into his inner breast pocket and remove his wallet. One of the men who had left before the fight came back. He looked at King as if he regretted missing it. He went to the curly-haired man and whispered urgently to him. Mickey nodded. King thought he heard the words "McCarthy" and "into his car."

Pat was back in the lounge now. "Get him out of here," he said. "I don't want this sort of trouble in my bar." He pointed to the door like the father of some violated virgin. King was bent over, barely able to keep on his feet, but they turned him toward the door and he went, feeling the breath laboring into his lungs. He saw the man called Mickey was carrying his wallet. Outside, a cold drizzle was falling.

"This your car?" They must have known the Hillman was his, for without waiting for an answer they bundled him into the driver's seat and slammed the door. Mickey went around and sat in the passenger seat next to him. The rest grouped around the driver's window, staring in. Mickey took out King's passport.

"King," he announced. "Peter David King. Born Gloucestershire, England, July 24, 1942. Fucking Englishman." The driver's window was down and he read out to the men outside, "Country of residence, U.S.A. He lives in America."

"English spy," one of the men said. Holding the wheel of the car, King looked out of the windows. It felt better sitting down. The streets, slick with wet, were dark and empty. No soldiers now.

"Hey, Mickey," one of the men outside started, "King. Wasn't that the name of the feller they took out—"

"Shut up," Mickey said. He looked at King. "Your brother was he, or something?"

King, his breath coming easier now, nodded.

"They killed him," he said. He discovered it also hurt when he talked.

"Yes, I heard about him," Mickey said. "Somebody shot him, up Forkhill way. You're here because of him?"

King nodded again. "They murdered him," he said.

It was bizarre. It was as though they had spent all their fury on him and were content. Like an amnesty. It was almost peaceful inside the car. He knew they were going to let him go.

"Sorry about your brother," Mickey said.

"Why are you sorry? He was English and you kill the English over here."

Mickey ignored the combative note in King's voice. "I told you I'm sorry about him," he said. "Now, leave it alone. This is a dangerous area. You shouldn't have come here."

One of the men outside said, "Okay, Mickey, let's go."

"All right, boyo," he said to King. "Best thing for you is to go down to the barracks and spend the night there, then get on the road in the morning. There's those around Crossmaglen who won't be as easy on you as us. Understand?"

"I think I'll stick around."

"That's up to you, but you'd be best off in the barracks tonight. There's nowhere else to stay." Mickey's voice was almost solicitous.

"All right. How do I get there?" He would talk to the 'army; he should have gone straight to them.

Mickey gave him directions and slid out of his side of the Hillman. With the door still open, he paused and poked his head back in.

"If I was you," he said, "I'd not get out of the car until you're safe in the barracks. 'Specially after dark, like it is. All right?"

King stared at him. Twenty minutes earlier, Mickey had been putting his boot into King's ribs. Now he was wet-nursing him. He shrugged, started the engine and put on the lights. The last he saw of Mickey and his buddies, they were walking off in a bunch down the street.

His headlights threw a white light on the wire that surrounded the walls of the barracks like a gigantic cat's cradle. Beyond the barricade, he could see movement and then a soldier, an automatic rifle in his hands, stepped forward.

"Put out those bloody headlights," somebody shouted. "Or I'll shoot them out." King switched them off. The soldier came to his window. He was a chunky man wearing a beret and combat fatigues.

"Identification," he said. King handed over his passport and his press card. The soldier examined them and handed them back.

"Are they expecting you?" he said, like a martial butler.

King shook his head. "I got into a bit of trouble down at the pub," he said. He pointed to his forehead where they had kicked him. "I need somewhere to sleep."

"Stay where you are," the soldier said. King could now make out the badge of the Fusiliers. His gun still at the ready, the man retreated back through a narrow path between a wire barricade. King felt as if he were marooned in the no-man's-land between two armies.

When the soldier returned, he had a young lieutenant at his side. The officer had the slightly disheveled, irritated look of a man whose slumber had been disturbed.

"Who are you?" he demanded. King again passed his press card and passport through the window. The lieutenant examined them.

"Where have you come from?"

"Belfast," King said. "Then I stopped for a drink down the road. Bit of a punchup, I'm afraid."

"In Crossmaglen? You were in a pub in Crossmaglen?" He leaned forward and King guessed he was trying to smell his breath. King began to feel annoyed.

"Listen," he said, "if you can't give me somewhere to sleep for the night, say so and I'll be on my way." The lieutenant ignored him. He turned to the soldier.

"Do a walkaround," he said. The Fusilier, his weapon still pointing in King's general direction, began to walk around the car at a distance of about ten feet.

"Not enough light, sir," he called. The lieutenant stepped back from the car and shouted, "Lights." Almost immediately, a beam of light shot out from the elevated machine-gun nest, centering on the Hillman. King was dazzled.

"What the hell's going on?" he demanded. Again the officer ignored him, but then he said very quietly, "Stay just where you are, if you don't mind. Don't move." He was looking toward the bottom of the driver's door. He had moved and was about six feet from King.

"Roberts," the lieutenant said, "come here." The Fusilier joined him and they stood there, staring down at the side of the car. "Don't move," the officer said to King again.

"It's attached to the bottom of the door," the soldier said. "Jesus Christ."

"What's attached . . . ?" King began. He could see the tension in the faces of the two men outside.

"Put quite simply," the lieutenant said, "there's a bomb under your car."

"Sir," the soldier said, "shall I fetch the captain?"

"Yes, do that please." The soldier vanished from the cone of light.

"It's probably wired to the door," the lieutenant said pleasantly. "Open the door and . . ."

Everything that followed assumed a heightened intensity for King. It was as though the fumes of alcohol had been swept away to be replaced by an impossibly brilliant magnification of his senses. He could smell the liquor on his own breath, the leather in the car, the gas in the tank. The driving wheel in his hands felt smooth and hard as it had never felt before. The night sounds came to him with exaggerated clarity, the distant clatter of a helicopter, the rustle of leaves and the noise of orders, urgent but controlled, from inside the fort.

"You're fortunate," the lieutenant said, as if in mockery of his plight. But then he went on, "There's a bomb disposal man in the barracks tonight. Captain Cray. He'll take care of this. No problem."

King realized the man was talking to him, almost crooning, trying to keep him calm, trying to instill some confidence.

Cray was a tall, balding man wearing gray slacks and a hacking jacket over a polo neck sweater. He was carrying a workbox like a plumber on assignment to deal with frozen pipes.

"Good evening to you," he said as he approached King. "Don't stir. Don't sneeze. Don't pick your nose. Nothing."

"Booby trap," the lieutenant said.

"Oh," Cray said. "How do you know that?"

"You can see it. Under the door there."

Cray vanished from King's view to kneel at the side of the car.

"I say again, how do you know it's a booby trap, Lieutenant?" Cray's voice issued weirdly from below the door.

"I've seen them before. There was an abandoned farmhouse on the Forkhill—"

"Well, you're a better man than me, Gunga Din," Cray said, still out of King's sight. "How d'you know it's not a timed device? A little clock ticking away in there? There's a wind on the heath, brother, tarah tarah."

"Sorry, sir." The lieutenant was offended.

"Yes, well, you may be right," Cray said abstractedly. "Wired to the door perhaps? Life is very sweet, brother, who would wish to die? Don't know if I've got the lines right, but I like them anyway. George Borrow."

He stood up and walked to the other side of the car. He seemed to be humming softly. He stared down again. "Tell them to put out that searchlight," he said finally. "I have a flashlight. And better send out a patrol, Lieutenant. I don't want to be picked off by some ambitious Paddy who wants to make a name for himself."

He vanished again from King's view to peer up at the underside of the car on the passenger's side. The light from the machine-gun post went out and King could see nothing, not even his hands in front of him, until his eyes refocused. He could feel the sweat coming from his armpits, draining down his sides. A patrol, men with black-greased faces and leopardskin-patterned fatigues, broke out of the barricade and went padding past on rubber-soled boots.

They stared curiously at King, sitting motionless in the Hillman, and then they were past him in the darkness.

Cray reappeared at King's window. "All right," he said, "now, young man, perhaps you'll tell me how you got yourself into this interesting situation."

King knew how they'd done it. He remembered the way the men from the bar had gathered at his window while Mickey went through his wallet at his side. He could imagine the bomb layer kneeling among their feet, attaching the device to the car under the chassis.

"For Chrissake," he said, "what does it matter how I got here? Get me out. Or do something about the bomb before the fucker goes off." He spoke still staring ahead, still motionless. He was getting a cramp in his right leg.

"I can understand your concern," Cray said with careful formality. "But, you see, if we're going to remove you from danger then we must know how the situation arose." The rain was coming harder now, streaming down Cray's balding pate and dripping off his eyebrows. It struck King as ironic that Cray and the soldiers were getting uncomfortably soaked while he remained dry. Yet he was the one trapped a few inches away from a primed explosive. He yearned for the feel of the rain on his face.

"I got into a fight at a pub," King said. "They knocked me about, then they took me out and put me in the car and suggested I come here. That's it."

"Which side did you get in?"

"This side. One of the Irishmen sat in the passenger's seat alongside me for a few moments. The rest of them stayed outside."

"How long did you sit there? Before they sent you off." Cray reminded King even more of a plumber now, slightly aggrieved as he asked the homeowner how the pipes came to be frozen.

"Two or three minutes," he said. "No more than five minutes."

"All right," Cray said, "that helps. They didn't have time to do anything sophisticated. That is, so long as they hadn't already set it up before they brought you out to the car. There's always that possibility. Of course, you can never tell with bombs. They're temperamental, especially the homemade variety."

"Jesus," King said. His nerves were screaming. "Do something instead of standing around as if you're at a town hall meeting."

"Be quiet," Cray said. "If you go up, I go as well. Let me think."
He vanished from King's sight and King knew he was back on the
ground examining the bomb with his flashlight. The lieutenant was
standing about twelve feet away, watching. Why didn't he get away,
King thought. He wasn't doing any good there, displaying his fortitude.

Cray reappeared. "No sign of any wiring to the other door," he
said. "First, let's see if we can get you out of there. This is what I
want you to do."

What he wanted King to do was move over to the passenger's seat
and leave the car by the passenger's door.

"I want you to move slowly and carefully," Cray said. "I can't hear
any ticking from the infernal machine so it's probable that the
detonator is connected to the bottom of the door. Open the door
and you make the contact and it all goes up. If you drove here,
there's a good chance that movement alone won't detonate it. All
right, when you're ready."

He started to move back toward the lieutenant, keeping his front
facing the car. He paused, then returned to King.

"What's your name?" he asked.

"Peter King."

"All right, Mr. King. You'd better give me your identification
papers." King handed his passport through the window. Beautiful,
he thought. If I go up, at least they can identify the corpse. "I'll go
around the other side," Cray said, "and see you out through the
door."

"No need for both of us to risk it," King said. He said it, but he
didn't mean it. At that moment, he didn't give a damn about Cray.

"Well, I might be of some help," Cray said vaguely. He tossed
King's passport to the lieutenant and went around the front of the
Hillman to the passenger's side.

King began to move.

He kept his hands on the wheel. He raised his left leg and pushed
it over to his left. Damn gear shift. He could feel his weight pressing
down hard on the seat above the bomb. What was it? Gelignite?
Dynamite? Mickey, with his concern for King's safety. Mickey the

killer. He took his hands from the wheel. He stretched his left arm out along the back of the passenger's seat. He could see Cray staring in at him. The bomb-disposal man said something, but King couldn't hear. The window on the passenger side was closed. Very slowly he edged his buttocks to the left side of the seat. Now he was almost straddling the center of the car. He put his right arm along the top of the driver's seat. He was already thinking about the passenger door. Suppose Cray was wrong. Suppose they had somehow managed to wire it. Suppose nothing. Get on with it. His hands, pressing on the top of the seats, were slick with sweat. He could feel the dampness along his hairline.

Newspaper stories came back to him. IRA bomb makers blowing themselves up. IRA bombers driving through city streets, bombs in their laps, and then the blue flash and the hurtling flesh minced by metal splinters. "You never can tell with bombs," Cray had said.

He pressed down with both hands and lifted himself completely from the driver's seat. He was splayed like a spider, his buttocks over the stubby gearshift. He shifted his weight to his left leg and very slowly sank into the passenger seat. He felt better. He felt better now, even if the risk of the car going up remained unaltered. Probably it was his genitals. However absurd, there was a particular horror in the subconscious thought that if the explosive detonated it was his genitals that would take the most shattering impact. Not that he would know anything about it.

He could make out what Cray was saying now. Cray wanted to know if he should open the door from the outside. It was the last hurdle.

King realized that, for the moment at least, control of the situation had passed to him. He was the one who had to act while the army watched. However reluctant, he was the star. He shook his head at Cray. He said, "Go away," then realized Cray couldn't hear him. He looked through the glass and mouthed the words twice. Finally Cray understood. He hesitated, shrugged, and retreated a dozen steps.

King put his hand on the door lever. The door lever wouldn't be connected, he was sure of that. No, he was sure of nothing. No thinking. Just do it. He pressed down.

He opened the door.

Cray was smiling at him. "Good boy," he said softly.

King pushed the door further open. He put his left leg out, then his right. "Slowly," Cray said. "Slowly."

King put his weight on his feet, stood up and walked away. He felt the rain on his head and looked up to let it soak his face. It felt good. Euphoria swept over him. In the car he had been stripped down to essentials. Life. Survival. Nothing else. Nothing else had mattered. Now the very breath he was sucking into his lungs tasted sweet and precious. For the first time since they had told him there was a bomb under him he felt again the pain from the beating in the pub. The pain felt good, too. It meant he was alive. The poor man's Descartes, he thought with buoyant self-derision.

"Sandbags," Cray shouted. "Quick as you like. Sandbags down here."

King went to the bomb-disposal man.

"Thanks," he said.

"Yes, well," Cray said. "That's all right then."

"What about a drink?" King needed a drink badly.

"Later, perhaps," Cray said. "I've not finished here yet."

Soldiers were coming through the barricade carrying sandbags. They began to pile them around the car at a distance of about two feet. They worked without direction as if they had done it before. The light in the machine-gun nest was switched on again so that once more the scene was eerily illuminated.

"You'd better get inside," Cray said. "No point in getting wet out here and you may suffer some reaction."

"I want to watch." King's eyes were on the Hillman. Before, it had just been another saloon car. Now, it looked sinister, as if awaiting a victim.

"Up to you," Cray said and he went around to the driver's side of the car. He seemed to be examining the door again.

"It's not locked, is it?" he called to King, who shook his head. The lieutenant joined him.

"Thanks for spotting it," King said. "Bit of luck."

"Not really. They tried it before up in Lurgan, only with a van. Taped the bomb under the door, just like they did with you. So we've been looking out for repeat performances. Not very original, the Paddies."

"What happened?"

"The driver stopped to take a leak. He opened the door and was blown to smithereens. So was the side of a public lavatory."

Cray had gone through the barricade back into the barracks. When he reappeared he was carrying a length of wire and he wore a raincoat over his soaking clothes. Too late, King thought. It had almost stopped raining.

"They booby-trap everything," the lieutenant said. "Milk churns, houses, cars, bridges. Half the bridges around here are mined. They sit and wait until an army vehicle goes over them, then they push the plunger and—boom. Bastards."

Half an hour later, a wall of sandbags five feet high surrounded the Hillman. Cray had attached the wire to the handle on the outside of the driver's door and run the length back behind the sandbags. He seemed to be singing. King listened. It was "Nearer My God to Thee." In the darkness beyond the floodlit scene, King caught glimpses of the black-faced patrol in doorways and against walls. Some crouched, some stood. All were watching the windows of the silent houses that overlooked the front of the barracks. King and the lieutenant walked back until they were at a corner, fifty feet from the car and the sandbags.

Cray now wore a steel helmet and he had replaced his raincoat with a shrapnel-proof jerkin. He looked like an actor on stage in a World War I drama about trench warfare. He was still singing. Peering around the corner, King felt as if he were watching from the wings. The whole thing had a theatrical flavor.

Cray crouched tightly against the sandbags on the driver's side and went from King's sight. Nothing happened for more than five minutes. King could imagine the bomb-disposal man pulling on his wire, fishing for the door catch like a late-night poacher.

The violet flash came first. Then the noise, a shattering roar that burst out of the piled sandbags. Then the metal began coming down like grapeshot. Then the dust, a great cloud of it rising through the beam of light from the machine-gun post.

Out of it all, Cray came walking toward them, taking off his steel helmet. He was no longer singing. He looked tired, like a workman on his way home after heavy labor.

"It's a funny old world we live in, but the world's not entirely to blame," he said. "All right. Now let's see if we can find that drink."

SEVEN

Two days before King reached Crossmaglen, two letters were mailed across the Atlantic to New York. One, sent from Dublin, was addressed to Detective John O'Hara at the Three-Two precinct. The other, bearing a London postmark and unsigned, was addressed to O'Hara's wife at their home in Forest Hills. Through the vagaries of the mail, the letter to O'Hara's wife, Ellen, reached her twenty-four hours before the other letter arrived at the precinct. O'Hara did not see his letter from Dublin until he went to the stationhouse the following day.

O'Hara was off duty and sleeping late when the letter to his wife arrived. She read it in the kitchen, sat thinking for a few moments, then telephoned the restaurant across the street from the Queens Criminal Court building where she had a part-time job as hostess for the lunch trade. She said she was feeling ill and would not be able to work. She put the telephone down, slipped the letter into her purse, and went out. She took the subway to Manhattan, where she got off at Forty-second Street and transferred to the southbound

IRT, which carried her to the City Hall stop. She walked the few blocks to a lawyer's office on Worth Street.

When she got home, O'Hara, unshaven and wearing slacks and a sweater, was watching television in the living room with the drapes half drawn to block out the thin early spring sunshine. He had eaten a hamburger and there was a can of beer at his elbow. She didn't mention the letter from London and they exchanged only a few words. She said there had been more customers than usual at the restaurant, but he hardly heard her. He was half asleep.

Later in the afternoon, O'Hara roused himself, shaved, and went to the local gas station to pick up his Rambler, which he had put in the night before for an oil change.

When he came back to the house, he sat in front of the television set again and was still watching when the network news program came on at seven o'clock. The first item was about a corruption investigation in Washington that seemed to be going nowhere. He paid it little attention. He was thinking about Lenane. Most of the time now he thought about Lenane and Internal Affairs. He tried not to because every time he did his thoughts led him into a maze from which there was no escape. There was nothing he could do. Even so, he couldn't stop thinking about Lenane. They were back on duty together, acting as a back-up team, but the atmosphere between them was foul with suspicion. Outside the words necessary to do the job, they didn't talk. O'Hara had thought of requesting a new partner, but they might give him Twinkletoes or some other rat fink. At least he knew Lenane.

During the last section of the news program, O'Hara's attention was drawn to the screen by the anchorman's reference to Dublin and the visit there of New York's senior senator, Jay McCloud, to receive an award from a human-rights organization.

McCloud came from the Bensonhurst section of Brooklyn. O'Hara had seen him once, campaigning in Elmhurst. He was a black-browed Irish-American who, armed with a good war record with the marines, had come up through the Democratic clubhouses, gone to Washington first as a congressman with a huge plurality, then six years later been returned as a senator. That was ten years ago.

During his political career, McCloud had never deviated from the Sinn Fein line that was the article of faith of any Irish-American politician who wished to survive in New York. McCloud never missed the Saint Patrick's Day parade up Fifth Avenue, wearing his badge: "England Get Out Of Ireland." He could be counted on at every dinner of the Ancient Order of Hibernians. That was how it always was.

Until six months ago.

In the previous October, McCloud and New York's Irish-American cardinal, Patrick Moran, had issued a joint statement condemning the violence in Ulster. The statement criticized all those involved in the strife—the Protestants, the British, and the Provisional wing of the IRA. To an outsider, it would have seemed unexceptional, a justified plea for peace. To Irish republicans, it was outrageous heresy. It specifically urged Americans not to send relief funds to Northern Ireland. It said, as the British had long claimed, that the money was being used for guns and explosives that were being smuggled into Catholic strongholds and then employed on the streets of Belfast and Londonderry.

Political analysts had suggested that the driving force behind the composition of the statement was Jay McCloud, rather than the cardinal, although they were unable to explain satisfactorily the reason for the policy change that appeared to imperil his political base.

There was no film from Dublin, but the screen showed a stock black and white picture of McCloud. He was smiling.

O'Hara stared at the picture, hating the man. While he had been risking his life for the cause, as hundreds of men before him had risked theirs, McCloud in the comfort of his privilege had turned his back on the martyrs and the heroes. Worse, he had attacked them as if he were an Englishman or an Orangeman. So had the cardinal.

O'Hara rarely thought of himself as a hero or as a potential martyr, although he would have accepted the description. The killings he had carried out in England and in Ireland were executions ordered by the leaders of the Ulster brigades and he, as a soldier, was merely following orders. They were jobs that had to be done, just as other

Irishmen had felt compelled to pick up guns in 1916 and in the 1920s to meet force with force.

He did not think of himself as an assassin, would not have recognized the word in connection with his work. He would have assaulted anybody who dared place him in the company of Lee Harvey Oswald or Sirhan Sirhan. They were psychotics. He was a soldier.

The anchorman was gazing into the camera, reading what McCloud had said at the dinner before he received his citation. O'Hara stared back. He could feel the fury washing over him.

The senator had attacked the Provisional wing of the IRA, describing them as killers, fomentors of death and destruction, perverters of children, fanatics struggling in a blind alley of hatred. "The senator said that the Provos could not exist without financial aid from the United States," the anchorman read. "He appealed to Americans to halt their fund raising for the IRA and instead to work for peace."

"Traitor," O'Hara said. "Fucking Irish traitor." He sat there while the announcer was replaced by a commercial. They had to do something. This senator and his comrade-in-betrayal, the cardinal, they would cut the lifeline of supplies, freeze the movement into immobility and frustration. The impact of their infamy was overwhelming. Jesus Christ, something had to be done about them.

"Filthy traitors," he said. Savagely, he remembered all the other betrayals of the dream, Mulcahy and Michael Collins and the rest Cahill had described as part of his education. The British must have bought off the pair of them. But how? Not money, but there must be other things. Somebody had to take care of them.

In his fury, he went to the telephone and called Cahill, but the inspector wasn't in his office. His assistant said he was at a police conference in Buffalo. He would be back the next day. "Who was calling?"

"Never mind," O'Hara said. He hung up and began to pace restlessly. Everything in his life was fucked up. Lenane. He knew for certain Lenane had ratted on him. Maybe he shouldn't have said anything to the prick. Maybe he should have let Lenane wear the wire with him and then he could have said things that would have cleared him with Internal Affairs, maybe even put Lenane further in the shit. Hell, it was too late for that now. Lenane would never bother with a wire anymore.

Nothing was happening. That was what was getting to him. They were just letting him stand there, the rope around his neck, until they were ready to kick the chair from under him and let him swing. Cahill. Cahill never seemed to be available anymore and when he was, he was vague about developments at headquarters, if there were any. He said he was still working on it. O'Hara shouldn't contact him unless it was absolutely essential. Was Cahill going to walk away, leave him to swing alone? He better not. Cahill was vulnerable, by God. It was Cahill who had led him into the movement, showed him the debt all Irishmen owed to Ireland and then called in the marker. Cahill was an accessory whichever way you looked at it. How would they like that in the commissioner's office?

But it was McCloud and his pussyfooting pal, the cardinal, who really destroyed him. Jesus, something had to be done about them and quick.

He looked out of the window. It was dark now. A boy and a girl were walking down the street hand in hand. He thought about Mary in Dublin. Whether they had another job for him or not he would go back soon. He could afford the trip. Jesus, Mary, and Joseph, a week, maybe more, with her. They would go out of Dublin into the country. Find a tavern and walk and eat plain Irish food and she would give him everything he craved. Jesus.

His wife came in.

"I'm going next door to see Sal," she said. "We might catch a movie. D'you want to come?" She knew he didn't enjoy movies.

"I'll watch TV," he said. She looked at him, shrugged, and went out. These days they never talked to each other. Looking back now, he didn't know why they had gotten married. She had been pretty then and it had seemed right. He had never expected love, not even when he was a youngster growing up and looking ahead. In one of their arguments, in the days when they bothered to argue, she had called him a cold man, cold and hard.

It could have been different if little John had lived. Crib death, they'd called it, but he had known it was her fault, had known she hadn't looked after the child properly. He came home from a midnight-to-eight tour and the ambulance was outside the house and he knew immediately. He didn't forgive her, didn't try. He got rid of every trace of the little boy—the photographs, the clothes, the toys he'd been too young to play with. He kept one photograph showing the boy full-face, the serious eyes, the determined chin; but after a while he'd burned it. When he looked at it, the pain was always there; so he'd burned it. She said that what had happened was just an excuse for his coldness. He didn't know if she was right.

Somebody handed him the letter when he went on duty at the Three-Two. He saw the Dublin postmark and he knew who it was from, could see her face smiling at him. He told Lenane to wait for him and he went out to a coffee shop. He couldn't read her letter in the grimy squad room, with all the noise of telephones and foul language and prisoners being interrogated.

As he walked along the street, he smelled the envelope, seeking the scent of her. When he sat down with his coffee, he didn't notice the dirty table still cluttered with cups and plates from the last customers.

He just looked at her writing on the envelope, letting the pleasure of it move into him like the warmth of the sun. By God, she didn't think he was a cold man.

Finally he opened the envelope, took out the sheet of notepaper and began to read.

She didn't even use his name.

Your friends paid me a visit. Three of them, there were, and all of them bastards. They knew you'd been to see me. Did you tell them? Not that it matters. They said we weren't to meet again, ever.

Oh, such brave boyos. They stood there in their dirty raincoats and they said that if I saw you again, they would break my kneecaps. Just like that, as if it was the most everyday thing.

Then they hit me. They knocked me over in my own home. And when little Tommy tried to stop them, they hit him, too. He's still got the bruise where they rapped him across the face and I've got an eye that looks like the sunset so I can't go to work.

Your colleagues, they said they were. Before they left they said that there was no place in your life for such as me because you had more important things to do with your time. They said it might be more than just broken kneecaps, it might be a bullet. Then out they go as if they've just stopped in for a cup of tea.

So that's it. Don't bother to try to contact me because you won't find me here. I've packed and we're off, Tommy and me, to London where nobody bullies you in the name of justice and freedom. You never told me you were one of them.

I wish I'd never met you.

She signed it simply, "Mary Bannion."

O'Hara put the letter into his pocket. His face was gray. It was in that moment that his perception shifted dangerously.

EIGHT

A report on King and the bombing of his car had gone to the Fusilier's headquarters at Bessbrook during the night. While drinking with Cray in the officer's mess, King had explained the reason for his visit and this information was included in the report.

Loughton, the contact man, came in by helicopter the next morning. He seemed to be suffering from a mixture of irritation and embarrassment at King's presence in the area. He introduced himself and they talked while they stood watching the remains of the Hillman being winched into a truck. King's luggage in the trunk had survived the blast remarkably well so that he had been able to shave with his own razor and change his clothes.

"There was no point in your coming down here," Loughton said. "But, if you felt you had to, why the hell did you go hanging around that pub? It may be a newspaper cliché that Crossmaglen is the most dangerous place in Europe, but that doesn't mean it isn't true. You were asking for trouble."

Almost as an afterthought, he said, "Everybody was very sorry about your brother. Good man, very good man."

"That's why I'm here," King said. "I'd like to know what happened to him."

"He was shot by the Paddies."

"I know that."

"Well, then—"

"I want to know the circumstances."

Loughton hesitated, staring at the ruins of the car, which were being lowered onto the bed of the truck. He looked tired, as if he hadn't slept well. "He was doing a job," he said finally. "The Paddies didn't approve of the particular job he was doing and so they killed him. Happens all the time, I'm afraid."

"What job?"

Again Loughton hesitated, seeming to be unwilling to commit himself. "I don't know all the details," he said. "But it involved intelligence. He knew the possibilities, the hazards. He accepted them. That's all."

"I'd still like to know what happened."

"Look," Loughton said, "the people running this thing aren't even in Ulster. They're in London. They're the people who can fill you in. As a matter of fact, I was on the phone to them during the night. They'd like to talk to you."

"I'm willing. Who are they?"

"Oh, government types," Loughton said vaguely. "They have some sort of input about what goes on over here. They can explain just what happened if anybody can."

"I'd also like to see the place where he was killed."

"All right, if you insist. Can't do any harm, I suppose."

"I know I'm being a terrible nuisance, wanting to find out what happened to my brother."

"Look," Loughton said, "I'm sorry. This isn't my sort of thing, intelligence and all that stuff, and I'm working under various restrictions." He sounded aggrieved like a rugby player forced to join a soccer team. "I'll show you where your brother was shot and I'll help you get to London, take care of the car-rental people and all that. But that's about all I can do."

King accepted that. The answers to his questions, it seemed, lay in London and he was anxious now to get there. First, however, he had to wait while Loughton ate breakfast in the mess.

They left Crossmaglen in the Bessbrook helicopter at ten o'clock in the morning. The rain had stopped and the air was fresh and clear over the mountains to the north and east.

After only a few minutes, the helicopter sank down to a narrow road alongside a slate-roofed cottage. There were no other buildings in sight.

Loughton, who had been examining the landscape through binoculars, led the way out of the shuddering helicopter. "He was living here, in this cottage," he said. "We found the body on this path after he failed to answer a telephone call. He'd been shot and left there."

King walked up the little path, Loughton trailing behind him. It was a lonely place to die. He noticed a stain on the front door and put out his hand to touch it. He looked over his shoulder at Loughton who shrugged uncomfortably. "Death is a messy business," he said.

The front door was unlocked and King walked inside. He looked into all the rooms but felt nothing of his brother's presence. It was just an unoccupied cottage, cleared of personal belongings. The wire of the telephone in the front room had been disconnected. Loughton stayed outside. Through a window, King caught a glimpse of him using his binoculars again.

When King rejoined him outside, Loughton looked at his watch and said, "All right? We should be on our way."

King was angry now. "Are you telling me that he was ordered to stay here on his own?" he demanded. "To live here, with no protection? Jesus Christ, what sort of game were they playing, Loughton?"

"No game," Loughton said. His embarrassment was back. "Over here, risks have to be taken and sometimes they don't work out. Your brother knew what he was up against."

"I bet he did," King said. "And there was nothing he could do about it, was there? Because he was under orders, bound to do what he was told or take a court martial. Isn't that right?"

Loughton said nothing, but turned and headed back for the helicopter. He turned at the doorway and looked at King. "I shouldn't have brought you here," he said. "You're only seeing one side of the picture. There are things you don't know about."

King's anger was such that he didn't speak to Loughton or the pilot on the flight to Bessbrook. The image was back in his mind now, slightly changed so that his brother was walking alone up the cottage path while behind him a man in a raincoat was raising a gun.

Another helicopter took him to Aldergrove and from there an RAF Hercules transport carried him to Northolt. He made his own way into London and registered at a hotel on a street running off the Strand. Loughton had booked him in there because, he said, it was not far from the office where he was expected at nine o'clock the following day.

King toured some pubs along Fleet Street but ran into nobody he knew. In the Stab in the Back they said that Purgavie was taking an early vacation. He picked up an early edition of the *Mail* and went back to the hotel. Another soldier had been shot in the Falls Road area of Belfast.

There were those in the Department who, later, said that none of it would have happened if the First Murderer hadn't decided to bring King into London for a meeting. They said that it was never good tactics to bring in an outsider because you never could be sure which way the cat would jump. Outsiders, civilians as they were known in the Department, were emotional and unpredictable.

And, they said, there were enough imponderables in their work without adding to them. The ones who said this were, of course, the Department officers who deprecated Toby East and his methods, the ones in fact who had given him his Shakespearean nickname. Right or wrong, they were biased.

Toby East's justification was that there were always prizes to be won in a fluid situation and, he said, Peter King's entry onto the scene created an extra element of fluidity in the New York operation. He welcomed it because, like the letter to O'Hara's wife, it changed things, gave an added dimension. An alert officer, he argued, could always seize an advantage from such a situation, so long as he was aware of the variation and had the ability to control it.

To that, his detractors replied that you can never control a civilian, that he is the wild card that can bring problems, quite unnecessary problems. East replied that the Department employees who argued this way were conservatives and that the conservative mentality didn't belong in their line of work. Of course, this didn't really answer the questions they raised. Finally, East fell back on the truism that it's always easier to criticize than to originate.

King's anger was still with him when he arrived at the address given him by Loughton. During his night's drinking along Fleet Street, he had been unable to shake the mental picture of his brother's lonely death in Armagh. It seemed to him that the men who had sent him to that cottage had risked a life with blind disregard of simple humanity. They had used Martin's loyalty.

A soldier, killed with a gun in his hand, in the company of his fellows, was a grievous matter but understandable. His brother's death was another thing entirely.

As instructed, he took the elevator in the nondescript building on Northumberland Avenue and went to the fourth floor. He stepped out into a reception area where a pale girl wearing spectacles was typing at a desk below a picture of the queen. To one side, a burly man in a blue suit, sitting in a hard-backed chair, looked at King impassively. He had the short haircut of a soldier. A watchdog? A kettle was simmering on a hot plate behind the girl.

"Mr. King?" she said. He nodded and she said, "You're very punctual. Would you like a cup of tea?" He said he would and she led him to a door on her right. She pressed a button and the door slid aside into a hollow wall. There was a metallic thud as it came to rest. Two men were sitting in the office. They both rose to their feet as King came in.

"I'm Orin Redder," one of them said, shaking his hand, "and this is Toby East, one of my assistants." East also took King's hand then strolled to a chair in a corner to the right of the desk. Redder motioned King to a seat and resumed his place behind the desk. The girl came in with tea, smiled at King and retreated to her post.

"I'm glad you could come to see us, Mr. King," Redder said. He was very much in charge of the situation and King could feel the force of his personality. It did nothing to quell the bitterness coiled inside him.

"I've just come from Crossmaglen," he said, "and I have some questions."

"Yes, I know," Redder said. "We'll do our best to answer them. But there's something I have to ask you to do first." He pushed a piece of paper across the desk toward King, then laid a fountain pen on top of the paper.

"I'm sure you've heard of the Official Secrets Act," he said. "Before I can tell you what you want to know, I must ask you to sign that form. It's all rather absurd, but government departments have rules and regulations and we have to abide by them."

King looked at the duplicated form presented to him. It said, "I have read the Official Secrets Act and understand the penalties attached thereto."

"I haven't read it," he said.

"Very few people have," Redder said. "There's no need. The effect of signing that bit of paper is that you agree to keep what we tell you to yourself. Yourself and your immediate family."

King shrugged, picked up the pen and signed.

"Who are you?" he said. "What's your connection with my brother and Ulster?"

Redder put the sheet of paper in a drawer of his desk and said, "This is a department of the Ministry of Defense. We work for the government, with particular reference to terrorist activities. It's a growing field." King thought he detected a thread of satisfaction in his voice in the same way that a manufacturer might take pleasure in an increased demand for his wares.

"Ulster, of course, is one of our items and, in particular, the border area through which arms and explosives are smuggled to the Provisional wing of the Irish Republican Army in the cities to the north. It is vital that this border be closed to arms smugglers.

"Now, you understand, I'm only able to tell you of this because we feel that you're entitled to know, you and your family, about the magnificent work Captain King did before his unfortunate death. It's a terrible shame that because of the nature of his work and its continuing effect we're unable to make it public. Believe me, there's nothing we would rather do."

King looked to his left at Toby East, who was sprawled comfortably in his chair. East looked completely relaxed except for his eyes, which were intent on King's face.

"Very well," Redder went on. "Now I must tell you about the Special Air Service, which is sometimes vulgarly known as the John Waynes, a reference to the American film star and his imaginary exploits. The SAS consists of a small group of men, headquartered in Hereford, whose mission is to counter military terror in the field, whether at home or abroad.

"A few weeks ago, the decision was made to put the SAS into the border area in an attempt to seal the seepage of arms.

"Your brother was sent in ahead of them to prepare the ground, so to speak. His job was to watch the border, divorced from the regular patrols, so that when the SAS came in they would know where to strike. You might call him a pathfinder."

"I'm sorry," King said, "but I don't understand. Why was Martin assigned to the job? He was an infantry officer, not a commando."

Toby East stirred. "He'd received training in counterterror," he said softly. "He was in Northern Ireland, available. He had a splendid record. He was the man for the job. He accepted it."

"What else could he do?" King demanded. "He was a soldier. He had to do what he was told."

"Exactly," East said. He had very white teeth. There was a physical grace to the man that, King realized, derived from the economy of his movements. As Redder gave off intimations of power, East exuded control and precision. He made Redder, with all his authority, appear gross.

"And so you put him, alone, with no protection, in a cottage surrounded by men who wanted nothing better than to be given the chance to kill a British soldier. Jesus."

"Soldiers are taking that sort of risk every day, right now, in Ulster," Redder said. "They're doing their duty without complaint. Every day they go out on patrol, offering themselves as targets to fanatics. You should be proud that your brother was one of them. And remember this, on the border as a result of your brother's work, the SAS is in place doing their job more effectively, saving lives, because he had led the way for them."

"Who killed him?"

"The Irish. The Provos."

"Has anybody been arrested?" Redder looked at East.

"No," East said. "But we know who killed him."

"Well, why haven't they been arrested?"

"Because he's no longer in Ulster, or Ireland for that matter."

"It was one man in particular?"

"Almost certainly there were others involved, but we believe that one man alone was given the task. He's done this sort of thing before."

"And he's no longer in Ireland?"

"That's our information."

"Where is he, then? Who is he?"

Redder looked at East. It seemed to King that there was an expression of disquiet, a warning even, in Redder's eyes. Was King supposed to notice? He remembered the good cop–bad cop ploy used by policemen.

"He's in New York," East said.

"And there's nothing you can do to bring him to justice?"

"Justice," East said. He seemed to be testing the sound of the word. To King now it sounded flat and self-conscious. Perhaps words always did when they concerned basics like life and death and revenge.

"There are things we can do," East said. "Oh, yes."

"The American government. Can he be extradited?"

"We could try that," East said. He sounded uninterested.

Redder said, "There are problems with that. There always are with extradition. In this case we don't have enough evidence to put him on trial, which means we don't have enough evidence to apply for extradition. You see, in this line of work, political action, it's not easy to produce clear-cut evidence. It's not Agatha Christie country. And then again, you see, it might not be in the best interests of the country to put him on trial. Publicity can be dangerous. There are some things we'd prefer to keep confidential—"

"Beautiful," King broke in. "So you sit here and let this man come in and out of Ireland, in and out of Ulster, killing whenever he wishes."

"It's difficult," Redder said. His voice was bland.

"Why was the D-notice issued?"

There was a momentary silence and again Redder's eyes flickered toward his assistant.

"How did you know about that?" he said.

"I heard."

"The issue of a D-notice is not a public matter."

"Tough." It was a childish triumph, seeing them shaken, but he didn't care. He felt the anger moving in him like a restless animal. Beyond that, he needed a drink. He wasn't used to dealing with men like these. He was out of practice. He'd been sitting at the rim of Burr's desk too long.

"I'll ask you again," he said. "Why was it issued? Why was Martin's death covered up?"

"I don't accept that definition," Redder said. "Look, Mr. King, we've already gone further than we should have into a very sensitive area. The Special Air Service is a most valuable organization and much of that value lies in its ability to operate out of the public eye."

"The D-notice."

"The D-notice was issued because it wasn't in the best interests of the country for word to get out that an army officer living alone close to the border was killed in Armagh the way your brother was. There are other men down there doing similar work, enduring similar hazards. Apart from that, almost certainly publicity would have affected the operations now being conducted by the SAS. We couldn't allow that."

East said, "It would have destroyed the value of your brother's sacrifice."

King looked at him. "That doesn't add," he said. "The Provos knew he was there and they killed him. They're supposed to be the enemy and they know what you won't allow the public to know. That's what I call a coverup."

Redder seemed about to say something, but then he changed his mind. King got the impression they both were moving carefully, trying to placate and maneuver him at the same time.

"Mr. King," East said, "we've told you how your brother died, why he was at Crossmaglen. We've told you about the killer. We simply can't go any further. The lives of other people still in Armagh are at risk."

"What about this man, the man in New York?"

This time, East looked across the desk at Redder before he spoke. Redder stirred as if to protest, but finally shrugged in consent. "Ironically enough," East said, "he's a policeman. He's an American and he's of Irish-Catholic descent. Evidently he believes in murder if it's ordered by the holy men of the Provos. His name is O'Hara, John O'Hara, and he has deep cover as a detective dealing with narcotics traffic. We believe he comes over here for specific assignments, to kill men who are particularly dangerous to the Provos. Such men as your brother. O'Hara's believed to have killed at least three other high-priority targets. Undoubtedly, the Provo reasoning is that such actions must bring about widespread manhunts, but there's little we can do if the killer has left the country."

"And so, what d'you propose to do about this O'Hara?"

"They're using unorthodox methods. We shall have to use unorthodox methods in response."

There was no need for them to spell it out.

"I want him in a courtroom on trial," King said.

"On trial," East said. Again it was as if he was trying out the words.

"Yes," Redder said, "that would be very nice. I'm afraid it's just not possible." He sounded more comfortable now, as if the difficult terrain had been negotiated.

"You see, Mr. King, we're confronting one of the many problems that arise from this type of terrorist activity. It's not just the IRA, though God knows they're bad enough. It's worldwide and ours is not the only government faced with the same questions."

East was staring out of the window as if he'd heard all this before.

Redder went on, "You know, somebody once said that dictatorships are like splendid ships with all sails set. They move majestically on, then when they hit a rock they sink forever. But a democracy is like a raft. It never sinks but, damn it, your feet are always in the water. Well, people like us are engaged in the task of trying to keep those feet just a little bit drier."

"Yeah, yeah," King said. He needed a drink more than ever. East raised his eyebrows at him.

"It's a question of moral collapse, moral collapse everywhere you look," Redder said. That justified everything, King thought. Violence and terror became acceptable to both sides.

"I don't want him iced, this man O'Hara," King said. "I want to see him in a courtroom on trial."

"In a courtroom on trial," East said.

"We've explained about that," Redder said. "It can't be done that way."

When King had gone, Redder looked at Toby East and said, "What's your opinion?"

"A drinker."

"Any use to the Department, d'you think?"

"No, sir. We've got drinkers, always have had. But he's naive as well. He wants a trial, for God's sake."

"All right," Redder said. "Now, Toby, you know I never question the methods of my case officers. If I had to do that, they wouldn't be case officers. But I confess to some curiosity in this matter. Why bring in Peter King? What does he add to the equation?"

"He carries the beauty of the unexpected."

"I don't have much time, Toby."

"Sorry, sir. Look at it this way. Suppose we take out O'Hara in New York. Suppose it's done very clean. Suppose it's assumed by the American authorities to be, say, an accident or even a mystery killing. Such things happen. That's all right. But we can be damn sure the Provo connections over there won't look at it that way. They'll see a motive all right and the most obvious motive as far as they're concerned belongs to the Brits. And they'll act on that. We can't know what they'll do, but they'll do something and who knows where that might lead? The takeout might not be clean after all."

"I follow."

"So we have to satisfy the Provo connection that there was a different motive for the takeout."

"Peter King."

"Exactly, sir. King lives in New York, works there. He will have been sniffing around asking questions about O'Hara."

"How do you know he will?" Redder was leading East like a teacher with a star pupil.

"Oh, we'll make sure of that. And we'll make sure he's in the area when O'Hara is taken out."

"And you think that will satisfy the Provos?"

"I'm sure of it. They can understand revenge. They can even accept it, one man killing the murderer of his brother. Tit for tat."

"They might take action against King. More tit for tat." Redder was smiling as if he knew the answer.

"They might. But that would be a private matter between them. Nothing to do with the Department or with British policy."

There was a silence.

"You have a devious mind, Toby," Redder said finally. It was an accolade. "All right," he went on. "Now, what's the status of the Bannion woman?"

"She's in London, with her boy. Staying at a hostel in Bayswater."

"She didn't go to the police in Dublin?"

"No. It seems the mention of kneecapping was enough. Funny thing is, the Provos are looking for her in Dublin right now."

"You didn't have to go over on that one, Toby."

"I wanted to. I quite like Dublin. And it tickled my sense of the ridiculous, playing a hard man, dirty raincoat and all. The odd thing is that probably we were doing exactly what the Provos would have done if they had reached her first. Anyway, she bought it. Might stir up O'Hara a bit. You never know."

NINE

That day, the day when all the doors closed on him, O'Hara got up at eight o'clock even though he was not assigned for duty until the afternoon. He wanted to get out of the house, out of New York, away from the cruddy place. He thought maybe a drive upstate would help him clear his head, help him face up to what lay ahead. Perhaps he would go as far as Cahill's little stone house outside Phoenicia. It was pretty up there, even now when the snow still lay in the hollows and on the mountaintops. If he used the thruway he could be there and back in comfortable time. Back to the crud.

She was sitting in the kitchen, drinking coffee and reading a newsweekly. He saw the pages were open to the foreign-affairs section. She wasn't interested in foreign affairs. He sensed a tension about the set of her thin shoulders.

"You're up early," she said. The tension was there in her voice, too.

"I'm going to take a run," he said. "Maybe up to Cahill's place."

"That's nice for you. What about us?"

"What d'you mean?"

"Johnny," she said, "I want a divorce."

"So get one," he said, moving toward the coffeepot.

"I want my freedom. We can't go on like this. You know we can't."

He shrugged and poured coffee into a cup. It didn't matter now. A week ago he would have welcomed her words. Now, with Mary Bannion lost to him, they meant nothing. He turned on the radio. A newscaster was forecasting a clear day. Upstate, the sun would be glinting through the bare branches, melting the ice off the lakes.

"What's the deal?" he said.

"You're not going to like it, Johnny. I want the house. I've paid my dues over these years and I'm not going empty-handed. The house is a start."

In another year it would be free of mortgage. It was worth at least forty thousand dollars. It was his financial stake.

"Like hell you get the house," he said. "I'll go see a lawyer and he can talk to your lawyer. Do it properly."

"I had a letter," she said, watching him. "About a woman in Dublin you've been seeing."

He went to the window and stared out at the unkempt backyard. He hadn't touched it since the summer before.

"What woman in Dublin?"

"Mary Bannion. A barmaid."

"What the fuck are you talking about?"

"You don't know a woman by that name, I suppose?"

"Never heard of her." Even as he said it, he thought, what's the use? Why bother?

"I suppose you've never been to Dublin."

"You know I've been there. That vacation Cahill arranged."

"This month."

"Sure," he said. "I popped over with the jet set for a hunt ball. With Bianca and Truman and the Astors. It was terrific fun. Super."

"You went over the other day, when you were supposed to be on that stakeout at the Hilton. I made inquiries."

"Inquiries," he said. "Who sent you this letter?"

"It's with my lawyer."

"I said, who sent it?" He was staring at her, thinking he'd never really known her, never had, never would now. He longed to be away, moving north on his own in the sunshine.

"It doesn't matter who sent it," she said. "As a matter of fact, I don't know. It was anonymous. One of your friends, I suppose. But whoever it was, he knew all about you and your Mary Bannion. You spent the night with her, didn't you, Johnny?"

"You're crazy."

"You spent the night with her and it wasn't the first time. Look, Johnny, d'you think I'm stupid? D'you think I don't know about your little trips over there for Cahill? I know about them and my lawyer knows about them and we have a theory about the reason you go over there—not just Mary Bannion. Would you like to hear it?"

"I don't want to hear anymore of your fucking ravings."

"The lawyer says it's all grounds for divorce and you wouldn't have much to say about the settlement, if anything."

He wanted to hit her, wanted to smash the cool facade she presented. The tension had resolved into triumph. She had him and she was enjoying it and if he hit her he would be in worse trouble. He turned from her and left the house.

As he got behind the wheel of the Rambler, his mind was raging with questions. Who had sent the letter? Who knew about his flights to Ireland, his connection with Mary Bannion? The same people who'd scared her away from Dublin? He felt as if enemies were all around him. Driving away from the house, he didn't notice the gray sedan parked halfway down the block, two men slumped low in the front seat.

O'Hara didn't go upstate. He drove into Manhattan and went to a four-story town house on East Sixty-second Street, between Madison and Park. Ivy had been allowed to grow unchecked over the walls and the lower windows were smothered with leaves. Vagrant newspaper pages and rubbish had collected in the corners of the steps up to the black front door.

O'Hara pressed the buzzer three times, then after a moment he pressed it twice. He heard the click of the electric lock being released and he pushed the door open. A woman was coming toward him. She was tall, in her early thirties, her plain features made attractive by careful makeup. She wore a severe white silk shirt and a calf-length black skirt. She looked like a woman who had done well in the business world, an executive who knew her way around.

"Johnny O'Hara," she said. "For God's sake, what—?"

"Hello, Lily," he said, "you're looking okay." It made him feel better just to look at her. Her world had nothing to do with guns in Ireland or arguments in Forest Hills.

"I'm fine," she said. "What are you doing here? You're much too early."

"I know," he said. "I wanted to have a word with you while nobody else was around. I took a chance you'd be here."

"I stayed over," she said. "Otherwise you'd have been unlucky. It was very busy last night and I didn't feel up to going home. Come in here."

She led the way into a ground-floor room, off the hallway. The heavy dark red drapes were drawn so that no daylight, even if it penetrated the ivy outside, could enter. In the corner a television set glowed, showing a soap opera. Every time O'Hara had been in the room, the television had been on, ignored, a part of the furniture. She turned on the lights. In this room it was always nighttime. The furniture didn't match the elegance of the address. There was a cracked leather couch, a scattering of plastic-covered chairs, and in one corner, a short bar constructed from pinewood. The fireplace was closed off with a piece of cardboard. On one wall hung an amateurish painting of a girl lifting her skirt to fiddle with her stockings. The atmosphere was that of a waiting room, which it was.

"Drink?" the woman asked.

He nodded and she brought him a whisky without ice. She poured a Perrier water into her glass.

"What is it, Johnny?" she said.

"Just wanted to see you, Lily. Have a talk."

"Is that all you wanted?" She was smiling at him.

He stared back at her, at her long legs under the demure skirt, at the smooth flow of her silk shirt.

"You're something," he said. She was. She was a New Jersey schoolteacher who had decided that life should offer her more than other people's moronic children. She had made a connection with people who had set her up in business. She was very good at it. Her ambition was to make enough money to establish her own place, free of outside control. With the profits from that, she planned to open a string of beauty parlors, using the girls who now worked for her on East Sixty-second Street. In her own way, she would redeem herself and the girls. She had set herself a target of two years. When she first told O'Hara about it, he had been amused, thinking it a dream, a fantasy. Now he wasn't sure she wouldn't make it. She was something.

He had been introduced to the house by two vice cops working out of the One-Nine. He had been back a half dozen times, usually after his duty tour, and on the last two occasions Lily, who had taken a liking to him, had entertained him personally. She would take no money, would have been insulted at the offer. She wanted it to be very clear that she was not one of the girls, some of them housewives, secretaries who wanted to make extra cash. She was respectable, she told O'Hara very seriously. If she took him to bed it was because she liked him, nothing more. Of course, he thought, it was always useful to have a good contact in the detective division.

Sitting there, he thought about his wife and about Mary Bannion. Lily was different from them both. Lily was a no-bullshit lady. She was tough and ambitious and clear-eyed. She knew the score. He couldn't imagine Lily using the word *love*. He liked her. Screwing her was a comfortable pleasure, not a task such as his wife presented or a high like Mary Bannion. For all Mary Bannion's open lust, he had known her no better than his wife.

He and Lily talked for a while, but O'Hara didn't raise the subject that had brought him to Sixty-second Street. He could tell she knew he had something on his mind, but she was content to let him go at his own pace. After she had poured him another drink she said, "Come on, Johnny. Let's go upstairs before everybody busts in. You know what a madhouse it is when the lunchtime crowd arrives."

They went up two flights. Carrying his drink, O'Hara felt a flush of excitement such as he had not experienced here before. Perhaps it was because there was nobody else in the building. There was something incendiary about the two of them alone in a brothel, using it for straightforward rutting with no business logic behind it.

She took him to a back room, also curtained against the daylight. It held a four-poster bed and two rocking chairs and not much else. There was a small bathroom. Lily called it the Colonial Room. She had names for all the bedrooms in the house.

She looked at her watch and said, "We have about half an hour." She undressed swiftly, smiling once at him across the bed. That was another spur, he thought, the transformation from the business-woman in austere clothes to a naked, smiling wanton. By the time he had taken off his clothes, she had pulled back the covers and was sprawled on the sheets. She handled him with lazy sensuousness but, in bed at least, she expected him to lead as if she were saying, "Okay, here I can be feminine, here I can forget that I'm trying to make it in a man's world."

For him, it was urgent and satisfactory. Like a good steak, he thought. In bed she called him darling but only in bed. Bed was a different compartment of her life. Afterward, they lay side by side smoking cigarettes, staring at the ceiling.

"You want some ice?" she said. There was a small refrigerator in the bathroom, one of the luxuries that attracted what Lily called her "class customers." She was genuinely proud of the place, would have been outraged to hear it called a cathouse.

"This is fine," he said. "How's it going?"

"Good. And getting better."

"That guy from City Hall still come here?"

"Once a week, regular. Pays with American Express."

"And Hook?"

"Who?"

"Hook, the assistant D.A."

"Oh, yes. He was here a few days back." She leaned on one elbow and looked down at him. "It's Hook you're interested in. Right? That's why you came round today."

"He was on my mind, yes."

"Why?"

"Maybe I need him. I don't know."

"Don't mess with my customers, Johnny. I don't need that."

"It won't happen," he said. "It's just that Hook could be useful to me. Which day did he come here last?"

"I'd have to look it up. Look through the books."

"Do me a favor, Lil. Look it up for me."

"All right. But you have to tell me why."

"I can't right now. It's just I may need some help, high up."

She went to the bathroom. When she returned and began to dress he was fascinated once more by the transformation, this time into a cool executive preparing for tough decisions, hard work, success.

"Don't bring the house into it, Johnny," she said. "I wouldn't forgive that."

"Don't worry," he said, starting to dress. "It just gives me the edge I need, that's all." She started to say something, but the bell rang, three and two.

She slipped on her shoes and went to answer it. To her it would be betrayal, but he didn't see it that way. It was simply a question of need. He needed the pressure on Hook more than he needed the madam of a cathouse. When he reached the ground floor two of the girls, Julie and Yvonne, were taking off their coats in the hallway. They turned and looked at him coming down the stairs.

"Hello, Johnny," Julie said. They were both grinning at him, guessing what had preceded their arrival. Lily appeared carrying a cloth-bound ledger.

"Time to get ready," she said, and the two went to a back room to change into their working outfits. Lily put the ledger on a table in the hall, opened it, and ran a red-tipped finger down the columns.

"Here's his last visit," she said. "Tuesday. He was here an hour that night. Had Amanda. He usually has her. Is that what you need?"

"That's it, Lil. You're a princess."

"I know," she said.

They were parked three cars behind the Rambler with their engine running to power the heater. They had secured a copy of the duty roster for the Three-Two so they knew he was scheduled for duty at 4:00 P.M. They would have to stay with him for another four hours. The team didn't have enough manpower to keep him under surveillance around the clock. It had been decided therefore, out of necessity, that he would be watched only off duty. They pulled away from the curb and followed him toward Park Avenue.

He telephoned from the squad room at the Three-Two. It was an appropriate place, he thought. The room was stained with deals, threats, promises, and betrayals. Hook was ready to brush him off. Until he mentioned the house on Sixty-second Street. He went quiet then.

O'Hara could imagine Hook looking around him in his office on Leonard Street.

"Who are you?" he said.

"I told you. I work narcotics out of the Three-Two. John O'Hara. Detective, second grade. I'm a friend of Lily's."

"I met you?"

"Let's get together. Have a talk."

"Do I know you? Talk about what?" He sounded edgy and O'Hara grinned, enjoying himself.

"How about Vincent's, down on Mott Street? You like shrimp?"

"Listen, I've got nothing to talk to you about."

"How about Amanda. Last Tuesday night? You talked to her didn't you? Why not talk to me? Or do I go to the D.A. and get him to set up an appointment?"

There was a silence. O'Hara could hear the man breathing at the other end of the line.

"What time? When?"

"Tomorrow. One-thirty. Be there." O'Hara put the phone down. He felt better.

That night, after their tour of duty, he dropped off Lenane at his apartment building. He watched his partner go into the lobby. Shithead. They still weren't talking except when essential. Still, nothing was happening. Perhaps Internal Affairs had given up. Perhaps there was nothing Schmidt could do. He just had to hang tough. What did they have, except the word of a three-time loser dope dealer and Lenane, who would do or say anything to save his skin? It was a week now and nothing had happened. Perhaps he had reached bottom. No way to go but up. And, with Hook, he had a hidden card.

But then he thought of what they had done to Mary Bannion and he remembered the anonymous letter to his wife and Cahill's reluctance to talk to him. It was no good. He was whistling in the dark. They were out to get him. He started to drive away, but the thought of his wife and the house in Forest Hills made him take his foot from the accelerator. He had no wish to go home.

He moved into a space by a fire hydrant, pulled down the "Police" I.D. on his sun visor and got out. P. J. Clarke's was just down the block. Outside the bar a horse-drawn carriage from Central Park was letting off a giggling young couple. It was after midnight and Clarke's was thick with an assortment of tourists, sportsmen, and regulars who displayed their status by calling the bartenders by name. He recognized two hit men from one of the Brooklyn families standing by the food counter near the door.

O'Hara found a suddenly opened space at the far end of the bar and ordered a Scotch. On his left, a blond young man, his eyes glazed, was listening to an older woman whose eyes were ranging restlessly over the crowd. Behind him, two men were arguing about the Giants. Down the bar he saw a famous, much-married actor with bruised, grieving eyes drinking tonic water. He was off the sauce, the actor had announced, but he still looked drunk, as if his alcohol-soaked system was turning the fizzy water into a highball. Ordinary people, O'Hara thought, not an idea in their heads beyond themselves. Had any of them risked their lives for other people? Like he had? For people whose response was ingratitude. He thought of Cahill and of Donovan, who expected him to follow orders without question. No reward, not even a pat on the back; just follow the orders. He didn't even have the camaraderie that should go with membership, active membership, by God, in the organization. He had nothing. What the hell had he gotten out of it all?

Once O'Hara had seen a picture painted by a freaky Spaniard who liked to parade around with a tiger or some such animal on a leash. The painting showed a flat wasteland littered with various artifacts —distorted, shadowless, and somehow threatening. He hadn't understood the picture, but it had chilled him. Now he felt as if he were in the center of that wasteland without the strength to move, trapped. Melting. He drank his Scotch and pulled himself straight. It was all bullshit, a complete crock. He was still capable of action.

O'Hara sensed a rustle of interest behind him and, turning, saw the broad, smoothly tailored back of a dark-haired man moving through the crowd toward the small room at the end of the bar. He saw Ransom, the police reporter who had a permanent late-night claim on one of the tables, standing to welcome the new arrival. O'Hara knew Ransom. Like many other detectives, he had fed the reporter stories hoping that the publicity would help his career.

He still couldn't see who Ransom was talking to. And then the new man turned and sat down and O'Hara saw it was the senator, McCloud. The traitor. He was smiling, nodding at those people in the crowd who had recognized him and were giving him the veiled look awarded to celebrities. There were two other men with him. McCloud sat with his back to the wall facing out into the bar area listening to the others talk. Once his eyes caught O'Hara's and then moved on. Looking for votes, counting the house, O'Hara thought bitterly.

He could act now. He could step forward, take out his .38, waste him, and be gone in the confusion. He could imagine the screams when the gun roared, the panic as people turned and twisted to get away. Only he would know at that moment what had happened. It was then that O'Hara realized he had decided positively to get McCloud. McCloud and the mighty priest. He would kill them, execute them for the crime of treason, betrayal of the cause. He would kill them because they deserved nothing but death. But not now. It was too late now. McCloud and his companions were getting to their feet and moving toward the restaurant area.

They were going to eat. O'Hara knew the dining room. It was much darker than the bar. You could spend five minutes wandering around in there before you found your man. And then you could be trapped for there was only one way out, through the narrow entrance. He would do it, but he would do it somewhere else. He finished his drink and ordered another. His mind was full of the killing of McCloud and the traitorous cardinal. Midway through his second drink he began to think of himself as Mr. Death. Say, Senator McCloud, he mused, I'd like to introduce you to Mr. Death. And you, Your Eminence, give Mr. Death a big hello.

He didn't notice the man drinking draught beer four shoulders away. There was no reason why he should. The man looked like an ordinary customer except that his eyes never strayed far from the mirror in which he could watch O'Hara.

The cops filled the two front rows of the courtroom seats. Two black patrolmen were in uniform, but most of the arresting officers were in slacks and sweaters, their badges pinned to their jackets or windbreakers. Most of them had been waiting since the court opened; one man was asleep, his mouth open, his head lolling. Another was eating a hot dog from the canteen on the first floor. All had the slack look of soldiers awaiting the convenience of others.

O'Hara sat in the second row. Like the others, he was tuned out. His thoughts concentrated on McCloud, the cardinal, and their destruction. He had found more than one reason for it. He knew it was Donovan who had scared Mary Bannion out of Dublin, and though he hated the Provo leader for it, in a perverse way he understood, even admired the ruthlessness of it. He still accepted the authority of the movement. It was, he thought, all he had left. Without the IRA he would be nothing. His career with the police department was over, he knew that.

Whatever happened, even if he escaped any penalties for the Lenane betrayal, he would be a marked man. A desk job, no more promotion. His marriage was nothing but wreckage. The Provos were all he had left. And he could build on that.

Gradually it was coming together, the way he would rehabilitate himself with Dublin. If he could do that, and he could, they would help him find Mary Bannion in London. They could find her, no doubt about it. They better.

McCloud and the cardinal, they were his tickets to a new life of respect. If he took them out, it would be one of the Provos' greatest coups and he would be owed a reward. It was the sort of thing that would go down in history, put him in the legends alongside Kevin

Barry and the men behind the wire. Maybe a song would be written about him. And he wanted to do it, Jesus, how he wanted to do it. Mr. Death, he thought, you've got a job to do.

"O'Hara. Are you O'Hara?"

He looked around. A patrolman in uniform was standing in the aisle looking at him.

"Yeah. What d'you want?"

"Phone call. In the office." The cop didn't bother to lower his voice and the judge banged his gavel in irritation.

O'Hara went with the patrolman. It had to be the precinct. They knew he was downtown.

"Detective John O'Hara?"

"Yeah."

"Shield number 12647?"

"Yeah, that's right. Who's this?"

"Internal Affairs. Deputy Inspector Clinton. We want you back at the Three-Two. Now."

"I got a case coming up here in court."

"We're talking to the D.A.'s office about that. They'll take care of it."

"Hey, listen—"

"Detective O'Hara, I must now tell you that you are suspended from duty as of this moment. You will go immediately to the Three-Two precinct, where you will turn in your shield and your gun to the desk sergeant. He will instruct you further."

"What is this bullshit?" O'Hara rasped. "What's the charge? Aren't I entitled to know what the charge is—" But the connection had been broken. Deputy Inspector Clinton had done his duty.

O'Hara hung up. It was, he thought, like bridges collapsing. He was on an island surrounded by snapping creatures and one by one the bridges were collapsing even as he put his feet on them. They were cutting him off, taking everything away from him and the creatures were coming nearer every moment. Well, by God, they weren't taking his gun from him, and they weren't taking his badge. They belonged to him. He had earned them. He picked up the phone. He would call Cahill. Then he thought, no way. Let Cahill sweat, too. Let him wonder what I'll do. Fuck every one of them. He wasn't finished. And he would start taking care of things right now.

O'Hara got to Vincent's early. He ordered the shrimp with the extra hot sauce and sat in a corner watching for Hook. When the assistant D.A. came down the steps from the counter area, he was carrying a glass and a bottle of beer. He was black, but he had thin lips and an aquiline nose and smooth hair so that he could be taken for a Latin. He looked around for a moment until O'Hara nodded at him. Hook stared at him for a moment, then shrugged and came to sit across from him.

"I haven't got long," Hook said. "What is it?"

"You've got as long as I need, pal," O'Hara said. Fucking nigger in his Cardin suit with the shirt cuffs showing, pretending to be an Italian. Even the label in his coat, which he had thrown across the next chair, had an Italian name on it.

"What d'you want?"

"All right, this is how it goes down. I need some help, an eye and an ear in the D.A.'s office. You're the eye and the ear."

The black stared at him. He hadn't touched his beer.

"Look, I'll give it to you straight. The bastards in Internal Affairs think they've got me by the balls on some crappy corruption charge. It'll likely end up in the D.A.'s office. All I need is for you to let me know what they've got on me. A look at the file."

A thought came to O'Hara. They were tricky bastards in the D.A.'s office. "Open your jacket," he said.

Hook laughed, genuine laughter. "No wire," he said. He flipped open the jacket of his suit. Underneath, he was wearing a fitted shirt through which O'Hara could see the play of powerful pectorals. O'Hara was conscious of a vague unease. It wasn't going right. Hook was too relaxed.

"Blackmail, right, goombah?" Hook said. "You seen me at Lily's?"

"A couple of times. The last was Tuesday. You had Amanda. Nice chick."

"You threatening me?"

"I'm asking your help, buddy, and you better give it. You know and I know that you've got problems if it gets out that an officer of the court, sworn to uphold the law, is a regular at an illegal house. Might make the papers. The evening news."

"Does Lily know about this, that you're talking to me?"

"She'll tell the story if she has to."

It would finish him with Lily. Hook would be onto her as soon as he left Vincent's. She would wet her pants. He didn't care. This was more important than a whore and her cathouse.

Hook looked down at his fingers, at the polished nails splayed before him flat on the table. "You know anything about me?" he asked.

"Enough."

"You ever worked two jobs at the same time?"

"Come on, Hook, don't bullshit me—"

"I did. For six years, Dee-tective O'Hara. I worked as a corrections officer. That's what they call it, 'stead of a zookeeper, which is really what it is. Only in the Tombs and on Riker's Island you're locked in with the animals, watching your back for a knife, smelling them, hearing them all around. And all the time I was studying, first at City College and then at Brooklyn Law. Because that was my way out of the zoo."

O'Hara put down his fork. "What d'you want me to do, join in a chorus of 'My Way'?" he said.

"And I passed the bar and I went to the district attorney's office and I got me a job with the Indictment Bureau so I could call myself an assistant D.A. and walk around like an ordinary human being. It was tough, O'Hara. You don't know how tough it was. But finally I took my wife and my two kids and I bought a house out on the Island and I started commuting. I'm on my way."

He paused, but still he didn't drink his beer. "And now you come along, Dee-tective O'Hara, and you'd take it all away from me? Just like that."

"I don't give a fuck about your fascinating history, Hook. You've been around. You know how things work. The D.A., your wife, none of them have to know. Just tell me what they have. That's all."

"You know what heart is?"

"I know what it is. It's got nothing to do with this. This is a business arrangement. No risk, no problem. Just cooperate."

"My wife. If you stick it to me—"

"She doesn't have to hear anything. Nobody does. I'm giving you a break. That's why we're sitting here. Just stay loose and I'll be in touch."

O'Hara grinned. "Listen," he said, "maybe nothing will develop, maybe you won't hear from me again. Only if they bring this bullshit case against me, if there's an indictment, that's when I'll need you. All you have to do is let me know what they have. Other than that I don't give a fuck. You can spend every night at Lily's as far as I'm concerned."

Now it was going the way it should. O'Hara felt better. He was halfway through his shrimp, feeling the abrasive sting of the hot sauce on his mouth. Vincent's was a good joint and this wasn't a bad day at all. All you had to do was have the edge on people.

"And if I help, you won't break my balls over Lily's?"

"That's exactly right."

"There's a problem. It's a nice setup, Dee-tective O'Hara. I'll give you that. Only, there's a problem."

"Don't fuck with me, Hook."

"That problem is that I can't find out anything from the office even if I wanted. Not after this weekend anyway."

"You better find a way."

"I can't. Because I quit the D.A.'s office. *Capisce?* I turned in my papers the same day I went to Lily's. It was a celebration, you mother. How d'you like them apples, O'Hara?"

Hook was getting to his feet, reaching for his coat, putting it on, grinning down at O'Hara.

"You know," he said casually, "you're a lousy cop. Cops like you, they're the reason we get hammered in court. The cop doesn't make sure of the evidence or it's tainted and he's screwed it up some way and we get stuck with cases that get thrown out as soon as we stand up in front of the judge. Assholes, all of you. And you, man, you just O.D.'d on stupidity."

O'Hara felt as if he had been physically assaulted, taken by a mugger who had come at him from a dark corner.

"I'm going into private practice," Hook said, "going to make some money for myself for a change. So I don't give a fuck if you run off to Rosenthal with your little story about Lily's. And I don't give a fuck if you tell my wife because I left her two months ago and that was because I wanted to go to places like Lily's whenever I felt like it, among other things."

Hook hadn't bothered to lower his voice and at the next table two girls had stopped eating and were staring at them.

"Is that yours?" Hook said, indicating O'Hara's car coat hanging on the wall behind him. O'Hara nodded. He couldn't speak.

Hook said, "Excuse me, goombah." He picked up O'Hara's plate, awash with the remains of his sauce and a couple of uneaten shrimp. A puddle of tepid oil lay in the middle. Hook casually tipped it toward the open pocket of O'Hara's coat. The viscous mess slid easily into the pocket. Hook let the whole plate follow the sauce and the shrimp until its width held it lodged in the pocket opening.

O'Hara stared at him, his eyes aflame. His hand moved instinctively to his gun, tucked in his belt. Hook put his right hand in the pocket of his coat and O'Hara saw something hard outlined by the material.

"You want to get it on, O'Hara?" Hook said. "I've got one of those as well and I can use it if I have to."

Watching the detective, he began to move away. The two girls and a waiter standing frozen at the top of the steps leading down to the dining room were staring in fascination. "You poor punk," Hook said. "You can't do anything right can you?" He turned and went up the steps and was gone. O'Hara knew he was going straight to the telephone. In five minutes, Internal Affairs would know exactly what had happened in Vincent's.

The waiter came toward him. "You want anything else?" he said.

TEN

The night he got back, King had the dream again. He hadn't had it for more than a month, but now here it was again. He was almost used to it, it had happened so many times, and usually in the midst of it he knew it was nothing but a dream. Still, it always left him sweating and shivering at the same time. He was looking through a window, surrounded by the darkness of night, but the room was moonlit somehow and across the room he could see a pair of legs. He couldn't see above the knees at first, but he knew they belonged to a girl. Ginny's legs. They were six inches off the floor and they were moving very gently together, making a small tapping sound as they touched the door behind them. One shoe had fallen off and lay on the floor.

Then the moonlight seemed to advance so that he could see more, see the thighs and the hips and the torso, and now it was as if he was hypnotized by the horror of it and he thought something was moving in the darkness behind him.

And then there was more light and he could see the shoulders and neck and then the face. Only there was no face. Just a round white blob, no features. Like a moon reflecting back the moonlight. That was when he always woke up and this night was no different.

He didn't go back to sleep. It was dawn anyway. He made some coffee and sat in the window overlooking Fifty-first Street, drinking the coffee and thinking about the dream. Then he thought about his brother and about Detective John O'Hara. And about his father.

He remembered the miserable scene. At first, when he had said he didn't want to follow him into the army, the general had not taken it seriously. Just a schoolboy phase, he had thought.

But then, with Sandhurst looming, the general had called him into the drawing room after breakfast.

Outside the tall windows, racing clouds were sending shadows scudding across the green wolds. The steeple of the village church was an admonitory finger sticking up from the trees that shrouded the roofs of cottages and shops in the valley. They were at the heart of an ordered, unchanging world, their world, yet King felt no kinship with it.

"Now, Peter, we have to discuss your future, get it sorted out," the general said. He was standing sideways to the windows so that he could see the shaggy lawns bordered by low walls of Cotswold stone. He had just returned from a NATO meeting in Brussels and he looked tired. The meeting had not been a success. Nowadays he wore glasses to eat and read, and they were still in place, giving him an unfamiliarly benign look as if he were a long-suffering schoolmaster.

"Your mother tells me you're being foolish still."

"I'm sorry," King said. "It's just that the army doesn't appeal to me. I've always felt this way."

"Appeal? What d'you mean, appeal?" Already there was anger in the old man's voice. "The army isn't supposed to appeal to you. It's the other way around. You have to make yourself appealing to the army. You have to work and struggle and learn until the army wants you, can use you."

"I'm sorry," he said again. "I don't want to do that. I want other things." Even as he said it, he knew the trouble was that he didn't really know what he did want. But he knew the army wasn't for him. That he knew.

His father, staring through the window, struggled with his emotions and then his tone became softer, conciliatory. "Try it, Peter," he said. "Give it a chance. Then, of course, if it doesn't work out, we can reconsider. It means a lot to me, and to your mother."

That almost did it. King had never disobeyed his father in anything important and now the note of pleading in the usually assured voice almost unmanned him. He stared silently over his father's head at the portrait of his grandfather as a young man in khaki with the vague outline of trenches and barbed wire behind him.

While he hesitated, his father went on speaking and the moment in which King might have bent was lost. The general had miscalculated, not realizing how close to victory he had been.

"It's a question of duty," the old man said. "The oldest son has always been an army man. That's the way it is in this family and I don't expect you to let me down. It's not just me. It's the family you'd be letting down." He spoke, King thought, as if the family was something sacred and, perhaps, to him it was.

"It's not what I want," King said. He looked away from the picture.

"All I hear from you is want," the general said, his voice rising. King knew how much it had cost him to plead and now the voice was bitter.

"Nowadays," the old man said, "all I hear is 'I want this' and 'I want that.' There are no standards anymore. People laugh at words like *loyalty* and *sacrifice* and *duty* as if they're bogus." He sounded angry and hurt. King quailed. The man had led an army and now he couldn't demand obedience of a simple order and he didn't understand it.

"I'm sorry," King said again. "But I don't want to learn how to kill." The general didn't seem to hear him.

"The words meant something in the western desert and on the beaches and on the Rhine," he said. "Now they mean nothing. Less than nothing. A joke."

"I know I wouldn't be happy in the army," King said.

"You wouldn't be happy," the general said scornfully. "Happiness is not the issue. Duty is the issue. It doesn't seem to occur to you that the time has arrived when you have to pay back what you owe.

You've had the best education any boy could hope for. You've had a home full of love and care. You've not gone short of anything. You've had advantages that most people in this country can only dream about. And now is the time you have to pay back what you owe. You have to accept the privilege of leadership that's being offered to you."

"I know what you've done for me," King said hopelessly. "But, in fairness, I didn't ask for it. You gave and I accepted, but I didn't know you planned a day of reckoning. It's a bargain I didn't agree to and that doesn't seem fair."

"It wasn't fair when your grandfather was killed at Passchendaele but, by God, he did his duty and he went to his death without complaint."

"I'm sorry, father," King said. He couldn't think of anything else to say. His father was no Colonel Blimp, but he believed in certain things that King couldn't accept and that was all there was to it.

The general stared at him for a long moment, then turned and left the room. After that, his father was courteous enough to King, but they didn't talk much, perhaps because they had little to say to each other. And Martin went to Sandhurst and became an army officer and went to Ireland where he was killed by a man with a gun in front of an ugly little cottage.

The Runyon trial was in its second week when King returned to the desk. Masters was doing what was required of him, clean copy always filed before the deadline, constantly on the telephone in case there were any queries.

Burr gave King the copy to edit as if to say, "That's the closest you'll get to New Orleans, buster." King didn't much care. He wouldn't have been able to go to Louisiana anyway, not after they killed Martin. The events in Ulster and London had made his life in the office, the jealousies and backstabbing, seem extraneous, unimportant.

"One grenade," Dancer said. Dancer was sitting along the rim, staring malevolently toward the news desk. He had spent two months hunkered down at Khe Sanh after the draft took him from the copyboys' bench. On his return to the paper, Dancer had gone to the library and settled himself in front of the microfilm machine to examine the paper's coverage of Vietnam during the period he was there. The coverage consisted mostly of leads that went: "Giant B-52 bombers today pounded targets . . ." This was because the paper's correspondent in Saigon—he had been there nearly ten years —had achieved a certain kind of fame by never stirring from the capital. His stories always came from briefings, never from the field. On his return to New York he had been made city editor.

"One grenade would frag them all," Dancer said. "Take out the lot of them. Roll it along the floor, around that desk, and you'd clean them out." King saw Dancer was staring at Burr, Anderson, at the Saigon cowboy and Riddle, the managing editor, who were gathered around the columnist, McEvoy, as if to draw warmth from his fame.

McEvoy wrote like a blue-collar Hemingway, his stories full of lonely times in Brooklyn bars while the rain misted down outside and the jukebox poured out the blues. Sometimes he launched violent attacks on the city's indifference to its poverty areas before going home to his tenth-floor duplex off Sutton Place. He wrote at the top of his voice. Every winter he took his column on the road to the Sunbelt to describe the Philistine wilderness that lay west of the Hudson. He was much appreciated by the liberals of Fifth Avenue.

And of course, while deploring violence, he used his column to stroke the bombers and gunmen of the Provisionals. He was, after all, a man of the faith, a true Irishman.

The newspaper reminded King of a glass-bottomed boat from which curiosity seekers could survey the exotic creatures, the politicians, killers, hustlers, saints, moving in a frenzy below. That didn't mean nothing happened aboard the boat. Riddle, the managing editor, liked to call the situation he had developed creative tension. The idea was to set reporters in competition with reporters, photographers against photographers, with the editors as judges. The result instead, it seemed to King, was barely contained rebellion. Favorites were elevated while the dissenters watched, scarcely concealing their venomous resentment.

He telephoned Ransom at police headquarters on the office line. Ransom was busy with a corruption scandal, but he promised to call back. He came on the line half an hour later.

"I hear you had a death in the family," he said. "I'm sorry about that." King had said nothing in the office about the cause of Martin's death, where it had happened, or even that his brother had been a soldier. He told Ransom he needed some help. He wanted background on a detective named John O'Hara. Ransom showed no surprise.

"Narcotics?" he said. "The guy in the Three-Two?"

"That sounds like him. You know him?"

"He's fed me some stuff. You working cityside now?"

"No. This is a personal matter. What d'you know about him?"

"I just filed a piece that will make page ninety-nine if I'm lucky. More likely the spike. He and his partner, fellow called Lenane, have just been suspended. Some narcotics payoff in Brooklyn last year, usual thing. All I know about him is in the piece."

"Can you find out anything more? Might be a good story at the end of it." Ransom was a dissident, but he would kill for a by-line.

"Give me a clue."

"The IRA. I'm interested in any connection O'Hara might have with the Provisionals."

"Fund raising?"

"I don't know what the connection is, but I need to know."

"This isn't for the paper?"

"Not right now. I have a personal interest, but it could become public and you could have a piece of it."

"Good enough. Don't expect too much, though, King. The department's still an Irish clan. They protect their own."

"You can do it if anybody can."

"Don't con me, King. I'm the con man, not you. Okay, I'll try the Bureau of Special Services. Cahill owes me a favor."

"Cahill?"

"He's in charge of BOSS."

King had enough left over from his withdrawal from his English account to pay off the tab at Jimmy's. He was into his third Scotch when the columnist McEvoy came in with Burr and the Saigon cowboy. McEvoy wore soft, expensive boots, but his jeans and woolen work shirt, open at the neck, were off the peg. He was just a glorified reporter, he always pointed out, just one of the boys.

He included King in the round he bought, then turned away to talk to his companions. King pulled the Scotch toward him. He was thinking about Detective O'Hara. He had told them in London that he wanted the man on trial, but that was nothing, not if they couldn't extradite him to put him on trial. What did you do then? Go after him with a gun? He knew that was what East and Redder were talking about. No good, he thought. No fucking good. There was no end to that. But what did you do?

The reverse side of Redder's coin was forgiveness, but King had always seen the turning of the other cheek as a form of self-indulgence. That way there was never a decision. It was too simple. Oddly, it was the perverse Puritan in him, King thought, that made him reject the later biblical teachings. Charity was easy.

Half an hour later, he found himself included in the circle around McEvoy. They were talking about the latest hijacking of an airplane that was sitting on a runway in an obscure African republic. The city editor from Saigon was bewailing his desk-bound fate. It was his sort of story, he said, he should be there. He was imagining himself on the telephone to New York while the bullets flew around him.

"Blow 'em up, hostages and all," Burr said. He didn't usually drink, wasn't good with alcohol. "Do that a couple of times and you wouldn't have any more problems."

"Not many people traveling by plane, either," King said.

"Go straight in with machine guns," somebody said. "Like the Israelis do."

"Hey, listen," McEvoy said. "These Palestinians, they've got a point. If they can't get justice what else do they do?"

King remembered East sitting in the office on Northumberland Avenue, trying out the word, examining it.

"Justice," he said softly.

"Yeah, justice," McEvoy said, turning to him. "They're another dispossessed minority. Like the Catholics in Northern Ireland."

"Here we go," Burr said.

King was silent. He didn't want to talk about that. But McEvoy wouldn't let it alone. It was part of his act, King thought. "The Six Counties, they're part of Ireland," the columnist said. "You don't need a map to see that. And in their own land, the Catholics face torture, imprisonment, exploitation. By foreigners."

He looked at King, challenging him. "They're at the mercy of soldiers from across the sea," he said. It was his sort of phrase.

"Nice and simple," King said. "Even if the Protestants don't think so."

"Justice is always simple," McEvoy said. "It's the politicians with their hidden motives who make it complicated."

"You're a windy man," King said. He could feel the alcohol drifting comfortably into his mind. "That's the trouble with your columns. They're great floating bags of wind. And they keep getting punctured by paragraphs in the paper that say that another soldier has been shot, another woman has been killed."

"Bloody Sunday was no bag of wind—" McEvoy said.

"Let's have another drink," Burr said. The telephone in the corner of the bar was ringing.

"Remove the British soldiers," McEvoy said, "and you'll remove the problem. No more violence, no more blood, no more funerals."

Freddy, behind the bar, gestured at King. "Phone," he said.

Glad to get away from the argument, King went to the corner. It was Ransom.

"Thought I'd find you there," he said. "I've got something on your friend O'Hara."

"Yes? Did you talk to BOSS?"

"Yeah, I got hold of Cahill. He said O'Hara's clean as far as any IRA connection. He ain't necessarily telling the truth, but there you are. That's not the thing, though. I've been having a drink with a couple of dicks from the safe-and-loft squad and they started talking about O'Hara. You know he was suspended, he and his partner."

"I saw your story. It made the spike."

"There, I told you it would. Well, anyway, the routine on suspension is that you have to turn in your shield and your gun. Then they usually give you a desk job until the thing has been settled. O'Hara didn't do that."

"Didn't do what?"

"He didn't show up to turn in his shield and gun. He took off. He's disappeared, with his badge and with his gun."

"When was this?"

"Today. Now, come on, King, tell me what gives. You say you have a personal interest in this guy and then he ups and vanishes. It makes a fellow curious."

"I can't, not just now. Have they looked for him?"

"Sure they have. He's not at home, he's gone. There's a message out on the teletype to all commands."

"Thanks. You doing a story on it?"

"Hell, no, not at this time of night. They can fill their spike with something else. They don't like stories about police corruption. They're not upbeat. I'll be in touch."

ELEVEN

From Vincent's, O'Hara drove straight to Forest Hills. He spent ten minutes in the local branch of his bank before going to the house. He left his coat, soaked with the shrimp and sauce, rolled up on the back seat of the Rambler. There was only one thing he needed from the house and that was in the desk in the front room. She wasn't home, wasn't due back from her lunchtime job at the restaurant for another fifteen minutes.

It wasn't where he had left it. He threw out the other documents, bank statements, mortgage papers, insurance policies. It had gone. He went to the chest in their bedroom where they kept their tax reports, birth certificates, the high school diploma of which she was so proud. It wasn't there. He slammed down the top of the chest as the telephone rang.

He stood, breathing heavily, listening. It rang and rang. He was beginning to sweat and he swore at the implacably ringing machine. Finally it stopped. He went to the window and looked out. There was no sign of her. He looked at his watch. Again he stared out of the window. His eyes passed over the gray sedan to his right, on the other side of the road, without pausing. He moved through the house, upstairs and down. It smelled stuffy, unused, as if they already had abandoned it.

She came, walking from the subway station, at three-fifteen. He was down at the front door when she came in.

"Where is it?" he demanded.

"Where's what?" she said, pushing past him. She didn't seem surprised that he was home, although she knew he wasn't scheduled to finish his tour until an hour later.

"The passport," he said. "My passport. It's not in the desk."

"What d'you need that for? Going to Hoboken?" She was taking off her coat.

"Never mind why I need it. I need it. Where is it?"

She stared at him. "Are you all right?" she said.

"Where is it?"

She hesitated, then as he came toward her, she flinched.

"It's on top of the wardrobe. On the ledge. I thought I'd make you ask for it. Check out your next little trip to Ireland."

He was already moving fast up the stairs. It was there, perched on the wardrobe. He thrust it into his inside breast pocket. Bitch. Stupid bitch. He was halfway down the stairs again when somebody knocked on the front door. First the telephone call and now the knock. He knew who it was. His failure to report back to the Three-Two would have been reported hours ago. Probably it was a patrolman from the local precinct, ordered to check. Or it could be Internal Affairs.

She was going to answer it.

"No," he shouted. He was still on the stairs, looking down at her. His gun was in his hand. "Stay away from that door."

"Johnny," she said, staring at the gun. He was crouching with both hands on the gun in combat position, pointing it at her. "Johnny," she said again. "Put that away." She backed away from the door. He could see the fear in her face and for a moment he enjoyed it. He had no intention of shooting. That would bring them at a run.

The gun still in his hands, he hustled down the stairs, turned past her and headed for the back door.

"Don't open up," he said. "I mean it." And then he was gone through the rear door. She heard it slam and went to the front door. There were two men there and she recognized one of them. Cahill.

"He's gone," she said. "Out the back."

O'Hara went through the backyard to the muddy lane that ran by the back of the houses. Some of his neighbors had built lean-tos where they kept their cars and for a moment he thought of taking an old Buick that he could see through an open door, a paint-splattered sheet covering its hood. He didn't have time. He shivered and thought of his fouled coat lying in the Rambler. He realized the gun was still in his hand. He looked around, but there was nobody in sight. Pushing the weapon into his belt, he broke out into the road which ran at right angles to his. The subway was two minutes away.

He wanted Manhattan. He yearned for the crowded, anonymous streets, the uncaring faces shifting ceaselessly by. Once he was there he could think, decide what to do. He began to run.

TWELVE

The upper jaw of His Eminence the cardinal archbishop of the New York diocese, Patrick Moran, was numb. For the past three days he had been troubled by a persistent toothache and finally, this morning, he had visited his dentist. Sometimes he thought he feared the dentist more than the wrath of God. As he sat in his office in the chancery at the back of Saint Patrick's waiting for some feeling to return to his anesthetized gums he smiled at the thought of the picture he must have presented in the dentist's chair. He wondered how many members of his flock would have been shocked to see him lying helplessly in the tilted chair, sweaty hands gripping the arm rests, his mouth pried open, episcopal moans emerging occasionally as the drill reached beyond the boundaries of the deadened nerves.

There were those among his parishioners who seemed to forget that his role was merely that of a shepherd. Even after eleven months in office, the awe in their voices when they talked to him conjured an un-Christian irritation within that he sometimes had trouble concealing. He looked at the leather-bound diary on his desk. McCloud at 10:00 A.M. At least with Jay McCloud he could relax.

They had known and liked each other for too long to allow any note of idolatry to come between them. Perhaps the dentist's drill was a God-sent reminder that he was merely a man among other men. Mischievously the thought came of His Holiness lying in similar bondage to the dentist's probe. The cardinal couldn't imagine it. Again he smiled and went to the window to gaze out at a traffic jam on Madison Avenue. Another reminder of man's frailty. He could see angry faces, hear the indignant blare of horns.

The cardinal was only forty-three, yet he held the second most powerful position in the church, with two million parishioners and jurisdiction over two thousand priests, more than four hundred churches. His rise had been swift for such a hierarchal institution. The first son of a sanitation worker who had emigrated from County Clare, Patrick Moran had become vice chancellor of the archdiocese while still in his twenties. Three years later he was appointed chancellor. He became prothonotary apostolic, secretary to the archbishop, and was vicar general of the diocese when Archbishop Dunigan suddenly died. Three months later, Rome named him archbishop-designate.

Money had much to do with his rise. Moran was good with it—good at finding it, good at assigning it where it would do most for the diocese. Dunigan had understood and appreciated his talent and taken him into the chancery as his protégé.

Moran's appointment as New York's ninth archbishop at first filled him with disquiet. It had come so fast and the responsibility seemed awesome, but quite swiftly he realized that in the last years of his predecessor he had already assumed much of the burden. It had happened so gradually that he hadn't realized the full extent of his control until he took the episcopal crosier in his hands and on looking around saw that the diocese was as streamlined and efficient as any corporation among the Fortune 500. Still, there were terrible problems—the devastation of the poorer parishes, the restlessness of the younger priests.

It had irritated him that such a peripheral matter as Ulster had spawned controversy. Far better for the arguments to revolve around the church's plans in Bedford-Stuyvesant, Harlem, or the South Bronx; but that was not the way of men. Poverty was insufferably boring for those not touched by it; Ireland now, Ireland was different. There was a fatal glamor.

As if in response to his thoughts, Jay McCloud appeared on Madison Avenue, dodging and weaving through the stalled cars and taxis and exhaust fumes toward the archbishop's residence. Fingering his gold cross, the cardinal watched the heavy-set figure with affection. The man had moral courage, even if there were hidden reasons for his arguments about Ulster and the Provos. The cardinal knew about politics; if he hadn't learned, his career would have felt the reins years ago.

He and McCloud were men of a kind; they would have been even if not for their discovery of common roots in the same small town in County Clare. Both were practical men, yet both had their dreams of the service they could offer.

He touched his upper lip. Some feeling was returning. Settling his red cap more securely on his balding head, he adjusted his cassock and stood smiling at the side of his desk as his secretary ushered in the senator. He offered his ring with its green jewel and McCloud bent to kiss it.

"Your Eminence," he said. The cardinal nodded to his secretary that he could go and the door closed behind him. Once they were alone the formalities could be ignored.

"I saw you risking your life outside," the cardinal said, gesturing toward the window behind him. "It's a good job Paul Maguire wasn't behind the wheel of one of those autos. It would have been an awful temptation to put in front of him."

"Maguire has a chauffeur now," McCloud said. "A Cadillac, of course, though I believe he would prefer a Rolls Royce if the truth were known. Impossible, of course, in view of the country where they're built."

They moved to sit on a couch under a portrait of Francis Cardinal Spellman.

"I was given a Memorandum of Protest from fifty-two priests," the cardinal said. "They said they didn't agree with violence in Ulster, but they said the blame lay with the Protestants. They seemed to think that the Protestants should just close up their homes and go away."

"That would make things simpler. Will these priests be a problem? A revolt?"

"Oh, gracious me, no. They're just showing their independence. I can understand it. You know, Jay, there was a time when I thought of becoming a worker priest. Even in the church, we're not immune to the charm of political activism."

"You'd make a very good politician, Pat," McCloud said. "You have the essential quality of being able to listen to bores without flinching."

"Well, there's one man who might fit that category who I don't have to listen to for a while. Paul Maguire. You know how seriously he takes his chairmanship of the Saint Pattie's Day parade. He always likes to come here a few days before to discuss the arrangements. Not this year, not after my speech. Here it is just forty-eight hours to the time they start marching and I haven't heard a peep from him."

"I'm sorry," McCloud said. "Not about persuading you to my views on Ulster, but sorry that you have to face the effects."

The cardinal waved away the regrets. "No problem," he said. "The heat in that particular kitchen is bearable. Now the liturgical arguments are another matter. They're really serious. And it wasn't your argument that persuaded me, Jay, as convincing as it was. It was those two women from Belfast you brought to talk to me."

The cardinal had been reluctant to talk to the peace women, one Catholic, one Protestant. He had read about them and he suspected them of seeking glory. He knew the insidious effects of publicity on those unused to it and these two had been interviewed as many times as Clark Gable—the cardinal wasn't familiar with the modern cinema.

Finally, under the pressure of the senator's pleas, he had agreed to receive them on condition that the visit was not announced. He would not become a part of their entourage.

And yet, when McCloud brought them to the chancery one evening, the cardinal had been beguiled. They were handsome women, unawed by him, able in fact to joke once or twice. Afterward he wondered wryly how much he had been affected by the Protestant's action in kneeling to kiss his ring.

But he had recognized the agony behind their sincerity. Both had lost relatives in the bloodletting, both had been threatened with death. He remembered the words of the Catholic woman from Flax Street: "The rights and wrongs of it don't matter anymore. Only life matters. The killing has to stop. It's turning our children into murderers. They're taking death into their innards with the morning milk."

When they left, he made no promises. But a week later at a City Club luncheon, he had spoken and now he was ranged publicly with McCloud, who was already on record against the Provos· and their supporters in the United States.

"Fine women," McCloud said. "And brave ones, too."

"They persuaded me," the cardinal said, "but they didn't persuade you. A greater power did that, Jay. In Washington."

McCloud grinned without embarrassment.

"I wondered how long it would be before you heard," he said.

"*Ad majorem Dei gloriam*—and the White House," the cardinal said. "Don't worry, Jay. I'm only too happy if the president's persuasive powers lead to the greater glory of God and in this case I believe they do. Whatever our motives, we must stop the killing."

"The White House wants an end to it. It's a distraction they can do without. That's why the president asked me to oppose the Provos and try to choke off their U.S. supply lines. The theory is that once things quiet down in the Six Counties we can step forward with some economic aid. Jobs, that's what is needed. It all stems from that, the hatred and the violence."

"How are you going to make sure that the Catholics get their fair share of these jobs?" the cardinal asked.

"There'll be strings attached to the package. At the moment, they're talking about a quota system, based on the proportion of Catholics to Protestants. Nothing has been settled yet. It's too early."

"There'll be a reward for Senator Jay McCloud's initiative?"

"I'm a politician," McCloud smiled. "And politics is the art of give and take. I would have told you, but I thought the truth from those two women would be more effective than some scheme cooked up in the Oval Office."

"I have to be a politician, too, Jay. The Church is in need, too."

"I know what's in your mind. The ghettoes. Your poverty parishes."

"They need the jobs, as well as Ulster," the cardinal said.

"Again our trains of thought are on parallel lines. I have a promise from the president."

The cardinal slapped his knee in a most unclerical fashion. "Magnificent," he said. "God has answered our prayers, as I knew He would. Oh, Jay, if you knew how many times I have prayed for the inner-city areas, that something could be done to ameliorate their plight. And now here is the answer."

He stood up, beaming, and went to the window overlooking Madison Avenue. "When, Jay?" he asked.

"It will take a long time. There are other forces to consider—Congress, other blighted areas, other cities. But it will happen. The president is determined and I will do everything in my power—"

"I shall say a mass," the cardinal said. "For peace in Northern Ireland. I'll arrange it for before the parade on Saint Patrick's Day. Will you come?"

"Of course," the senator said. He was smiling, enjoying the cardinal's exultation.

"You know, Jay, all this reminds me of that chaplain at the Ohio State Penitentiary. His superior was being bothered with complaints by certain state legislators. They were grumbling that this priest who spent his time with known criminals was seeking to outlaw the death penalty. The bishop had this young priest brought before him and he said: 'I know you consort with criminals. You must continue to do so. But from now on stay away from legislators.' That does not apply in this case, Jay. There's something else I should add, though. I must confess that at the time you brought those two women to see me, I already knew you had other motives."

The senator grinned. "Perhaps I also should disclose that at that time I suspected you were already aware of that fact." For a moment they stared at each other and then both laughed out loud.

"When the decision to help Ulster is revealed, you will make the announcement?" the cardinal suggested.

"It will be my pleasant duty. The president insisted."

"I'm sure he did," the cardinal said. "With full press, radio, and TV coverage no doubt."

"I expect there will be some reporters on hand."

"Well, Jay, you'll deserve the glory of it. It can't have been easy for you, the past few months, with all the Irish patriots issuing their denunciations."

"We've both been getting it, Pat. I hear that at the Ancient Hibernians' dinner they were fighting for the mike so that they could declare what rogues we are. The word *traitor* must have been used a score of times."

"I expect old Maguire was there first."

"He was, he was indeed."

"I've been getting some letters," the cardinal said. "The usual nasty stuff. And phone calls. For God's sake, I wish their tempers would be aroused as much by the thought of starving children along Lenox Avenue."

"Have they been threatening you then, Pat?"

"I haven't seen them. My secretary has been burning the letters, but I believe there were a couple promising sudden death."

"Probably the same people who've been sending me love notes. Ah, well, that's what the mail is for. If they get it down on paper they feel better and they don't pick up the gun."

"Have you been reading that columnist, McEvoy—the professional Irishman from Brooklyn who's always writing about the hard men in their raincoats going out into the dangerous streets of Belfast to tackle the brutal British soldiery? He doesn't like us at all now."

"He's just a romantic," the senator said wryly. "So long as he can be romantic with other people's blood."

"It'll pass. These fusses always do," the cardinal said. From the window he was watching workmen unload police barriers from a truck in preparation for Thursday's parade. The papers were talking about a record number of marchers, more than 125,000 of them. The crowds would be commensurate. Standing there, he wondered about the value of the parade, and particularly the aftermath. The night of Saint Patrick's Day sometimes seemed more like Walpurgis Night. Drunks staggering out of the bars and heaving up in the gutter. Teenage girls coming into Manhattan from the other boroughs and behaving as they never would in Bay Ridge or Corona. Normally respectable men and women seemed to seize the time with the utmost joyousness for a loosening of all restraints. All under the banner of the wearing of the green. He sighed. It had turned into a heathen celebration under the cloak of a saint's name. For different reasons he found himself sympathizing with the merchants of Fifth Avenue who were issuing their annual protests at the loss of business and the damages they would suffer.

They wanted the parade held in the park. To the cardinal it seemed like a not unreasonable suggestion. Those who wanted to watch would be able to do so. The city's business wouldn't be interrupted. And perhaps from the park the celebrators would be less likely to fall into the bars. Still, it would never happen. The Irish were too powerful in the city. On Wednesday night they'd be painting the green line down Fifth Avenue again, wishing bad cess to John Vliet Lindsay, obviously an Orangeman, who once had forbade it.

"Are you marching on Thursday, Jay?" he said, noting with amusement that the very thought of the parade had brought a touch of brogue to his voice. The parade was a powerful idea.

"I haven't been invited," the senator said. "Paul Maguire wouldn't want me within a hundred miles on the big day."

"Perhaps it's for the best. Where will you be? In Washington?"

"Oh, dear me, no. Maguire won't chase me away. For a New York politician not to attend is akin to giving up his career. I'll be there."

"At Sixty-sixth Street? On the reviewing stand?"

"Well, I don't know. There's a problem with that. Certainly the other pols wouldn't want me there. With all the photographers around, they'd be fighting not to appear in the same viewfinder with me. Not on Saint Patrick's Day."

"I'd pay to see it," the cardinal said, turning from the window. "I've had my toes trodden on more than once by politicians trying to make sure they get in a picture with me. They're quite ruthless. As a matter of fact, Jay, I seem to remember the imprint of your shoes. Size eleven aren't they?"

"I plead guilty."

"So what will you do?"

"You'll be on the steps of the cathedral as usual?"

"I will. Not even Paul Maguire can stop me standing on the steps of my own cathedral. You'd like to join me, is that it?"

"It was in my mind, I must admit."

"Jay, you'd be very welcome. We'll make a couple of fine martyrs. We'll retreat only if we see them bringing out the rope, the stake, and a box of matches."

"They'll say I'm hiding behind your red hat and episcopal crosier, Pat."

"They'll have something to say whatever you do. We'll stand shoulder to shoulder against the storm. You'll come to the mass, then we'll have a cup of coffee here before we go out to the steps."

"It'll be interesting to see how old Maguire handles it when he reaches the cathedral," the senator said. "Just for that it'll be a day to remember."

The cardinal touched his mouth. The numbness was almost completely gone.

THIRTEEN

The newspaper was lying on the seat across the subway car from O'Hara, abandoned by some passenger. He could see the front-page headline: "Sanit Workers Balk at Contract." O'Hara moved across and picked it up. He flipped the pages, wondering if there was anything about his suspension and disappearance. Nothing. He was small stuff, he thought sourly.

He was about to toss it aside when he saw the headline at the bottom of page 5. "The Big Parade." It was a description of preparations for the Saint Patrick's Day parade in two days' time. The names came at him from the middle of the story. Cardinal Moran. Senator Jay McCloud.

The cardinal, the story said, would be standing on the steps of the cathedral to greet the marchers, as every cardinal always did. The reference to McCloud came a couple of paragraphs later.

"Observers were wondering if the senator would show up during the parade, in view of Irish-American hostility to his recent statements about U.S. support of IRA activities in Ulster," the story said. "McCloud was unavailable for comment, but parade chairman Paul

Maguire said, 'Whether he appears in public on this sacred day is a matter for his own conscience. I can't say anything more.' "

For some reason, O'Hara remembered the slogans he had spotted in the Protestant areas of Belfast after Bloody Sunday. Painted on walls and fences, they had proclaimed, "Paras 13, Bogside 0." As if the slaughter of thirteen unarmed Catholics was a game, a deadly football match in which the paratroopers had emerged bloodily victorious.

That was a game Mr. Death could play. How about "Mr. Death 2, Traitors 0"? How would it be if he destroyed the cardinal on the steps of his own cathedral? How would they like that? I'm going to hijack their fucking parade, he thought. I'll take it away from them. The excitement of it came at him. Suddenly he felt as if he were living in two dimensions, suffering the paranoia of the hunted, yet at the same time enjoying his hunt for his own quarry. The cardinal, he was offering himself to O'Hara. As for the turncoat senator, O'Hara would find him somehow. McCloud would feel the anger of the Provos, by God, he would.

Beyond that, he thought, I'm going to steal Saint Patrick's Day from these bland, uncaring Irish New Yorkers. His murderous thoughts urged the rattling train faster, faster, into Manhattan and the killing ground.

O'Hara started his reconnaisance at Fifth Avenue and Forty-fourth Street, where the marchers would assemble for the start of the parade. To replace his abandoned, food-soaked coat, he had bought a black windcheater at an army-surplus store on Forty-second Street. He turned up the fur collar against the bitter wind coming down the avenues from the north and pushed his hands into his pockets. It would be a long, cold walk, twenty blocks at least.

He started up the east side of Fifth. As he went he studied the walls of the central Manhattan canyon, searching out the ambush points; but even as he walked, his eyes restlessly ranging upwards, he knew there was only one place where he could hope to target the cardinal and the senator together. If McCloud marched, there would be a moment when both of them would be subject to his just anger. Outside the cathedral.

The gray ramparts of Rockefeller Center were coming up on his left. As he remembered it, the Center included a building directly across from the cathedral steps. Suddenly he recalled the bomb threat. What was it, three or four years ago, when he was assigned to Midtown North? Sure. That old fool Matson had been the captain. Retired long ago after that trouble with the politician's son, the hit-and-run driver. Yeah, there had been a bomb alert at the Center and Matson had sent O'Hara and a couple of other detectives to help out in the search. An impossible job. They had gone through the motions like they always did, but there was no way you could search that enormous complex of buildings. It was a city within a city. He remembered the jokes about searching the drawers of the Rockettes.

For want of anything better to do, O'Hara had looked over the International Building, between Fiftieth and Fifty-first. He had gone to an office on the twenty-sixth floor, some kind of book publisher. Full of gorgeous, college-type broads. The building had not been evacuated and the staff were at their desks. During the sham of a search, O'Hara found himself talking to an accountant in an office overlooking Fifth Avenue. From the window there was a magnificent view of Saint Patrick's, the gray spires and the structure that lay in the form of a great cross, the merchant towers pressing in from all sides as if to overwhelm this symbol of the scourge of the marketplace.

And there was a perfect view of the steps running in front of the great metal doors.

Moving up the avenue now, O'Hara felt a tremor of excitement. He could strike and be gone before anybody knew where the bullet had been fired from. The crowds would hinder any attempt at pursuit.

He considered his flight from this city, which to him had become as putrid as a cesspool. He would ditch his weapon and then there would be no more reason to suspect him than eight million other New Yorkers. Just dump it in a trash can. By the time it was found he would be long gone. His shield would help. The shuttle to Boston, he thought. That would be best. At the most there would be an hour's wait at La Guardia, probably much less. They wouldn't be looking for him in Boston, not at first anyway. From Boston he could get a plane across the Atlantic. He thought of Ireland and suddenly the pleasure of it overwhelmed him. He would be going home. More than that, he would be going home as a hero who had risked all for the movement and succeeded in striking a mighty blow. He had no thought of failure.

He was outside Saks now. The windows were full of deck chairs and sunshades, of mannequins in beach robes and swimsuits. He went across Fiftieth Street with the lights, a tall, thin-faced man, the poison working in him, a bitter twist to his lips. There were a few people on the cathedral steps and he went among them, staring up at the great carved doors and then at the passing throng as if he were a tourist. Almost immediately though, his eyes were drawn across Fifth to the mass of Rockefeller Center. Beyond the sidewalk on the west side of the avenue was a forecourt with an art deco statue of a muscle-bound Atlas, wearing something that looked like an Egyptian headdress and carrying a skeletal circle representing the globe. On either side of the forecourt, jutting out to the edge of the sidewalk, were buildings of only a few stories.

Behind them and enclosing the forecourt reared the multistoried International Building, one of the tallest in the Rockefeller Center complex. O'Hara's gaze moved up the gray facade, stained with the city's filth, until he found the twenty-sixth floor.

There were the windows from which he had looked down during the bomb alert. He wondered if the same firm still occupied those offices. But why go that high? From a lower window the shots would be more accurate, his accomplishment surer. Half twenty-six was thirteen. Unlucky thirteen, he thought. Unlucky for the traitors. He found the thirteenth floor and he gauged the distance between the windows and the cathedral steps where he stood. Never before, he thought, had he been allowed the luxury of scouting the terrain before he struck. Always in Ulster, in England, his orders had been to come in, make the hit and get out immediately. Now he was standing where his target would stand, seeing what his target would see if the cardinal should lift his eyes above the heads of the marchers. Less than one hundred yards. Poised on the steps, he already knew what he would do.

He went across the avenue and through the doors behind the Atlas statue. The building, with its escalators, lobbies, ground-floor stores, was so vast that he had trouble finding the elevator that would carry him to the thirteenth floor. Finally he located it. When the elevator door opened, he halted and stared for a moment until a girl brushed impatiently past him into the car. Jesus, the car was manned by a uniformed operator. He had forgotten that. He had assumed the elevators would be automatic.

He walked in after the girl and said, "Thirteen." The doors closed and the car began its climb. Fuck. An elevator operator was an additional complication, somebody who could identify him. He looked at the man. Black, uninterested in his passengers. He must see a thousand people in his elevator every day, day after day. Their faces must merge into a great blank. Why would he notice O'Hara on Saint Patrick's Day?

At the thirteenth floor, he stepped out with the confidence of a visitor who knew exactly where he was going. He went around a corner away from the elevator bank. He was alone in the brightly lit corridor. He paused to regain his sense of direction. The elevator faced west. The offices overlooking Fifth had to be at the end of this corridor. Suddenly a door to his right opened.

A man said, "Have a good trip, Johnny." For a moment, befuddled, he thought the words were aimed at him. A gray-haired man carrying a briefcase came out, back first, saying, "Oh, sure, Dan. Detroit's my favorite city." He closed the door and without looking at O'Hara walked toward the elevators. O'Hara moved on.

In the middle of the corridor that ran north to south on the east side of the building was a pair of wooden doors. The office behind them must overlook the front of the cathedral. O'Hara pushed the doors open and went in.

A uniformed policeman, his cap peak pulled low over a saturnine face, was staring at him. Beyond him, another cop was turning to look at O'Hara. They both looked grim, tense. O'Hara felt disoriented. Instinctively, his hand moved toward the .38 under his jacket. Christ, right into a trap. Like a stupid amateur.

The cops were frozen in position. There were desks and mail trolleys and scales and, along one wall, a series of mailboxes. There were other people in the room. Three young blacks. A middle-aged man. Two girls. It was some sort of mail room.

"Who are you?" It was the cop closest to him. He had a Zapata moustache shadowing a low-slung jaw.

Jesus, O'Hara thought, he doesn't know. He really doesn't know. His hammering heart began to steady. He looked toward the windows. The cathedral spires. But this place was no good. Too open. Too many people working in it.

"What's going on?" he said.

"I'll ask the questions," the cop said, moving closer. There was something odd about him. O'Hara couldn't make it out and then he recognized it. The cop was scared, almost as scared as O'Hara had been a moment earlier.

"Joe," the cop said over his shoulder. "Come here. We may have something."

O'Hara knew what it was. They were on some sort of scam. Bagmen, maybe, collecting a payoff. The second cop's hand was hovering over his gun. He wore it low on his thigh like some sort of Western gunslinger.

"I'm on the job," O'Hara said. He watched their reaction, beginning to enjoy himself. He took his shield from his pocket and flashed it. The two uniformed men looked even unhappier.

The men and women in the room had given up any pretense of working and were staring openly at the scene by the door.

Suddenly, O'Hara was impatient. He didn't have time to mess with these scumbags. "Outside," he said.

He opened the door and the patrolmen walked through like truant schoolboys. In the corridor, the door closed behind them, the two cops stood in front of him, almost at attention, awaiting the sentence, the end of their careers.

"What's the con?" O'Hara said.

They stared at him dumbly.

"Oh, shit," he said. "Get the fuck out of here. Don't you realize you're in the middle of a stakeout? There's gonna be more brass along here in a moment than you'd see at an Academy graduation."

Still, they stood staring at him. They couldn't believe he was going to let them go.

"This is what you're going to do," O'Hara said slowly and clearly as if he were addressing retarded children. "You're going to walk down this corridor to the elevators and you're going to press the button and when the elevator car arrives you're going to step in, the both of you, and you're going down to the street and you're going to resume your posts. Got it?"

They turned as if in a dream and moved along the corridor. O'Hara watched them go. Just before they went around the corner, the cop with the moustache turned and said, "Thanks." Then they had gone.

O'Hara waited two minutes. Further along from the mail room was a door inlaid with glass. He looked at the lettering on the glazed glass. An employment agency. "Jobs for the Boys. President, Sam Jiras." It had to overlook the cathedral. He went in.

There was a counter, a glass barrier, and a woman sitting at a switchboard. She was reading a paperback book and she ignored him. He looked past her and saw what he hungered to see. Beyond an open door was a window and outside the window he could make out the edge of one of the cathedral spires.

O'Hara turned to leave. Immediately, the woman put down her book and said, "Yes? You want to register?"

He kept his back to her. "Wrong office," he said, his hand already on the door. "It must be down the corridor. Sorry."

Without looking back, he went out. Sam Jiras, president, he thought. Okay, Sam, you don't know it, but you just joined the Provos. He moved swiftly back down the corridor to the elevators. He felt exultant.

Luck, hell, he thought as he waited for the elevator. Luck had nothing to do with it. It hadn't been luck in Ireland. You had to seize the moment and act, take the chance, make your own breaks, and he'd done it. The plan was already forming, the way he would use the Jobs for the Boys Employment Agency. He had one thing your average assassin didn't have. He had a police detective's shield. He stepped into the elevator, ignoring the operator. Let the operator identify him and see how much good that would do them when he was safe within the protection of the Provos.

*   *   *

142

The three men were waiting in the lobby when O'Hara stepped out of the elevator. They went into their routine with the easy expertise of professionals who had worked together before. While two of them followed O'Hara to the Fifth Avenue exit, the third approached the elevator operator who was standing at his controls inside the car.

"Floor?" the operator said.

"Ten."

The operator punched a button but waited for more passengers. "That gentleman you just brought down. Wasn't it Bill Sigrist?" The operator shrugged, bored. "I don't know him," he said.

"I was sure it was Bill Sigrist. He has an office on the ninth floor."

"He got on at the thirteenth floor. I don't know his name."

"Funny," the man said. "I could have sworn it was Sigrist."

He would have paid for the information, but now he didn't have to and that gave him a special satisfaction.

It wasn't a question of the money. It gave the man pleasure to know that he had the technique still to get what he wanted for nothing. It was the sort of thing for which Toby East employed him. Okay, so what had O'Hara wanted on the thirteenth floor?

O'Hara stood for a moment in the forecourt of the International Building with the Atlas statue looming over him. He could continue his reconnaisance up Fifth to Sixty-sixth Street, where the politicians would review the parade on Thursday. If the traitor McCloud dared to appear there with the borough presidents, the mayor, the governor, and their hacks, then O'Hara could take him out like he would take out the cardinal.

First, the turncoat cleric and then the senator. The trouble was that once he had killed the cardinal, McCloud would bolt for cover. There was little hope that O'Hara could move fast enough to waste both of them if they were nearly twenty blocks apart. He pondered murder like a mathematician faced with a new problem in integral calculus. It was no good, he decided. Mr. Death would have to introduce himself to the cardinal outside the cathedral and hope that McCloud would march in the parade. That way he might leave his calling card with both.

A fear was growing in O'Hara. It blossomed in him like some

terrible malignant tumor. He feared that a patrolman, a detective, would tap him on the shoulder, say, "They're looking for you downtown," and take him in before he could act against the betrayers of the dream. He shivered, looked around, and began to move, his steps quickening.

He went across Fifth to the office of Thomas Cook, the English travel agent.

It pleased him to use this enemy organization to help him strike against two of London's allies. He asked about flights from Boston to Ireland for the following Thursday.

The girl flicked through her books. "There's an Aer Lingus 707 from Boston to Dublin that night," she said. She was young, yet she had the husky voice of a spirit drinker. "Flight EI 116. It leaves Boston at nine thirty-five and gets into Dublin at ten-thirty the following morning. Is that any good?"

There were seats available and he paid with cash—$279 for an economy seat, plus $3 head tax. Three days, he thought. Three days and he'd be breathing Irish air, Mr. Death's work completed. He put the ticket in his breast pocket and walked out. Beautiful. He'd be in Boston by early afternoon. Plenty of time to catch the 707, not enough time for anybody to follow his spoor. Now he had to kill some time, first the time and then the traitors. He knew exactly where he would go to do that.

O'Hara was walking to the ticket counter of the Adirondack Trailways Bus Company in the Port Authority terminal on the West Side when he saw Minelli. He knew Minelli was with the Vice Squad these days, chasing pimps around the terminal, taking when he could, arresting when he couldn't. Fucking Vinnie Minelli who'd taken him to the cathouse on East Sixty-second Street. Minelli would know they were looking for him downtown. Minelli would take him in as soon as spit. The vice detective was leaning against a wall near one of the Greyhound counters, watching the throng with his hard, spiteful little eyes. There was no way O'Hara could reach the Adirondack Trailways counter without going past Minelli. He stopped to look in the window of a candy store.

If Minelli was there, Nick Carter wouldn't be far away. Carter knew him as well; he'd come to O'Hara's wedding without being invited. Shit, the bus was leaving in twenty minutes and he couldn't move. He turned to take a quick look up to the second floor of the terminal. Yeah, there was Carter, standing at the top of the escalator so that people had to edge past him. Nick Carter in his pie-shaped hat standing there as if he owned the whole fucking terminal. Goiters, both of them. Even if he got past Minelli, Nick Carter would spot him and give his partner the high sign. He fought the paranoia that threatened to take control.

Slowly O'Hara drifted away from them, back toward Eighth Avenue. He had fifteen, sixteen minutes to get his ticket and make it to the gate downstairs. He went into a liquor store. There were no other customers. He bought a bottle of cheap California brandy. As he came out of the store he took off the cap. About ten minutes left.

He walked directly to a trash basket against a wall. He let some of the brandy spill out onto the pile of old newspapers, candy wrappers, empty cigarette packs in the basket. He dropped the bottle into the trash. He took out his matches and lit a cigarette, his eyes passing swiftly over the unheeding crowds moving past.

Now. He tossed the flaming match and the cigarette into the trash can. He was moving swiftly away when it caught. First the flicker of flame, then a whoosh as the fire fed on the brandy. A shopping-bag lady, one of the city's tattered vagrants, was staring past him and he looked again over his shoulder. Just then the bottle exploded and a blue pillar of incandescence leaped up from the trash. Pointing at O'Hara, the shopping-bag lady screamed, "I saw him. I saw him." But her words were lost in other shouts, shrieks. People were running away from the flaming trash can.

O'Hara went with the pack. Ahead he could see Minelli walking quickly into the onrush, swearing, elbowing aside the panic-stricken mob, forcing his way toward the glow of the trash can. Nick Carter was running down one of the escalators. Six steps from the bottom he leaped over the handrail and as he landed he was running. Fucking Errol Flynn to the rescue, O'Hara thought, but now they were past him. He could hear the shopping-bag lady still yelling, "I saw him. I saw him." Nobody would take any notice of her. He slipped into the Adirondack Trailways area and asked for a ticket.

"What the hell's going on out there?" the agent said.

"Trash-can fire."

"Shit. This place is a madhouse. That'll be seventeen fifty. Gate thirty-seven downstairs."

O'Hara pushed the money across, took the ticket, and went down to Gate thirty-seven. He caught the bus with three minutes to spare. It left on time and O'Hara found a seat at the back where he could smoke. Minelli and Nick Carter, he thought, a couple of real shmucks. You had to make your own breaks. Luck had nothing to do with it.

The bus had stopped in the center of Woodstock to let off passengers when the thought hit O'Hara. Christ, he didn't know about the windows in Rockefeller Center. Did they open? Or were they permanently closed, the interior climate controlled by heating and air conditioning? If they were sealed he couldn't smash one without drawing attention and he couldn't risk firing through the glass. It would distort the path of the bullet. Again he felt the blossom of fear, the paranoia that threatened to overwhelm him.

If the windows did not open, he would have to abort his plan to use the International Building as a sniper's nest. Yet the skyscrapers surrounding Rockefeller Center were more modern, even more likely to have windows that would not open. He wondered about the roofs of the two shoulder buildings that jutted out to the sidewalk from the International Building. From the twenty-sixth floor, he remembered, he had seen roof gardens on both structures. Perhaps he could use them. But they were overlooked by thousands of windows. And, almost inevitably, there would be people on the roofs to watch the parade.

The bus began to move. O'Hara stared at the village, quiet now out of the tourist season, and saw that, as if to compound his malaise, Woodstock had received a fresh fall of snow. There were two inches here and probably it would be deeper when he left the bus in the mountains fifteen miles further west. He cursed himself for his failure to check the windows; he could think of nobody else to blame and it infuriated him. If he telephoned the management of Rockefeller Center, even if he called "Jobs for the Boys" to ask about the windows, he would arouse suspicions. He swore again. He would have to leave it until the morning of Saint Patrick's Day, find out then. He would have to trust to his luck. He had forgotten now that he believed in making his own luck.

With a hiss of air brakes, the bus pulled into Phoenicia just two and a half hours after leaving Manhattan. Most of the passengers had already left at intermediate stops and he was the only one to step out. The driver called out a loud "good-night," as if to emphasize his thankfulness that he could remain in the warm bus. O'Hara ignored him. He trudged down the street, his light city shoes sinking into the soft, wet snow.

Phoenicia, in spite of its exotic name, was little more than a single street lined by a handful of stores and Victorian-era houses, surrounded by steep, pine-clothed mountains. There was a rope-tow ski area just outside the town, but most skiers bypassed the place, heading along Route 28 for the trails of Belleayre and Hunter. In the summer, white-water enthusiasts contended with the currents and rocks of the river that scoured the bottom of the valley that held the village.

Now, at night, nobody stirred along the main street. O'Hara headed for the neon lights of a bar. A Schlitz beer sign flickered uncertainly in the window amidst dusty Christmas decorations. He could have set off directly for the cottage, Cahill's cottage, nearly two miles away in the mountains, but he didn't know how many eyes might have noted his arrival on the bus. He knew the village, knew that for some residents the passage of the Trailways bus through the village was the most exciting thing that happened, one of the few tangible signs that there was another world beyond the mountains. He didn't want anybody watching him plodding toward the cottage, wondering who he was, why he was there.

The bar smelled of disinfectant and failure. The jukebox was playing something from the 1950s and O'Hara saw two figures swaying in the center of the linoleum floor before he took a seat at the bar. Two men were on barstools, watching a television set lodged on a platform above the door. They could have been brothers, both burly, blond, red-faced, both wearing heavy red lumber jackets. They stared at O'Hara for a moment, said nothing, resumed their contemplation of a comedienne in Hollywood whose voice was drowned by the music of the jukebox.

The bar was commanded by a sad-faced woman, pregnant, wearing a man's hunting shirt and elastic-topped jeans sagging below the bulge of her belly.

She looked at O'Hara with an aggrieved lifting of her eyebrows, as if he somehow was responsible for her shapelessness.

"Scotch on the rocks," O'Hara said. "Cutty Sark."

"We're out of that. Not much call for it around here." She made it sound as though there had been a town meeting and by unanimous vote it had been decided that Phoenicia didn't like Cutty Sark.

"Okay," O'Hara said. "Anything you've got."

"Bus was late tonight," one of the men said to show he knew O'Hara had been aboard.

"Not often late," the other man said, his stare unwaveringly on the television screen.

"It was tonight," the first man said.

O'Hara took a swallow of his whisky and turned away from them. Thumb-sucking hicks. The two dancers were holding each other close, belly hard against belly, hands roving over backs and buttocks. They both wore tight jeans and sweaters. As they languidly turned, O'Hara saw they were both girls. A long-haired blonde and a brunette with a boyish bob. Dykes, he thought disgustedly. Still, they weren't like the Greenwich Village crowd. They were attractive, fresh-faced, slender. Girl-next-door stuff. They were grinding into each other. The blonde's hands were now clenched around the high tight buttocks of her partner who had pushed a hand under the blonde's black sweater. From Woodstock, O'Hara thought. Everything went in Woodstock. Watching their open sexual play, he felt his loins come alive.

"Groovy place," the blonde said to him, over the brunette's shoulder. She was smiling at him, smiling while the other girl played with her breasts.

"That's enough of that," the woman behind the bar said.

She turned and pressed a button under the counter. The music faded, the rhythm fading away into a sigh. The girls still swayed in each other's arms. Their hair was clean and shining as if just shampooed.

"Take a hike, both of you," the woman behind the bar said.

Still the girls held each other, slender body tight against slender body. "We're out of the closet," the blonde said to O'Hara, "and they want us back with the mothballs."

The backs of the two men at the bar were taut with disapproval.

"Call the cops," one of them said.

At that, the dancers pulled apart and the blonde reached down to lift the cuff of her jeans. She wore brown cowboy boots. When she straightened up, there was a knife in her right hand. Below the fringe of gleaming hair, her eyes had a crazy glint. High on something, O'Hara thought.

"Anybody calls the cops get this," she said. "Anybody touches Chrissie gets it, too." The men at the bar, the woman behind it, didn't move. They stared at the knife as if at a cobra. It was a dull, evil-looking blue.

O'Hara watched the scene with cold detachment. His first brief instinct had been to act, act as if he had been on 116th Street. That had gone. Even if he had been unconcerned about drawing attention to himself, he realized, he would have done nothing. He still had the badge and the gun, but he was no longer thinking like a cop. He had moved over the line.

"Okay, sweetheart, let's go," the blonde said. She was trying to imitate Humphrey Bogart's lisp.

Grinning, the brunette moved behind her, clasping her around the waist, pressing her breasts and belly against the blonde's back. As they began to move in lockstep toward the door, Chrissie's hands moved up under the blonde's sweater and she began to fondle the breasts again. O'Hara could see the fingers flicking at the nipples. All the time, the blonde kept the knife in front of her as if to repel a dozen ravishers although nobody had stirred since she pulled the knife. Nobody had even spoken.

At the door, the blonde took the knife in both hands and bent it. It was made of rubber.

"Here's looking at you, sweethearts," the blonde said. Both of them shrieked with laughter. They turned through the door and were gone. O'Hara could hear them laughing on the street outside.

Behind the bar, the woman was on the telephone asking for the sheriff's office. The men in the lumber jackets went to the sooty windows to stare after the girls.

"Gone down toward the bridge," one of them said. "They're dancing again. In the middle of the street."

"You want we should grab them?" the other one said.

"You stay right here," the woman said. "Jack said he'll be up in a minute. Dirty dykes. He'll take care of them."

"Got to go," O'Hara said. The deputies would be on their way and they'd want to know who he was, maybe call him as a witness if they decided to lock up the lesbians. He finished his drink and headed for the door. Sometimes, he was almost glad little John had not lived, had left a world with so much crap in it. Sometimes he thought he hated people. Hated them individually and together. He wanted to be alone in the cottage, alone with the warmth of his thoughts about the approaching moment of reckoning. The crud was everywhere where there were people, even up here.

He left the bar, ignored by the woman, the two men. Down the street, the girls were bent over the bridge staring at the ice-rimmed river. The night was damp but windless. Above freezing, so that the snow was turning slushy. O'Hara slipped into the side street that ran up into the mountains. Fucking morons, he thought. How many were there like that in Ireland, crazy idiots who would never understand what he was doing for them?

The three men watched O'Hara plod off into the darkness.

They were sitting in a black Ford, which they'd parked, lights out, in front of a closed grocery store while the New York bus let off its lone arrival. One of them, the man in the rear seat, got out and stood for a moment looking down toward the bridge. He could see the girls embracing, kissing. They parted and went toward a white Corvette. The man moved across the icy sidewalk and into the bar.

By the time he reached the cottage, O'Hara had thrown off the depression that attacked him after the incident in the bar. He had walked in the ploughed center of the road so that he would leave no tracks.

There were no other houses in sight. Two hundred yards before the cottage, which was perched in front of a stand of timber overlooking a small valley, he left the road and walked across a field that once had been a sheep pasture until the farmer had admitted defeat. O'Hara wanted no tracks leading up the rough path to the cottage. Coming this way he approached the solitary building from the side. Twenty yards away, standing under a pine, he stopped and listened. Other than a light wind soughing through its branches, he could hear nothing but his own breathing. It was as though the valley had been stripped of all life.

He stared at the sharp slope of the cottage roof, coated with snow, and at the walls constructed from stones torn from a miniature quarry higher up the hillside. Deserted. He knew it would be. Cahill had talked of renting it to skiers in the winter, had even advertised in the local paper, but it was too far from the ski slopes and a heavy fall of snow on the drive frustrated all but the largest ploughs.

Still, he approached carefully and circled the place before finally confronting the heavy wooden front door. He opened the storm door and rammed his elbow through the glass panel directly above the lock. The first time, it cracked. A second blow smashed it and O'Hara reached inside. By stretching his arm, he could just reach the latch that controlled the lock. It turned easily.

Inside, he felt his way through the living room and into the kitchen. Cahill usually kept a flashlight in a cupboard above the sink and it was there that O'Hara found it. The kitchen windows faced away from the road and he flicked the switch on and off to test the battery. Okay. He drew the kitchen curtains, then moved carefully back into the living room. He didn't use the flashlight until he had drawn the heavy drapes across the windows.

The cottage had been built in the 1920s. Its rough stone walls, plastered on the interior, were ten inches thick, broken by windows so narrow that they would have served as seige embrasures. The living room ceiling was supported by black box beams and a large stone fireplace dominated one end of the room. O'Hara saw that Cahill had left a pile of wood alongside the grate and he began to build a fire. While the flames caught, he went into the basement and punched the button on the oil furnace. The engine came to life with a roar. He was chilled and his shoes and trouser cuffs were sodden from the snow.

In the kitchen he found cans containing potato soup, meat loaf, and peas. The electric stove was working and he set about cooking a meal in the light of a candle he had found on the mantelpiece in the living room. He discovered a bottle of Johnny Walker Red Label, kept for visitors. Cahill didn't drink. O'Hara poured himself a glass, lifted it in salute and said, "To you, uncle. You douche bag."

By the time he had finished preparing his meal, warm air pouring through the floor grids from the furnace, together with heat from the fire, had driven the clammy chill from the cottage. He ate sitting by the fireplace, staring into the leaping flames. Now he felt pretty good. The problem of the windows in Rockefeller Center was something that he'd solve. He would solve it because he was driven by something that ordinary people, like those in the village tavern, wouldn't understand. An irony struck him. The English spy, King, he had been living in a cottage not so different from this, outside Crossmaglen, until he had opened the door to a stranger. English fool, he thought. He had been a pigeon fat for the plucking.

They wouldn't get O'Hara as easily. They wouldn't get O'Hara at all. He was the hunter, not the hunted.

Suddenly he swore and put aside his plate. He had forgotten the most important thing, the chief reason he had come to this godforsaken house in the Catskills. It wasn't just to wait for the moment to strike. He went into the small bedroom that opened off the living room. The glass-fronted cabinet was still there and through the glass he saw it. No problem, it was waiting for him. Where else would it have been? Still, he was angry with himself once more for not going straight to the cabinet as soon as he had broken into the place. Was he losing his street smarts now that he was in the boondocks far from the danger of his hunting ground? He looked at his face, reflected from the glass doors in a flicker of light from the candle in his hand. Mr. Death, he thought, you need to keep your wits. His gaze focused on the interior of the cabinet and he forgot his self-doubt.

It was a 99 Savage, a lever-action hunting rifle known by buffs as the take-down model because the stock and action could be detached from the barrel. The style had been more common before World War II when hunters traveled into the mountain by rail rather than auto and needed an easily portable weapon. There were other guns in the cabinet, but they didn't break down. The Savage could be reduced from a total length of forty-two inches to only twenty-two inches. He could carry it around Manhattan in a bag and nobody would raise an eyebrow. With its Bausch and Lomb scope, it weighed only about seven pounds. He pulled open a cabinet drawer. Yes, there was a box of the 30/30 ammunition it fired.

He remembered the first time he had seen the gun. It was on his eighteenth birthday. Cahill had brought him up to the cottage and, the next day, making a mystery of where they were headed, he had driven them north. The goal was Albany, the state capital.

Cahill took O'Hara to lunch at the Sheraton Ten-Eyck on State Street, below the capital building. O'Hara was allowed a whisky sour. "You're a man now, John," his uncle said. Even Cahill took a drink, although O'Hara noticed he didn't finish it. Cahill had no taste for alcohol.

After lunch they went to the Gut, the main artery of the skid-row area that lay close to the Hudson River below the hill on which the old capitol stood. The gun store was at the corner of Green and Beaver streets. O'Hara clearly remembered the man behind the counter that day, a giant with a shaven head and tattoos on his hamlike forearms. Evidently he knew Cahill, because as soon as they walked into the store, he bent to take something from under the counter. It was the Savage. Cahill must have ordered it. Later O'Hara would learn that the man was a power in the O'Connell political machine, which controlled the town, and a ranking member of the movement.

"A beauty," the man said. "Take a doe's nipple off at a hundred fifty yards and she wouldn't even notice." He handed it over the counter for inspection.

Cahill hefted it for a moment, then turned to O'Hara.

"It's yours," he said. "For your birthday. It's a good gun and it's time you had one of your own. I'll teach you to use it and you'll take a few deer, maybe other things, with it before you're finished."

"His eighteenth birthday, is it then?" the man behind the counter said. He snickered. "You going to Marion's?"

Cahill said something but the young O'Hara wasn't listening. He was getting the feel of the Savage, putting it to his shoulder and aiming at a target at the end of the store.

"You'll want a scope," the man said.

Cahill bought him a Bausch and Lomb and they watched as the shaven-headed man fitted it to the rifle. O'Hara was delighted with the deadly appearance of the weapon. That day, that gun, was one of the many reasons why Cahill had succeeded in binding O'Hara to his ideas and to the movement. Cahill had no children, his wife had died before O'Hara was born, but Cahill knew how to mold a young man to his wishes. He molded O'Hara.

Later, after they had locked the gun in Cahill's car, the two of them went to Marion's. It was a brothel.

Now, nearly twenty years later in the shadowy bedroom, O'Hara reached out to put his hands on the gun once more. There had been no better place to leave it than in this cottage where it was always ready in the hunting season. The cabinet was locked. O'Hara looked in the cabinet drawer for the key. Even as he did so he knew that Cahill wouldn't leave it there, for if it was so easily available, then why bother to lock the cabinet?

He went to the kitchen and came back with a knife. He slipped it between the two glass doors and twisted until the small lock cracked away from the wood. The doors swung open and he reached in for the gun. Now he had what he needed to answer betrayal. He would test-fire it tomorrow in the woods.

He carried it into the living room and began to clean it. He wondered about a silencer. He knew where he could get one, but it would do little to muffle the sound of the shot from a rifle. Another fucking problem.

Thoughts of the parade conjured up images of Saint Patrick's Day. The red-faced kids with their drums and bugles, the girls' thighs well covered by decent skirts unless the vagrant breezes caught them. The green uniformed stewardesses from Aer Lingus smiling and waving. The grim, lined faces of the IRA veterans who now lived in Canarsie and Bayside and Flushing. And the pipes, always the pipes and the beating of the drums. He paused in his cleaning of the barrel and stared into the flames. Of course, the bands. They came crashing through the center of Manhattan like a triumphant army and when they were alongside you couldn't hear yourself sneeze. If he fired when a band was passing the cathedral he would need no silencer. The sound of the shot would be swallowed by the savage wave of the drums and the pipes and the bugles, ay, and the cheers.

He resumed the cleaning of his weapon. A fierce grin twisted his mouth. The music of Ireland would be his ally, lead him into battle as it had the tribes those centuries past.

"It's all coming together," he told himself softly. A few minutes later, satisfied, he put down the gun and stretched out on the flower-patterned sofa that flanked the fireplace. He lay there watching the flames chasing shadows between the black beams. O'Hara saw the gun coming up before him, tracking onto its target, and he heard the music thundering up to him, shielding him, urging him on. The music of his homeland.

The three men were back together in the car in Phoenicia. They had learned that the road to the cottage led nowhere. He would have to come back into the village.

Two of them were sleeping; the third was on watch.

Tomorrow they would find out if O'Hara owned the cottage or, if not, who did. Tomorrow they would telephone London.

Sucking on a piece of hard candy, the man on watch thought about London. The orders to switch to full-time surveillance had come through just in time, just before O'Hara went underground. He winced at the thought of the reaction in the office overlooking Trafalgar Square if they had lost him, if they hadn't been close by when he went to the bus terminal and bought his ticket for this godforsaken spot in the mountains.

It had been easy enough to follow the bus, knowing where O'Hara was headed, but then there had been the scene in the bar, the deputies coming in almost on his heels. At first the men in the car had thought O'Hara had called the police, knew he was being followed. That didn't make sense, though. And the swaggering men in the fur-trimmed hats weren't interested in anything but a couple of lesbians. The deputies were going to give them a hard time when they caught up with them.

O'Hara, he thought, sinking back into his seat, was holed up for the night. The sparks from the cottage chimney proved he was staying, at least until tomorrow. There would be no action until then. The man on watch wondered idly if London would order a takeout. It was the perfect place—isolated, forgotten in the winter. The body might not be found for a month. That decision would have to come down from Toby East. In London, it would be 4:00 A.M. No need to disturb them. The bird was settled in for the night. Even so, the watcher didn't shift his gaze from the road down which O'Hara might come.

FOURTEEN

Two show girls wearing plumes, skimpy jackets, and tights were parading through the city room followed by a doleful press agent who once had been at the right hand of the governor but now was reduced to plugging a failing nightclub on Fifty-second Street. King watched their neat buttocks swaying toward the office of one of the paper's gossip writers. Greatorex would have their pictures taken by one of the photographers, allow himself to be entertained at lunch, and publish nothing about the club in his Broadway column. The press agent didn't expect him to. It was enough that he could prove to his employer that he had made the contact with Greatorex, bought him lunch. He would report that the story had been forced out by late-breaking chitchat.

"Get on with it," Burr said. "There's a big news hole today."

King looked down at the copy in front of him. Another load of rubbish from the Washington bureau. The Senate Foreign Relations Committee this time. The lead was in the sixth paragraph. He didn't bother to suggest a rewrite.

The phone rang and Burr, painting a picture of a harassed executive, swore distractedly and answered it.

"It's for you, King," he said. "Don't be long. There's a big news hole to fill and you're getting personal calls and fucking Dancer has called in sick and they're screaming for Master's copy."

King punched the button on his phone and took the call. It was Ransom, from police headquarters.

"Hey, King," he said. "You still interested in that cop, O'Hara?"

"What've you got?"

"Something funny's going on and I think it's about time you told me what it's all about."

"Soon, soon. Just as soon as I can. What's funny?"

"Don't screw me on this, King. I want a piece of it."

"You will, Ransom, you will. Now tell me."

"All right. But, remember, never try to con me. I've been over talking to Schmidt, the guy who runs the shooflies, Internal Affairs. He owes me."

"Everybody owes you, Ransom. That's why you're the greatest police reporter in the world."

"Big joke. As a matter of fact I am. If the paper realized the importance of crime stories, I'd be on page one every day. You see what they did with that shootout down on Mulberry Street? Page fucking ten."

"Disgraceful," King said, glancing at Burr, who was growing restless. "What did Schmidt say?"

"Okay, now listen. This O'Hara had a partner, a shithead called Lenane who thinks he's a reincarnation of Jimmy Walker. East Side pad, broads, fancy Porsche, and he thinks the Knapp Commission was some study of the sleeping habits of night workers. On the pad, like O'Hara. He gets suspended the same time as O'Hara, but now they're no longer buddies. Lenane decides he doesn't want to take the rap so he starts singing to Schmidt. There's some talk he was around wearing a wire for Internal Affairs—"

"Hold it," King said. Burr had put down his pencil and was staring coldly at King.

Putting his hand over the mouthpiece, King said, "Two minutes and I'll be through. It may be a story."

"You're alleged to be a deskman, not a reporter," Burr said. "Get on with it, for chrissake, King." He could hear Ransom saying, "Tell that moron, Burr, to go back to licking Anderson's ass." He took his hand away from the mouthpiece.

"Okay," he said, "go ahead. You were talking about O'Hara's partner, this Lenane."

"Right. Okay, so the jig is up and Lenane and Schmidt are holding hands. Okay, so I'm talking to Schmidt and he owes me 'cause of that nice profile I did on him and he starts rapping on about O'Hara. I'd bought him a couple of drinks, too, see because that helps you get information in my line of work."

"Yes, I'd heard that," King said.

"Anyway, Schmidt lets slip that Lenane says he's been covering up for O'Hara."

"What d'you mean, covering up?"

"My exact words. I said, what d'you mean? Schmidt says that, for more than a year, O'Hara has been making covert trips to Ireland, something to do with the IRA. While he's been out of the country, Lenane has been covering for him as if he's been on duty right here in New York all the time. So now they've got three strikes on O'Hara —the bribery charge out in Brooklyn, his failure to turn in his shield and gun, and now unauthorized absences from duty. They're gonna throw the book at him when they catch up with him and bring him downtown. Schmidt is real pissed off."

"Did Schmidt report all this?"

"Sure, that's what's interesting. Among other places his report went to was BOSS, where they deal with nuts like the IRA mob and the Weathermen and the Puerto Rican bombers."

"I thought BOSS said O'Hara was clean of any IRA connection."

"That's what Cahill said. And at the time I spoke to him he must have had this report from Schmidt. It went to him more than a week ago."

"So Cahill was lying."

"He wasn't telling the truth."

"What d'you make of it then?"

"I don't know. Maybe he was keeping it under wraps for some reason or other. But I can't see why Cahill would want to protect this gonif O'Hara. Not when he owes me like he does. Still, sometimes people owe me and they don't come through. You can't trust people."

"It's interesting."

"Yeah, and now you owe me, King. When are you gonna pay off?"

"You can trust me, Ransom."

"Yeah."

"It's just too early yet."

"Yeah."

King hung up and returned to the Senate Foreign Relations Committee. In spite of what Burr said, he thought, it was time he returned to some investigative reporting.

King took the subway to Forest Hills. It was dark when he reached O'Hara's house. He rang the bell and, standing there waiting, he thought of all the other times he had prepared for door-step interviews. Once, in Battersea, a delinquent wife had emptied a bowl of washing-up water on him from an upstairs window.

In Forest Hills, the woman who came to the door was a wan-looking blonde with thyroid eyes. She wore a blue housecoat with a man's belt around the waist. Well-worn clogs showed at the hem. She looked at King without interest.

"Detective O'Hara home?" King said.

"He hasn't been back. The precinct called only an hour ago. I already told Inspector Cahill I'll phone if he shows." Jesus, King thought, she takes me for a cop. It wouldn't last, not with his accent.

"Cahill?" he said.

"That's what I said. He gave me the special number to call so there's no point in you bothering me. I've got things to do. Anyway, he won't come back here."

"Any idea where he went?" An attempt at a Boston accent was the best he could do.

"Look," she said, "I already told them. He took his passport and usually you need your passport when you're planning to leave the country so you'd better check the airports or the airlines. You with Internal Affairs or the precinct?"

"Suppose he doesn't go abroad. Where else could he go?"

"You with Internal Affairs?"

"I'll tell you the truth, Mrs. O'Hara. I'm not a cop. I'm a reporter." And that would be the end of that, he thought.

She nodded, unsurprised. "I was just starting to think you're no cop," she said. "That accent. What are you, English?"

"Yes, I am, but I'm working for the *Chronicle.*"

"I'm English," she said. She said it proudly. "At least, two of my grandparents were English. Irish on the other side. I traced the English side. I've got the family coat of arms inside. I'll fetch the plaque if you like. It's interesting."

When she went to get the plaque, she left the door open and King stepped inside. The old foot in the door, he thought. You never could tell. You went to interview somebody who was being hailed as a hero and he slammed the door in your face. You went to interview an accused mass murderer and he was as charming and welcoming as a maitre d'. Luck had more to do with scoops than persistence and ability. The philosopher, King, he thought cheerfully.

She came back carrying a small wooden shield bearing a colored insignia. "The house of Butler," she said. "That was my maiden name, Butler. I sent away for it, some place in the Midwest where they're experts. There's a scroll goeᶜ with it. Says the Butler family's connected with royalty, so I guess I am too."

King carefully admired the coat of arms.

"Very impressive," he said. "But I thought your husband didn't like the English. I don't suppose it meant much to him, did it?"

"I never told him about getting the plaque. It was none of his business, that was the way I looked at it. You do think it's genuine, don't you?" There was a tinge of doubt in her voice.

King considered the gap that sometimes yawned between strict honesty and good manners. His need for information weighed the balance in favor of good manners.

"Undoubtedly," he said. "I'm no expert on these things, but the name Butler is very highly respected in England. You should be very proud. Even in England not many people have coats of arms."

She smiled and for a second King could see the pretty girl she once had been. "I don't believe you for a second," she said. "But it's nice to have dreams, isn't it?" He was silent. She was shrewder than he'd thought.

He handed back the plaque. "Where did your family come from?" he said.

"Liverpool. It's north of London somewhere. I've never been there, probably never will."

"And your husband?"

"He's all Irish. Why are you interested in him? He's just another cop on the take." The years had returned to her pinched, dissatisfied features.

"We heard he's on the run, didn't turn in his gun and shield when they suspended him."

"He took off all right. Cahill came in the front, he went out the back. He's probably in Ireland now." She shrugged. "He can be in hell as far as I'm concerned."

"Suppose he didn't go abroad, is there anywhere else where he might hide out?"

She was no longer interested. She reached for the door latch, ready to close it behind him. "He could be anywhere," she said. "He didn't tell me everything he did. In fact, he didn't tell me much about himself in all the years we were married. He's a secret sort of man, secret and cold."

King moved through the door to the front step. "Nothing comes to mind?" he said.

"Nothing. Well, there's one place you might check out if you're really interested. His uncle has a place upstate, outside Phoenicia. He might have gone there. He likes it up in the country, God knows why. He likes to look at the wild creatures and then kill them."

"Phoenicia?"

"Yes. It's about a hundred miles north of New York."

"Did you mention it to the cops?" The door was almost closed to him now. She stared at him through the gap.

"Why would I do that?" she said. "It's Cahill's house."

"I thought you said it was his uncle's."

"I did. Oh, of course, you wouldn't know. Cahill is his uncle.

Cahill will have checked out the place so there's not much point in your trying it."

"Inspector Cahill, the Bureau chief, he's your husband's uncle?"

"That's right," she said. "All in the family, isn't it?"

King's first thought was, Jesus, what a story. A high-ranking officer of the NYPD protecting a rogue cop because of their secret relationship. But there were other, more personal, implications. On the subway ride back to Manhattan, King thought that it explained why Cahill had claimed the detective was free of any connection with the IRA. He was taking care of his own in a very special way. And there could be more to it. Did Cahill know that his nephew was a long-range assassin, that he sometimes slipped away to kill enemies of the Provos? Had he helped protect him from discovery? Certainly he was in a critical post where he could watch out for his nephew.

That led ineluctably to another thought. Was Cahill an IRA sympathizer? Did he approve of O'Hara's extracurricular activities? Did he applaud the shooting of British army captains? Christ, if O'Hara had gone, perhaps the answers lay with Cahill. Certainly he had some questions to answer.

King stared at an army-recruiting poster stuck on the side of the swaying subway car. What about Phoenicia?

It seemed unlikely that O'Hara would have gone there. If he had taken his passport it could only be because he planned to leave the country. Maybe he was already back in Ulster carrying out another assassination. King could warn Redder. He didn't like Redder or what Redder stood for, yet he should tell him. Maybe the Brits could pick up O'Hara in Northern Ireland. Put him on trial for Martin's murder.

Or, he thought, the passport might be a false clue. Perhaps Phoenicia was still a possibility. King's thoughts went back to his reporting days. Success followed the man who persisted, checked out the unlikely. Yes, he thought, and had luck at his elbow. Well, he'd been lucky enough with the woman in the housecoat. But then, he thought, she was right. If Cahill knew O'Hara might be at the cottage it was the first place he'd look. There was no point in trudging along in the tracks of the cops.

Maybe he could get Ransom to find out if they'd come across any trace of O'Hara upstate. Maybe he could start paying off Ransom with the news that Cahill was kin to O'Hara.

The train came into Manhattan and King got to his feet and headed for the door. It was years, he thought, since he'd done any reporting.

The following evening, he was on the desk when a call came through for him. It was after the first edition and Burr had gone home. King punched the button to take the call and he recognized the voice immediately. It was Toby East. He said he was in New York, had just arrived. What about a drink?

FIFTEEN

There were those in the Department in London who said that the whole thing happened the way it did because Toby East lacked a sense of timing. They, of course, were the dissenters who resented the ascendancy of the First Murderer.

They didn't know that Redder had specifically ordered East to go to New York to take charge of the O'Hara case and so they whispered that the case got out of hand simply because the First Murderer insisted on being on the scene when there was no need, when he could have judged the situation from his desk on Northumberland Avenue and issued his orders accordingly without any personal intervention. Smollet, said the dissenters, was perfectly capable of leading the New York team on this case as he had done on a score of other occasions, just as significant. It was poaching, they said, unconsciously echoing the charge that East so indifferently had suggested would be made. And a gentleman didn't poach.

The core of the complaints against Toby East, who of course was no gentleman, was that he had allowed a shining opportunity for the painless elimination of O'Hara to slip by because he was not available when the team telephoned London from the little town of Phoenicia, a name that produced a number of arcane jokes around the Department.

He was not available because he was on a plane crossing the Atlantic to New York. The call had gone to Redder finally, but he had said that the matter was in Toby East's hands. It was Toby East's responsibility and Redder had every faith that the matter would be pursued by East to a satisfactory conclusion. He declined to go under his head, he announced, enjoying his humor.

In fact, there was a further explanation for Redder's remarkable hands-off attitude. At that time he was engaged in one of those ferocious political battles that every so often wracked the secret world, and he simply didn't have the time to follow the O'Hara case and make the appropriate decision. MI5, as if testing Redder's power and fortitude, was attempting to oust the Department from any involvement in the Ulster situation and take sole control. Seeing an end to the troubles in Northern Ireland, the counterespionage office understandably wished to collect all available credit. Similarly, Redder could not afford to relinquish the Department's role in Britain's last battleground at such a crucial time. And so he refused to involve himself directly in a ground operation. It was a decision for which, later, he would pay dearly.

At any rate, the result was that no assault on O'Hara was launched while he was at his most vulnerable. By the time Toby East landed in New York and made contact with the team, the situation had changed irrevocably.

Toby East wanted King to meet him for a drink and a chat. King looked at the city-room clock. He could leave the office in another forty-five minutes, after the second edition had been cleared up. East was staying at the St. Regis and they agreed to meet in the King Cole Bar.

When King walked in, East was already in place at a corner table, lounging in his chair just as he had during the London meeting. He wore a blue pinstripe suit and a guards tie. He looked utterly composed, as if there was nothing more on his mind than the question of where to dine. King ordered a Scotch.

"When did you get in?" he asked.

"This afternoon. It's more than a year since I've been here. Everything's just as vulgar as I remember it though. Astonishing radio programs they have here. The announcers scream all the time."

"It's for emphasis," King said. He wondered what East was up to in New York. Had he come over especially to deal with O'Hara? He seemed an unlikely killer.

"Yes, well, different people, different cultures," East said. "I thought I'd bring you up to date on the matter we were talking about in London. We were wondering, however, if you'd made any inquiries about this O'Hara fellow. Perhaps we could pool our information, d'you think?"

"I haven't had the time," King said. "But I did hear that he'd been suspended and then had vanished. Something to do with an accusation of corruption in Brooklyn." At this point he hadn't decided what to do with his discovery of the relationship between O'Hara and Cahill. It was a card he would withhold for the moment.

"You seem to have lost some of your interest in the matter," East said lazily. "In London, you were much keener on gathering information about our Yankee Provo. You may remember we told you all we knew, although there was no compulsion beyond humanity to do so."

"Very good of you," King said. East stared at him and then smiled gently. Lounging there, he reminded King of a riverboat gambler in spite of his formal outfit. Under the negligent facade there was something reckless, nihilistic.

"Well," East said, "we've been a little more energetic."

"We?"

"My associates over here. They managed to discover where our man has gone to ground."

"He hasn't gone abroad?"

"Why would you think that?"

"It was a possibility. I heard he took his passport." That was a mistake. He wondered if Toby East had noticed it.

"Where did you think he might have gone?"

"Ulster perhaps. Maybe another assassination. I was going to tell Redder to look out for him."

"Thoughtful of you. Well, he hasn't gone out of the country. Or even the state."

"Where is he?"

"I wonder, have you ever heard of a little town called Phoenicia? It's north of Manhattan somewhere. One wonders if the Phoenicians are good traders."

"I've heard of it," King said.

"Have you now? It's supposed to be very small. A little spot in the mountains. I was wondering if you'd like to take a trip up there with me. Have a talk with our friend."

"I didn't think talking was what you had in mind."

Toby East shrugged. "We could have a look at him anyway," he said. "I thought you wanted to make contact."

"I do. How did you find out he was in Phoenicia?"

"We have our methods," East said. He didn't stir, but King felt as if he were a schoolboy having a finger shaken at him for asking the wrong question.

"When?"

"Tomorrow morning suit you? I've reserved a rental car. That's one thing they do well over here. Have you ever tried to hire one in England?"

"What time would you leave?"

"Oh, about nine. All right?"

King said, "I'd like to, but I have to work. Tell you what. If I can get the time off, I'll call you before nine. If I can't, you won't hear from me and you'll have to go up on your own."

"You surprise me, King," East said. "Here I'm offering you a chance to make contact with the man who killed your brother and you're too busy with your job. Has something happened, altered your views? It distresses me that you adopt this detached attitude toward an assassin when he's within our reach."

"Perhaps I suspect what you will do. Perhaps I don't want want to be a part of it."

"You think I'm some sort of Murder Inc. operator? My dear fellow, government departments don't do that sort of thing, whatever stories you may hear. Too unimaginative."

"The thing is, East, that I don't know, do I? You're part of a world about which I know nothing. Ordinary people don't, unless some-body like Philby clears off and all the dirt about betrayals and killings comes out."

Toby East grinned engagingly. "Oh, Philby," he said. "There's been a lot of nonsense written about him."

"So you say. But I can't know, can I? So there we are."

East looked around at the well-fed, well-clothed customers. "D'you know those lines by Brecht?" he said. " *'Sink down in the slime/Embrace the butcher/But change the world; it needs it.'*

"That's the philosophy of the Provos and the rest of the terror mobs. Not ours. You shouldn't take what Redder says too seriously. He likes to dramatize."

King grinned and East raised an inquiring eyebrow.

"I was just thinking," King said, "that it's probably the first time Bertolt Brecht has been quoted in the King Cole Bar."

East shrugged. "All right," he said. "Give me a call if you want to come tomorrow. But don't make it any later than eight-thirty. They tell me the Saint Patrick's Day parade is on tomorrow and the streets are liable to be somewhat jammed. Another drink?"

King shook his head. He already knew what he would do. He looked at his watch. It was eight forty-five.

He stood up. "Tell me," he said. "What will you do when you see O'Hara?"

East shrugged again. "I honestly don't know," he said. "A bit of questioning perhaps. Make sure we've got the right man. Perhaps I'll try to persuade him he ought to come back and face the music. Be a man, all that sort of thing." He smiled. He could have been a club member discussing the best way to deal with a spot of naughti-ness, a minor infraction of the club rules.

King didn't bother to telephone. He went straight to the Hertz office on East Forty-eighth Street. A car was available, a light blue sedan. By the time he drove onto the FDR Drive, it was after nine. It would be about midnight when he got there.

He took the George Washington Bridge and then the Palisades Parkway on to the thruway at Suffern. It was clear and dry and the traffic was light. He reached the Kingston exit at eleven and pulled over to look at the map the rental people had given him. He went west on Route 28, past the Ashocan Reservoir and into the mountains. He got to Phoenicia at eleven-thirty.

A tavern on the main street was still open. He went in and ordered a Scotch from the pregnant woman behind the bar. He realized he was hungry but was too impatient to eat.

"I'm looking for the Cahill cottage," he said to the woman. "You know it?"

"Nobody there at this time of the year," she said. "What is it, up for sale or something?"

"I might buy it."

"Funny time to take a look at it."

The only other customer, a man in a lumber jacket, had been playing with a pinball machine. He stopped, obviously listening.

"All I'm asking is, where is the place?" King said.

The man in the lumber jacket was looking at him curiously. "English, ain't you?" he said.

"Yes, I am."

"Thought so," the man said. He was red-faced, blond, and in need of a shave. "We get some Frenchmen up here, couple of good French restaurants up the way, and they come up from New York, but now it seems it's all English. Can't turn around without falling over an Englishman, is the way it seems."

"There've been other Englishmen up here?"

"Last night, about this time," the woman said. "Fellow came in and asked the same questions you're asking. Not long after that man came in off the bus, right, Petey?"

The man nodded. "The Englishman, he ordered a beer. Didn't finish it." One of Toby East's associates, King thought. He wondered if they had talked to O'Hara's wife, found out what he found out. Had they discussed her coat of arms?

"It's a bit too complicated to explain," he said. "But I'd appreciate it if you'd tell me where the Cahill cottage is. How about a drink?"

"That's what the other fellow said, and I had a bourbon and water, if that's all right with you."

"A bourbon and water," King said.

"Well now, it's up this road runs alongside the tavern. A mile or so. Stands back up the hillside, a stone cottage with a steep roof. On the right, you can't miss it."

"Can't miss it," the woman echoed.

King paid and left. He hadn't finished his drink, either. He drove up the side road and found the cottage without difficulty.

He drove slowly past, staring up the hillside toward the cottage. A quarter moon was out and he could see the gray stonework, narrow windows and snow-whitened roof behind a scrim of pine trees and saplings that partly shielded the building from the road. The place was in darkness. O'Hara must be asleep.

A hundred yards past the driveway, he pulled over and parked tight to a snowbank thrown up by a plough. After locking the sedan, he walked back. The snow was a day or so old; it was muddied at the side of the road and he could tell that during the day it had melted a little. If Toby East was right, if his associates had tracked O'Hara, then there would be tracks up the snow-covered driveway.

But when he reached the entrance to the property he saw there was no sign of any human passage. There were animal tracks, probably deer, leading across the driveway ten feet in from the road but no human prints. For a moment he wondered if he had come to the wrong place. He dismissed the thought. This cottage fitted perfectly with the description they had given him in the tavern.

He began to walk up the steep, curving drive. He was at the top, where it widened into a parking area, before he saw the footprints. The snow was about four inches deep and, bending down, he saw in the light of the moon that they led both toward and away from the cottage. During the drive north, he had pondered what he would do when he found O'Hara. Standing there in the moonlight, he still didn't know. He would have to take it as it came. He moved toward the front of the building. There were five stone steps running up toward the front door and the prints were on all of them. O'Hara must have come across the fields.

King reached the top step and, leaning to his left, tried to look through the glass of the closest window. He could see nothing. Suddenly he was startled by the sound of a machine starting up inside the house. It settled down to a steady humming and he realized it was probably the furnace. The cottage was heated. Why would the place be heated unless it was occupied? O'Hara must be inside.

It was then that he noticed, through the storm door, that a pane of glass in the heavy wooden door was broken. He was about to reach through to disengage the lock when it occurred to him that the door might be unlocked. He tried the latch and it swung open with a slight creak. A wave of warmth touched his chilled face. He slipped inside.

Except for the steady drone of the heating system, the house was silent. He stood there allowing his eyes to adjust to the darkness, but even after several minutes he could see nothing but the vague outline of furniture and the blackness of the beams set against the white ceiling. But then he saw a glow across the room, low down. Carefully feeling his way, he approached it and realized it came from hot wood ash in the large stone fireplace. He touched the stones of the chimney; they were warm.

King turned and reconnoitered to his left. There was a leather chaise longue and beyond that a standard lamp. He moved with his hands seeking contact in front of him. He went through a narrow entrance into another room. The dripping of a tap, the smell of food told him it was the kitchen. Off the kitchen was another small room. The bathroom.

He turned and maneuvered his way back to the other end of the living room, where he found another door.

From his memory of the exterior architecture of the cottage, he judged this must be the remaining room. The roof was so steep that it could only shelter an attic. If O'Hara was still in the cottage he must be in this last ground-floor room.

The door was open. King stood just outside, listening. Nothing, no sounds of slumber or of breathing. He sensed the room was as empty as the rest of the house. O'Hara could be inside, waiting for him, waiting with a weapon and murder in mind, but King didn't think so. Still, if he lit a match, he would be at a disadvantage, an easy target outlined by the sputtering sulphur. A lamb stepping into the lair of the wolf. For a moment he thought of his brother in the cottage outside Crossmaglen.

He hesitated. He felt the wall at his left and his fingers immediately encountered a light switch. He pressed it down, but the room remained as dark as before. Perhaps the electricity had been turned off. King swore softly and reached for his matches.

In the flare of the sulphur he saw that there was a bed, a table, and a chair. There was some sort of glass-fronted cabinet against one wall. The room was unoccupied. The cottage was deserted.

King returned to the glow in the living room. Perhaps O'Hara would return. If he did, he would certainly see King's tracks joining his at the top of the driveway. He would know there was an intruder in the cottage. King considered his options. He could leave, drive away, find somewhere to sleep and return in the morning in the hopes of coming across O'Hara, for he was sure it was O'Hara who had been using the cottage. The approach across the fields indicated clearly that his predecessor in the place had been there covertly.

Yet if he left the place, O'Hara might return and be awaiting him when he came back in the daylight. There was another aspect to be considered. Toby East might decide to leave New York for Phoenicia earlier than the scheduled 9:00 A.M. Indeed, when he didn't hear from King, he might suspect that King had left ahead of him and come in pursuit. He might already be on the way. King couldn't afford to abandon the cottage, not if he wanted to discover what he would do if he found O'Hara. He had nothing else.

He settled in a chair close to the fading glow of the ashes and settled down to wait. After five minutes he got up and went to the door. He locked it so that the noise of it being opened would alert him. He returned to his chair and his vigil.

King awoke suddenly at seven-thirty in the morning. The narrow windows partly masked the daylight, and for a moment he was disoriented. He stood up, grimacing at the cramp that had crept into his left leg. In spite of the furnace, he felt cold and stiff. He swiftly checked that the front door remained locked, then went to the kitchen. He needed something hot to drink.

He saw there was an electric stove. If the lights weren't working, it seemed unlikely that the stove would be, but he turned one of the knobs. While he waited for it to show signs of heat, he flicked on the kitchen light. It worked. He went back into the living room and tried the lights there. They all were in operation. The bulb in the bedroom light must have blown. He replaced it with one from the bathroom.

Fully awake now, he drew the curtains to shield the lights from the road and he began to look around the cottage. In the kitchen there were signs of O'Hara's occupation.

The plastic garbage pail held emptied food cans, tea bags, still damp, and a crumpled cigarette pack. Dirty dishes had been piled carelessly in the sink. King turned on the kitchen faucet. Nothing. He wondered how O'Hara had managed tea; melted snow from outside, perhaps.

He went back to the bedroom and now he saw the gun cabinet, its lock ripped away from the wood. The cabinet held three hunting rifles. Why had O'Hara, if indeed it was O'Hara, broken into the cabinet? King looked more closely. Tacked to the wood behind one of the empty racks was a yellowing card: "99 Savage—John O'Hara, 1958."

King moved so that the ceiling light fell without shadow on the interior of the cabinet. Now he saw that a thin layer of dust covered everything inside. But the slot beneath the card was free of dust. O'Hara had taken his own gun.

Surely he didn't use the weapon from the cabinet for his hits in Ulster? He would never get it through the search machines at the airports and certainly he wouldn't risk a customs search. And yet he could only have taken the gun if he meant to use it. For hunting? At nighttime, in the late winter?

King moved restlessly back into the living room. He looked at a half-full bottle of Scotch standing on the table, a used glass alongside. For a moment he was tempted. It would warm him, perhaps get his brain moving. He went to pour himself a shot and then, on a chair pulled up to the table, he saw the newspaper. It was the country edition of his own paper, the skeletized version that carried no city advertising. He recognized the front-page headline immediately and confirmed it with the date. It was a copy of the edition published twenty-four hours earlier.

He put down the Scotch bottle. Here was more unassailable

evidence that somebody had been in the cottage a few hours before his arrival. O'Hara—it had to be O'Hara—must have bought it in the village that day. He stared at the front page head: a mine disaster in West Virginia, eleven dead. Idly he flicked through the pages. Another judge indicted, more Cubans in Africa, a McEvoy column, one of those pointless short stories that he obviously hoped to compile in a book. At page 5 he stopped. There was no page 5. It had been ripped out. Why? To help start the fire? Why use one tabloid page?

King tried to remember what stories had been in that area of the paper. As far as he could recall, it had been used as a depository for Washington bureau stories, but this was a country edition and sometimes they switched pages around.

Without much hope, he looked around for a telephone. If one was installed, it wasn't in the living room. He went into the kitchen. Not only was there a telephone on the wall, but it was working.

There would be nobody on the national desk at this time, but an overnight man would be snoozing on the city desk. It was Mandrake and he sounded churlish at being disturbed.

"I want a favor," King said.

"D'you know what time it is?" Mandrake said, outraged.

"I know and I'm sorry. I'd have left it until later, but it's urgent. You're on duty, aren't you?"

"That's not the point. You don't even work for the city desk, King. Christ, I might be directing a big story and you start bothering me."

"Oh, are you?"

"No, but I might be."

"I'm doing a special feature for Anderson," King said. "And I need some help. Of course, if you don't want to give a hand, I guess I'll have to give him a call at home. He'll probably be up by now."

"Jesus," Mandrake said, horrified. "Don't do that. Why didn't you say it was an Anderson assignment. What d'you want?"

"Got a copy of yesterday's paper? The country edition, two star?"

"Hold on. I'll find one." While he waited, King gazed out of the kitchen window. Dark clouds threatening rain were massed over the stand of pines and maples running up the hillside above the cottage.

"I got it," Mandrake said. "The two star."

"Right. What are the stories on pages five and six?"

"Page six is all advertisements. Page five, let's see. There's a picture of a fucking cute dog with a fucking cute little boy. Ugh! A fire in the Bronx. Arson probably. And there's a load of rubbish about the Paddy's Day parade today."

"What does the parade story say?"

"Christ, King, it says the parade is going to be held today. What d'you think it says? It's by that shithead, Cromwell. He owes me five dollars."

"Read it to me."

"Read it? All of it?"

"All of it."

Swearing and sighing, Mandrake read the story, gabbling through it as fast as he could. He sounded as though he was trying to humor an idiot child.

It must have been the fifth or sixth paragraph. The cardinal, Mandrake read, was going to stand with Senator McCloud on the steps of the cathedral to watch the parade, greet the marchers.

The article went on to say that the cardinal had invited the senator to join him on the steps, thus avoiding embarrassment for the politicians who wouldn't welcome his presence on the reviewing stand at Sixty-sixth Street. The section concluded with a reference to parade chairman Maguire, who was only too happy to describe the arrangements for the big day but declined comment on his attitude toward the outspoken senator and his ally, the cardinal.

"What the fuck is all this about?" Mandrake demanded. "Doesn't sound like anything to do with a feature to me. Where are you anyway?"

"I'm out of town. What time does the parade start?" King said. The suspicion was already forming in his mind.

"Christ, King, it's in the story I just read. Noon. It's in the first fucking paragraph."

"No change since then? How about this morning's paper. There must be another story. Does it still say noon?"

"Hold it. Let me find . . . yeah, it's still noon. Good-bye, King."

King hung up. He stared out of the window at the hillside. It didn't take much deduction to see what was coming up, he thought. Put all the pieces together and you could get only one result. An IRA assassin on the loose with a hunting rifle. Two well-known men, both harshly opposed to his movement, appearing together in public on the day the Irish took over the city. O'Hara wouldn't be coming back to the cottage. He would be busy killing people.

The telephone rang. The sudden noise in the silence of the cottage stopped his breathing. O'Hara? But why would he call the cottage? Somebody trying to reach O'Hara? His uncle? The police?

The telephone continued its insistent noise. King picked it up. He recognized the voice immediately.

"King?" Toby East said. "You're up early." His voice was calm and soft, almost amused.

"It's me."

"Have you found O'Hara?"

"He's gone. He was here, but he's gone."

"I know."

"How d'you know?" King realized that East had known that O'Hara wouldn't be the one who answered the phone.

"That's not important now. As our American friends say, King, you double-crossed me. Very naughty, stealing a march like this."

"I wanted to find him before you did."

"Indeed. And what would you have done, had you been so fortunate?"

King was silent. He still didn't know what he would have done. Talked to him? Asked him why he had killed Martin?

"Never mind," East said. "Perhaps we'll never know. But if you want to be in at the kill, you'd better get back to New York."

"In at the kill?"

"Merely a figure of speech, though it might hold some truth. O'Hara's on the rampage. He's got a gun, I think, and he plans to use it."

"McCloud and the cardinal."

"Clever lad. Sherlock Holmes the second. You'd better get down here quickly."

"He's going to try to kill them at the cathedral."

"I know."

"How d'you know?"

"Never mind all that. We don't have time. It'll take you about three hours. I'll meet you at Rockefeller Center, across from Saint Patrick's."

"Where? It's a big place."

"The building across from the cathedral is called the International Building. I'll be waiting for you in the lobby. By the elevator bank."

King didn't bother to turn off the lights in the cottage or close the door. He went out down the steps and then down the icy driveway at a sliding run. His thoughts were whirling. Part of it was the knowledge that O'Hara was his brother's killer and he might soon catch up with him. But he knew there was something else that was sending him helter-skelter back to his car and the drive south.

Almost guiltily, he admitted it to himself. It was the story, he thought. Jesus, what a hell of a story.

He had turned the car and was pressing the accelerator when the thought of Cahill came to him. However much Cahill might have protected his nephew before, he wouldn't go along with this murderous project. Not with a cardinal and a senator as the targets. Cahill, he thought, was the key; he would telephone him, warn him, from somewhere on the drive back to New York.

But as the car moved away from the cottage on the hill, its tires spinning on the ice, King's overriding thought was, Christ, what a story. He was on the thruway when he came to see the excitement as a dreadful sickness, a fever that still held him when he thought it had long since broken.

The memory of Ginny and of his father came back to him. Both my victims, he thought. It occurred to him that he was not a pleasant man. But then it wasn't the first time he had thought that.

SIXTEEN

O' Hara came out of the Port Authority bus terminal on Eighth Avenue at 9:25 A.M. on Saint Patrick's Day. He felt the same stimulating tension that had suffused him on the jobs in England and in Northern Ireland. It was the same emotion he experienced when he went after deer in the mountains, only sharpened to a degree beyond the understanding of ordinary people who had never gone after the greatest quarry of them all.

Growing restless and bored in the cottage, a prey to fears that Cahill might check out the place, he had left at dusk and caught a bus to Kingston. He had spent the night at a motel there and taken the Trailways express to New York in the early morning. He still wore his black windcheater. The hunting rifle, broken down into its two sections, was in a canvas bag he had found, covered with dust, on the floor of the bedroom closet at the cottage.

The last of the New Jersey commuters were pouring out of the terminal and he went with them. No sign of Minelli or Nick Carter today. They had been easy, he thought. It was just a question of intelligence, quick thinking. That's what would carry him through today, just as it had on Bond Street and in Crossmaglen and the other places. Get ready, Mr. Death. If there was any question that fortune followed the daring, it had been answered by the folded page of newsprint that he carried in his pocket like a talisman. Both of them standing there together. The filthy hypocritical churchman and the blackguard senator side by side as if fate was saying, "Go ahead, Mr. Death, they're all yours." Beautiful.

But then he thought of the windows in Rockefeller Center and his lips tightened. A young woman walking toward him saw the bleakness cover his features and she felt a sudden chill.

A fanciful girl, she told herself that the face looked like knuckles drawn back to strike. She hurried on. O'Hara stared around for a cab but the commuters were lining up to take their turns. Impatiently, he turned south against the traffic on Eighth.

Two blocks down, he got a Checker and told the driver to go to Fiftieth and Fifth Avenue. The windows, he thought, so much depended on the windows. As the cab went uptown, he saw that although the start of the parade was more than two hours away, the marchers were already gathering. The side streets were blocked with chartered buses dropping off men, women, and teenagers, most of them in uniforms ranging from kilts to the black habits of nuns. In the Forties, he heard the clangor of bandsmen tuning up their instruments, the sounds ricocheting from the walls of the crosstown ravines. The music of Ireland, he thought, that would guard him while he struck.

At Fiftieth Street, he left the cab and walked toward the main entrance of the International Building. Police barricades were up along Fifth Avenue and the crowds were already massing behind them thickly across from the cathedral. Mr. Death will give you something to gawk at, he thought.

At the corner of Fiftieth, a group of blue-uniformed firemen, some holding beer cans, was singing "Does Your Mother Come from Ireland?" A girl stood with them, wearing a fireman's hat with the peak turned to the back. She was shrieking with laughter. All around, hucksters were selling green flags and paper hats and buttons bearing the slogan "Kiss me, I'm Irish." A man in a green jacket and kilt was staggering drunkenly, bumping into the crowds without apology.

O'Hara paused and stared at the scene. A great disgust seized him. All of this had nothing to do with the real tormented Ireland.

He remembered the story in the paper he'd bought in Phoenicia, the story that lay in his pocket. It had reported that the organizers had decided to allow only one "England Get Out of Ireland" banner. They didn't want to spoil the day with the hard truth.

This was a lark, an excuse for drinking and shouting and screwing and taking over the city. It was a perversion when it should have been a shriek of rage. By God, if these people wouldn't do it, then his gun would speak for Ireland.

Moving through the thickening crowds, he found his way into the International Building barred by a rope barrier. When he stepped over the rope and headed for the revolving door, a guard in the uniform of Rockefeller Center motioned him away.

"These doors are locked this morning," he said. "Go around to the side."

O'Hara got into the building through an entrance on Fifty-first Street. He scouted the huge, echoing lobbies until he came across the office that arranged tours of the Center. It was closed. He looked at his watch—9:55. Too early.

Impatience swept through him. He turned and went away, the skin tight on his narrow cheekbones. Once again, the fear of failure settled on him like some black and dusty carrion-eating bird. If the windows didn't open, he would have to shoot through them. Jesus, he had to find out. He strode toward the entrance to the NBC studios, where people were lining up for a tour.

A girl sat behind an NBC information desk. "Excuse me," O'Hara said. "Can you help me? I'm trying to get some information about Rockefeller Center. D'you have a brochure, anything like that?"

"Down the hall," she said. "The tour office is down the hall." She didn't even bother to look at him. He could have hit her bored face, taken her by the neck—

"It's closed," he said.

"Come back," she said. "They'll be open later."

"Fuck you," he said, and at that she looked up in outrage, but he had gone. He went to the locked front doors. A guard was standing there, explaining to anybody who approached that they couldn't use the exit today. O'Hara walked up to him.

"Sorry, sir," the man said. "Have to use one of the other exits."

"What is it, the parade?"

"That's right. We always close these doors on Saint Patrick's Day." He was wearing a lapel button carrying the message "It's a Great Day for the Irish."

"I'm Irish myself," O'Hara said. "I came down for the parade, but I thought I would take a tour around Rockefeller Center while I'm waiting."

"Too early, sir. They don't start the tours until later."

"Well, maybe I could get a brochure, something that'd give me the background on the Center, the size of it and so on."

"Yes, they have something like that. But you'll have to wait until they open."

"How about watching the parade from one of the windows? Do they allow that?"

"No way, they don't. You see, all those windows on Fifth belong to the offices that rent space from us. They've got their work to do, even on Saint Patrick's Day." The guard was explaining it to him as if he were a child.

"Oh, well, I'll watch it from the sidewalk. The thing is, my son's marching. He's with the Cardinal Spellman High School Band and I want to be sure I spot him."

"Yes, well, a lot of the marchers have relatives in the crowd."

"I expect some of the office workers here take a break and look through the windows."

"Oh, yes," the guard said comfortably. "It's a sight hard to resist."

"Pity the windows don't open in these modern buildings," O'Hara said. "I don't suppose they can hear the music with the windows closed."

"Oh, but they do open," the man said proudly as if it was one of the many assets of Rockefeller Center. "Indeed, yes, and some of the office people open them so they can hear the music."

"That's nice," O'Hara said. "Well, I must be on my way if I want to find a good spot to see my boy go by."

"Good luck," the guard said.

"And good luck to you."

O'Hara went away. His face was expressionless, but an exultation was growing in him. It was meant to be, by God, it was. First, the two traitors joining together in front of his sights and now the windows, the windows that opened. He could have shouted with triumph.

He found an empty telephone kiosk built into the angle below a bank of escalators. Not long now, Mr. Death.

This was one telephone call he was going to enjoy. He got through almost immediately.

"Cahill."

"It's John."

"Hold on a moment, John." O'Hara guessed his uncle had gone to close the door to his office. When he came back on the line, he said, "Where are you, John? I want to talk to you."

"We can talk right now."

"No, I want to see you. Where are you?"

"That's not important."

"John, you're in trouble. You need help."

"It's nothing I can't handle."

"Are you all right? You sound strange—"

"I'm all right. I'm in very good shape, thank you, Uncle. In training, you might say."

"Now, listen to me. Just listen. I'm talking to you now not as an uncle, and not as a senior officer of the police department. I'm talking to you as your commanding officer in the movement. D'you understand?"

"Go ahead."

"I'm ordering you to come to police headquarters, directly to my office. And that order carries the authority of the movement. D'you understand me, John?"

"I'm afraid I can't do that just now." Jesus, this was good, O'Hara thought. He could hear the strain beneath the controlled voice from downtown. "The thing is, I'm very busy at the moment and when my task is completed I'll have to go away."

"What task? Where are you going? John, you're disobeying the army and you know the penalties. I won't be able to protect you. Not any more."

O'Hara grinned without humor into the telephone. "I won't need your protection," he said.

"They know about your trips to Ireland, John. It's Lenane. He squealed to Schmidt, to Internal Affairs. I have the report in front of me now. And Ransom, that reporter, has been asking about any connection between you and the Provos."

"It's all spit in the wind," O'Hara said. "None of it matters. Not after today."

"Where are you, John? What d'you mean, 'not after today'?"

"Today I'm going to take care of two of the movement's biggest problems. Right here, in New York."

"You'll do nothing without orders, John. You're under my orders. Listen, I'll help you get out of the country. Meet me. Are you in town?"

O'Hara was hardly listening. In spite of the pleasure he got from listening to the anxiety in his uncle's voice, now it seemed irrelevant. He felt free as he had never felt before. Reborn, he thought, his own man, acting out of his own strength.

"I have to go," he said. "Get in touch with Donovan and tell him I'm coming over tomorrow."

"You're going to Ireland?" O'Hara grinned again at the relief in Cahill's voice.

"After I've stolen Saint Patrick's Day in New York," he said. "After I've struck my blow for Ireland on Saint Patrick's Day."

"Listen to me, boy. You'll do nothing without my agreement. You're subject to Provo discipline—"

O'Hara hung up. He sat there in the stuffy booth and already Cahill was forgotten. A man in a business suit, a briefcase in his hand, was staring impatiently in at him. O'Hara ignored him.

There was one more hurdle, a man named Sam Jiras, a man he'd never met. But he felt supremely confident. Success, he thought, followed talent and he had a talent for killing.

Cahill sat in his fifth-floor office staring across the plaza toward the Municipal Building. Sometimes the traffic shooting off the ramps of the Brooklyn Bridge reminded him of the metal pellets coming into play on a pinball machine, but now he could think of nothing but the potential for disaster building up somewhere out of his sight.

It had always been there, ever since the decision had been made on his recommendation that O'Hara should be used as a weapon in the hands of the Provos. At first his shaping of his nephew's life and beliefs had been little more than an expression of his own dedication to the movement. During the fifties and sixties there had been no use to which he could have put his creation; the IRA was withering like a plant left without water. It needed the nourishment of anger and blood to flourish.

In 1969, when the civil-rights marchers were hammered, it had burst into flower once more. And O'Hara could be used. The years of patient teaching had not been wasted. His nephew followed the orders; he never wavered in his commitment to the cause. But then he had met that ever-damned woman in Dublin and for the first time he had disobeyed. It was like a corruption, dirty and evil-smelling, a gangrene, which had crept through some unnoticed crack into the figure he had sculpted. Inevitably, it had spread.

And now O'Hara was out of control, a rogue killer talking wildly about striking his own blow for Ireland.

There was appalling danger here for Cahill. His secret life could be exposed just as he was about to retire, his public and private tasks completed. But, more perilous, the Provos would blame him, O'Hara's controller, for any unauthorized act carried out in the name of the movement. The army was not a forgiving organization. The implication of O'Hara's words on the telephone was paralyzing.

It was the sense of things happening beyond Cahill's comprehension that caused him the deepest dread. It had been a mistake perhaps to cut off contact with O'Hara while the corruption investigation went forward, but he had feared wire taps and, beyond that, there was little he could do in the matter. It was a question of patience, a time for lying low. O'Hara should have seen that.

Then there had been the inquiry from Ransom about O'Hara's links with the Provos. Ransom, as always playing the hard-nosed investigator, had refused to explain his interest. All he would say was, "We're very interested in Detective John O'Hara." Jesus Christ, who was "we"?

It got worse. The report had come through from Schmidt and now senior officers knew that O'Hara had been traveling to Ireland, sometimes during his tour of duty, for unknown purposes. Any inquiry into O'Hara's background would inevitably touch on Cahill's blood relationship with the detective. Cahill could imagine the expressions on the faces of his peers when that word got out, most of them maliciously enjoying the discomfiture of the paragon, Inspector Timothy Cahill. Suppose they learned the rest of it . . .

Cahill knew he was in a trap, a trap of his own making. If he alerted the department to the danger O'Hara presented and asked for a full-scale hunt with every resource of the NYPD, the first question from the commissioner would be: "Inspector, just where did you learn about all this? What is the source of your information?"

He couldn't do it. Cahill stood up and began to pace like a convict in his cell. He was due at a meeting called to discuss the second report of an undercover man who had penetrated to the leadership of the Puerto Rican bombers.

They would sit there in the conference room and talk and talk, every one of them trying to take the credit for the breakthrough—Narcotics, which had supplied the undercover man; Manhattan North; the pompous chief of detectives. And all the time, O'Hara was on the loose carrying out some insane project that could bring the roof down on Cahill. The phone rang.

"Cahill."

"Inspector Cahill?"

"Yes."

"My name's King. Peter King. I'm with the *Chronicle*."

"Yeah. What can I do for you?"

"I have some information. I heard about you through our crime man, Ransom, so I thought I should give it to you."

"What is it?"

"It's about your nephew, Detective John O'Hara. The thing is, I think he's going to try and kill Cardinal Moran and Senator McCloud today. During the parade. Hello? . . ."

It was like a punch to the gut that drove all the air out of you, Cahill thought. And then, when you were wheezing for breath, the right cross came out of nowhere and your eyeballs turned up and you staggered helplessly, waiting for the knockout. As he sat there, his face was impassive, but the dreadful sense of foreboding came over him like a gust of foul air.

"Who told you he was my nephew?"

"Never mind. That's not important."

"Who told you?"

"His wife. I went to see her in Forest Hills."

"You told anybody else?"

"No, not so far. But listen to me, Cahill. He's going after the cardinal and McCloud. He's got a hunting rifle."

Of course, Cahill thought, that had to be it. The two of them were going to be standing on the cathedral steps. Oh, my God, he thinks he's doing it for the Provos. That's what he'll say.

"Where did you get this information, Mr. King?"

"Why do you go on with these questions, Inspector? I'm telling you I'm certain of it. He's going to assassinate Moran and McCloud."

Cahill made a sudden decision. It had to go this way.

"We know about it," Cahill said. "Action is already being taken. He'll be arrested very soon. Where are you?"

"At a gas station on the Palisades Parkway."

"All right, you can leave it with us. But I'd like to see you as soon as possible. Are you coming into the city?"

"Yes. You say you know all about it?"

"We do. Now, I must warn you not to tell anybody else about this. It could have terrible consequences if it gets out. Don't mention it to anybody. Absolutely nobody. You understand?"

"I'm a newspaperman, Inspector. You expect me to hold this back from my paper?"

"A couple of hours, that's all. Then you'll get the full story. In the meantime, tell nobody. We'll discuss it."

"I'll come and see you. At your office?"

"Right. You're English, aren't you?"

"Yes." And you helped O'Hara kill my brother, King thought, either actively or passively, it didn't really matter which. He hung up. That was another thing that would have to be discussed.

SEVENTEEN

Sam Jiras examined the three potted plants arrayed along the window sill of his office. The upper leaves of the rubber plant were tipped with brown. He put his fingers into humus below the shiny leaves and frowned. It was dry and hard. He went to the intercom on his desk and flipped down a switch.

"Sally," he said. "Come in here, would you? And bring the watering can."

When his secretary came in, he didn't realize at first that her hands were empty. He was busy with his morning mail. Three checks, the rest bills. And there was bound to be an IRS audit.

"Water the plants," he said, without looking up. "They're parched."

"I'm sorry, Mr. Jiras," the secretary said. She was a fat woman with unhealthily white skin. "I can't do it. I've thought it over and I've decided I must make a stand."

Jiras looked up, puzzled. He was still thinking about the IRS. Two years running now they'd audited him. "Can't do what?" he said.

"I'm not going to water those plants." She wouldn't look at him.

She was staring over his head out of the window.

"The plants?" he said. "Why not, for heaven's sake?"

"I was hired as a secretary," she said. "Not a horticulturist."

"I get it. Women's lib. Right?"

"I like you, Mr. Jiras, I really do, but—"

"But you went to a meeting of your group last night. First it was the coffee and now it's the plants. Everybody has chores they don't like doing, Sally. I don't like taking out the garbage at home, but I do it."

"That's your job, Mr. Jiras. Making coffee and watering your plants isn't my job."

"What d'you mean, my job? Why should I have to take out . . . oh, God. All right, Sally, I'll water the plants from now on." Now she looked at him and smiled in victory. When she smiled she was almost pretty.

"No, I'll water them," she said. "I just wanted to make the point that it's not part of my job." He was staring at her in bewilderment when the telephone rang.

"All right, I'll take it," he said. "You run along."

As she closed the door behind her, he picked up the phone and swung around in his seat to stare out of the window. The gray spires of the cathedral poked through a light drizzle leading the eye down to the massive doors. A small group of people was already huddled on the steps although the parade wouldn't start for another hour.

"Jiras," he said.

"Is that the Jobs for the Boys Employment Agency?"

"Yeah. This is Sam Jiras."

"This is the Midtown Precinct East. Inspector Kennedy, of Special Events."

"Yes? What can I do for you, Inspector?"

"We need your help, Mr. Jiras, in a dangerous situation that has developed in the midtown area."

"What's the problem?"

"I must ask you to keep this confidential. Lives could depend on it."

"Sure, go ahead." Jiras was intrigued. He reached out and clipped off the brown edge of a leaf with his fingernails.

"Mr. Jiras, we've received intelligence reports suggesting that during today's parade an attempt will be made on the lives of Cardinal Moran and Senator McCloud."

"Good God."

"If you're willing, we would like to place a man in one of your offices overlooking the cathedral to maintain surveillance of the situation."

"Sure, no problem. But why don't you handle the matter by keeping the cardinal and the senator off the steps? That way they couldn't be killed."

"That has been discussed, Mr. Jiras, and I appreciate your quick-wittedness. However, they're brave men and they simply refuse to knuckle under to any potential killer. They're insisting on taking their places to watch the parade."

Sitting in his office, Jiras was smiling. Earlier, he had been thinking about the crowds gathering for the parade, about the way they would impede his efforts to reach the East Side at lunchtime. For Sam Jiras had a mistress who lived in a high rise on East Fifty-eighth Street and lunchtimes, plus the occasional evening, were the only times he could visit her. Jiras's wife out on Long Island expected him home at 6:45 every evening and he complied with her wishes. His wife was cool and demanding. His mistress was warm and understanding.

"Tell you what I'll do, inspector," he said. "Your man can have my office. It looks right down on the cathedral steps and nobody will bother him."

"That's very good of you, Mr. Jiras. I hope it won't be too much of an inconvenience." For a moment, Jiras was puzzled by the depth of gratitude that showed in his caller's voice.

But that was of no importance compared with the prospect that now invited him. He could have four hours in the big, modern apartment over the East River, in the king-sized bed with the ivory-colored sheets, which, she believed, enhanced her skin tones. He looked at his watch. Only eleven. She would still be in her nightgown, drinking coffee, still in bed. His pulse quickened.

"What time were you thinking of sending your man over, Inspector?" he said.

"Immediately, sir, if we may."

"That's okay with me. I'll be waiting."

He hung up. He would tell his wife that the police had commandeered his office, that he had decided to take the opportunity to call on a couple of his client firms. He picked up the telephone to call the apartment on Fifty-eighth Street. She wouldn't even have to get out of bed.

O'Hara left the phone booth in the lobby of the International Building. There had been two dangers: that Jiras might discover "Inspector Kennedy" was calling from a pay phone and that he might try to check back on his caller. He was ready for both. If the employment agency president had realized he was using a pay phone, O'Hara would have explained that he was on the street organizing the surveillance. And if Jiras tried to telephone the precinct he would have trouble getting through because there was no such unit as Midtown Precinct East.

He hefted the grip carrying his hunting rifle and walked toward the elevator bank. Not long now, Mr. Death.

King was driving fast down the FDR Drive.

Through the toll booths at the end of the Palisades Parkway, over the George Washington Bridge, coming down the hill onto the Harlem River Drive, he had been playing the conversation with Cahill over and over in his mind as if it were a record. There was something wrong, he knew it. It wasn't so much Cahill's words as a sense of artifice that he thought he had detected in the policeman's tone.

There was something out of kilter there.

King found a radio station offering live coverage of the parade and the man covering the cathedral said the cardinal and the senator were attending a mass for peace in Northern Ireland. After that, they would take their places on the Fifth Avenue steps. If Cahill and the police were aware of the assassination plan, why were the two targets still at Saint Patrick's? O'Hara could be sitting in one of the pews at this moment, preparing to raise his gun.

King dismissed any thought of going to see Cahill at police headquarters. Whatever was happening was happening on Fifth Avenue. He swung over into the center lane where the highway was clearer and he pressed the accelerator. A quarter of a mile before the Triborough Bridge exit, though, the traffic slowed. Ahead, he could see hundreds of red braking lights. He swore viciously. And then he realized he was thinking, Christ, I'm going to miss a hell of a story. He wanted to be there when his brother's killer went into his act again. It was a dreadful sickness. He wondered if, given the chance, he would abandon Ginny again.

The sound of the crowds gathering for the parade, the cries of the hucksters, the distant noise of drums, arose from the streets of midtown Manhattan like the stirring of some enormous beast. Some sections of the Fifth Avenue sidewalks were impassable because of the throngs. O'Hara stared through the locked doors of the International Building at the backs of the spectators lining the avenue and prepared to go to work.

He took his gold shield, attached it to the front of his windcheater and, carrying his canvas bag, went to the elevator bank.

Ten blocks to the south, Police Officer Michael Farley, born in Ballyjamesduff in County Cavan, fingered the green plastic whistle he would blow to signal the start of the parade. A traffic cop, he had been selected by his precinct for the duty and the privilege because of his work for the police department's Emerald Society.

There would be 120,000 marchers, including 194 bands, representing 240 Irish organizations. There would be politicians and schoolchildren, soldiers and priests, judges and air hostesses, wolfhounds and horses. In the staging area along Forty-fourth, fifth, sixth, seventh, and eighth streets, they were sorting out the line of march, so that organizations with seniority in the parade would be in the fore. The 219th Annual Saint Patrick's Day Parade was almost ready to move off.

O'Hara introduced himself to the receptionist as Detective Mulhare and asked to see Sam Jiras. Her eyes went from his shield to his face, but if she recognized him from his earlier visit she said nothing. She led him into the office overlooking the front of the cathedral. Even as he shook hands with Jiras, O'Hara gazed past him through the windows at the target area. A thin drizzle had started, but the view of the cathedral steps was peerless. A bleak smile touched his lips as he remembered standing below looking up just a few days earlier.

"The office is yours," Jiras said, locking the drawers of his desk. "If you need anything, just press this button and my secretary will take care of you. Would you like some coffee?"

O'Hara shook his head. "I just had a cup," he said. "I have to cut it out. Makes me hypertense."

"I know what you mean," Jiras said. He seemed distracted, his thoughts clearly elsewhere. "Well, is there anything else I can do for you? If not, I'll get out of your way. Go and visit some clients."

O'Hara moved until he was standing at the window. He made a pretense of studying the windows of the surrounding skyscrapers. Spectators had started to gather on the roof of the section of the building below that jutted out around the forecourt.

"This window open?" he asked.

Jiras was putting on his coat by the door. He bustled over and started to lift the sash. "It opens," he said. "But it's a long time since . . . damn thing won't budge."

O'Hara moved alongside him and together they struggled to lift the window. "It's been painted in," Jiras said. "Gave us a new paint job just before Christmas. D'you have to have it open?"

"Vital," O'Hara said. "I've got to be able to lean out, look around." The window wouldn't move.

"Hold on," Jiras said. He unlocked one of his desk drawers and took out a screw driver. He started to jab at the paint around the windows. By the time he had finished, he was sweating and irritable, but when they tugged together at the handles on the bottom of the sash, the window slowly began to move up.

When it was chest high, O'Hara said, "Fine, that's just fine, Mr. Jiras." A gust of wind brought a spray of rain into his face. To his right, down the avenue, he could hear the sound of music.

Jiras looked at his watch. "Must go," he muttered. An anxious little man, O'Hara thought. He felt cool and controlled.

"If you could tell your secretary not to disturb me," he said, "I'd appreciate it. For the next few hours, I'm going to have to concentrate on what's happening outside. It'd be better if there was nothing to distract me. In that moment, it could happen."

Jiras nodded in understanding. His eyes went to O'Hara's side and the canvas bag on the floor. O'Hara leaned down and lifted it.

"Binoculars," he said. "And a few other things I might need."

"Tell you what," Jiras said. "Here's the key to the office. Lock yourself in and then nobody can bother you. How's that?"

"Very good, Mr. Jiras," O'Hara said. "Will you be coming back later?"

"Not until four or five. Everything should be pretty well over by then. I'll call out to you, if you're still here. Okay?" He gave O'Hara the key and a moment later he had gone. O'Hara locked the door and looked around the office. Two chairs, a gray metal desk, two filing cabinets, a coat stand, abstract reproductions on the walls. The wind coming through the window was lifting some sheets of paper on the desk.

O'Hara moved over and pushed the sash down until it left a gap of about eighteen inches above the sill. He stared down at the cathedral steps, where a group of priests and men and women in civilian clothes had gathered, guarded by policemen who were checking passes of people trying to reach the steps. About one hundred yards. For the Savage that would be nothing.

He went to work. He took one of the chairs and tilted it against the door so that the top was jammed against the door knob. He swept the papers off the desk. Pens, pencils, paper clips tumbled to the carpet. He pulled the desk back from the window.

After placing it against the far wall, he turned to one of the filing cabinets and tried to move it. Too heavy. He swore softly and began to pull out the drawers, piling them one on top of the other in a corner of the room. Thus lightened, the cabinet could be moved and he eased it toward the center of the room until it stood about six feet from the open window.

There was a tap on the door. "Are you okay?" a woman's hesitant voice called. O'Hara froze. The secretary must have heard him shifting the furniture about.

"No problem," he said. "Just settling in."

He waited, but there was no further sound from the other side of the door. O'Hara stood behind the filing cabinet, leaning his elbows on the smooth gray top. He looked through the window. The sidewalk was cut off by the window ledge but he could see the rows of steps clearly, yet he was deep enough in the room that nobody looking up would be able to spot him.

Satisfied, he opened the canvas bag. The two sections of the rifle lay wrapped in a towel he had taken from the bathroom at the cottage. He had test-fired it deep in the woods the day before and adjusted the sights to take care of a tendency to pull to the right. Removing the towel, he took the two sections and carefully assembled them. He slipped on the scope and clipped it fast. The gun was ready.

Holding it with steady hands, he leaned forward and stared through the magnifying lens, his elbows resting on the filing cabinet. The scene on the cathedral steps leaped into close view. It was as if he was amidst the men and women who stood talking and staring about them. A man in a top hat and a cutaway coat was looking up at the International Building, but his gaze was idle, incurious.

O'Hara swung the rifle in an arc to cover the length of the steps and found that one of the potted plants on the sill intruded into his vision. He laid down the Savage and went to move the pot. When he returned, he carried a cushion from Jiras's chair. This he placed on the cabinet to give his elbows a resting place.

He took the box of 30/30 cartridges and loaded the gun. He looked at his watch—three minutes to noon. He was ready.

Traffic Officer Michael Farley lifted his whistle to his lips and blew. The first marchers stepped off behind the mounted police unit, its pennants snapping in the wet, gusty wind. On Forty-fifth Street, a knot of politicians, candidates for congressional seats, were being interviewed by bedraggled-looking reporters who treated their targets with the easy familiarity of experts who knew all the details of the hustings scam. Close by, a cameraman was having an argument with a rubicund-cheeked official who was trying to move the politicians out of the way of the Saint Camillus Fife and Drum Band.

At the cathedral, Senator McCloud and Cardinal Moran were

finishing their coffee following the mass for peace.

"The things we do for Ireland," McCloud said. "It's going to be cold and windy on the steps. They should hold the parade in the summer. Better still, in the fall when the air is crisp but the wind doesn't come at you like a deadly enemy."

"I have my electric socks on," the cardinal said. "They're a blessing indeed."

"Electric socks?"

"Why, yes. They're wonderful. A little battery on each leg and I can stand there in perfect composure as if only lesser men are bothered by the cold. There's a trick to every trade and electric socks is mine."

McCloud smiled. "I have always believed," he said, "that the princes of the church are shrewder than political leaders and you have just given me the proof."

The cardinal put down his cup. "Come," he said. "We must take our places with the multitude and find out how Chairman Maguire handles the delicate situation in which we have placed him." It was five minutes after noon.

King came off the FDR Drive at Fifty-third Street, and, double-parking, abandoned the car in heavy traffic on Lexington Avenue. At first, he tried to run toward Rockefeller Center, but the crowds were so thick west of Park that he could only walk, pushing his way through the throng, twisting and turning to make progress. He bumped into a man who swore at him and then suddenly, a surprised expression on his face, toppled and fell to the sidewalk. He held a beer can in his hand and the beer spurted from the can as it rolled away. King pushed on.

To the south he could hear the thump of drums and the skirl of pipes. When, finally, he reached Fifth Avenue, a block north of the cathedral, the air was filled with the notes of "Danny Boy" and applause from the spectators. O'Hara couldn't have acted yet, he thought. If he had, they would have halted the parade.

There was a gap in the crowd where the cross street met the avenue and King plunged through it. Immediately, he was confronted by a uniformed policeman who ordered him back to the sidewalk. Beyond him, King could see the gray mass of the International Building. Spectators were leaning over the ledge on the roof of the two arms that surrounded the forecourt.

King fumbled for his press card. Issued by the police department, it allowed the bearer to cross police lines.

Evidently, the patrolman didn't like reporters. "You'll have to go around," he shouted above the clamor of music and cheers. "Goddam press, always getting in the way."

King turned away, as if obeying, and then darted forward into the midst of the marchers. He heard an angry shout behind him and then he was surrounded by uniformed teenagers from a Catholic high school in Harlem. Black faces grinned at him.

"Go, man," a fat boy with an Afro said. "The mother's gonna arrest you for breaking into a parade."

Moving sideways, breaking up the ranks, King reached the west side of the avenue and ducked below the police barrier and into the crowd on the sidewalk. He was a block away from the International Building.

O'Hara watched through the scope as the cardinal, wearing a scarlet cloak, and Senator McCloud, in a dark business suit, emerged from the cathedral to take their places with the invited guests on the steps. Some of those closest to the prelate knelt to kiss his ring.

Between the assassin and his targets, a line of mounted policemen bobbed up and down as their horses, in perfect formation, trotted forward in a jingle of bridles and equipment. Behind them came the green mass of the "Fighting Irish 69th," silver helmets gleaming in the drizzle, escorting the grand marshal.

O'Hara could hear the cheers as he steadied his weapon on the cushioned top of the filing cabinet. While he had waited for the parade to start, he had decided on the sequence. First the cardinal, then the senator. Now, through the lens, he could see the gold cross gleaming on the churchman's chest. Beautiful.

Now all he needed was the alliance of a marching band immediately below. "And the rattle of the Thompson gun," he said softly, raising his head from the stock. He was tempted to go to the window to look for the next band, but he counseled himself to stay where he was, out of view. He was free of suspicion. He could afford to wait for the perfect moment.

More than five minutes passed before he lowered his eyes to the telescopic sight again. From his right, a band was approaching. Bugles and drums were playing "Minstrel Boy" at full pitch. The sound was booming and blaring and echoing up from the avenue.

Squinting through the scope, O'Hara centered the cross hairs on the cardinal's breast. He held his breath. His finger tightened on the trigger. He was a sculpture of deadly concentration. Then he swore venomously. The cardinal had moved, was no longer in the scope.

Cardinal Moran was enjoying himself. In spite of the hostility that he felt from some hard-line Irish-Americans, in spite of the logic that told him the parade was a cover for licentious behavior, a disruption of the city's business, he had to admit there was a haunting magic to the marching and the music, to the memories, good and bad, that it resurrected. He could remember all the times he had marched, as a child, as a boy, and as a priest. Logic and the parade, he thought, didn't mix.

"Here comes Maguire," McCloud murmured to him. They were almost shoulder to shoulder. "What's he going to choose—religion or Irish patriotism? The Church or the old sod?"

"We'll soon know," the cardinal smiled.

Evidently, Maguire had made up his mind. A shining top hat on his round head, a wide sash around his middle, he stepped out of the line of march and headed directly for the cathedral steps.

The cardinal, just as O'Hara on the thirteenth floor was tightening his finger on the trigger, went quickly down the steps to meet the approaching Maguire. He stood on the sidewalk, glad of the comfort of his electric socks, and put out his hand.

Maguire had chosen religion. Sinking on his knees on the wet sidewalk, he kissed the cardinal's ring. On the steps above, the senator was openly grinning, glad for his friend's sake that there had been no public snub to be noted by the press.

Still, Maguire would go only so far. After releasing the cardinal's hand, he would not stop to chat. He turned and stepped back among the marchers. His Eminence stood on the sidewalk and waved in response to the cheers that arose from both the spectators and the marchers. Perhaps, he thought, the magic of the parade encompassed reconciliation.

When King reached the elevator bank in the International Building, Toby East was standing there as he had promised. For the first time in their brief meetings, King thought he detected a note of concern in East's manner.

"You're late," East said shortly. "And we don't have much time."

"The crowds," King said, conscious that he was disheveled and sweating. "They held me up."

"Come on," East said. An elevator car was open, the operator peering out at them. They stepped hurriedly inside.

"The thirteenth floor. Quick as you like," East said.

"This elevator has only one speed," the operator replied. But he closed the door and the car began to rise. At the fifth floor, though, it stopped and a girl carrying styrofoam cups on a plastic tray stepped isnide.

"How're you doing, Matthew?" she said. "See anything of the parade?" She was wearing a green blouse and a green skirt.

"Too busy with the elevator, miss," the operator said. "The usual?"

"Yes, please. The old ogre will be shouting for his coffee. Got a hangover again." The operator pressed a button.

"I hate to be a nuisance," East said icily, "but we're in a hurry. It's important we get to the thirteenth floor immediately."

"Don't get in a lather," the girl said. "I'm getting out on the next floor and then it's all yours. If I were you, though, with an accent like that I'd keep quiet on Saint Paddy's Day."

On the sixth floor, she left them and the car moved up again. King stared at the floor indicator: 7, 8, 9 . . .

On the thirteenth floor, O'Hara could hear another band approaching. Again he leaned forward and again, through the scope, he brought the cross hairs up until they centered on the chest of the cardinal, who had returned to his position alongside the senator.

They were laughing at something the senator had said. O'Hara released the safety catch.

Below, up the avenue came the bugles and drums of the Saint Aloysius Cadet Corps, from Great Neck, Long Island. The sound of its music came up to the windows of Rockefeller Center like a thunderous wave. One part of O'Hara's brain registered that a bugler was off key but all else was excluded as he concentrated on the gold cross glittering on the cardinal's breast.

Motionless, breath held, he fired.

Enclosed by the office walls, the sound of the shot overwhelmed the music from the street. O'Hara didn't wait to see the result. He moved the Savage fractionally and immediately the stocky figure of the senator swam into view.

Pumping the lever to bring another cartridge into the chamber, O'Hara saw that McCloud was looking away from his traitorous ally, south toward another unit of the parade. For a moment, a terrible doubt seized him. Surely McCloud realized the cardinal had been shot. O'Hara couldn't have missed, not at that range, not with a hunting rifle, not when he was a first-class marksman.

Forcing back his dread, he brought the cross hairs onto McCloud's belly. Let him suffer before he died like they suffered in Long Kesh and along the Falls Road. He pressed the trigger and again the room was full of reverberating fury. Immediately, he swung the length of the barrel back toward the cardinal.

He was appalled. The man was still standing. And then O'Hara saw the reason. The bullet had gone true but the cardinal was still on his feet because the crowd around him was so tight that there was no place for him to fall. His head was back and even as O'Hara watched, the scarlet-cloaked figure crumpled, sank to the steps of the cathedral.

Back to the senator. No doubt there. He had been flung back by the impact of the bullet into the crowd, which was now swirling in confusion. O'Hara gave the scene no more than a glance. He had things to do. Conscious now of the acrid smell of cordite in the room, he swiftly slid the latch on the tapered forearm of his weapon and turned the hot barrel ninety degrees to free it. He tossed the sections into his canvas bag, zipped it, and then turned to stare at the door. Somebody was shouting on the other side.

He looked around. The once-neat office was a shambles. One glance would show it had been used as the sniper's nest. No time to straighten it. He went to the door, now shaking under heavy knocking from the other side. O'Hara pulled the chair away from the doorknob, kicked it to one side. Turning the key, he opened the door to find a group of men and women standing gawking at him.

An office worker in shirt sleeves started toward him. "What the hell is going on?" he demanded. His tone was blustering, but there was a tandem note of fear in his voice.

O'Hara pulled out his .38 and the man stopped, staring at the dull gray metal. O'Hara tapped the gold shield on his windcheater.

"Police," he said. "On surveillance duty. The shots came from the floor below. Anybody know who occupies the offices there?"

There was a gabble of voices.

"Never mind," O'Hara said. "All of you, stay right here." He knew his voice was strong, commanding. He was going to make it, he knew he was. He still had the key in his hand. He turned and locked the door of Jiras's office.

"Nobody goes in there until I come back," he said. "You understand?"

"Right," the shirt-sleeved man said. "I'll make sure of that, officer."

"Detective Mulhare," O'Hara said. He saw Jiras's secretary using the telephone. "What're you doing?" he said.

"I've got nine one one," she said. It was too late to stop her. She was giving the location of the office, reporting that shots had been fired. He had to move fast now.

"Right," he said. "I'm going down to the next floor. You all stay here." He went into the corridor, gun still in hand. Away from the Jobs for the Boys office, he holstered his weapon and went at a dead run for the elevator bank.

In front of the cathedral, the situation was chaotic.

Police had pushed the invited guests on the steps away from the sprawled bodies of the cardinal and the senator. The cardinal's scarlet cloak had fallen away and lay like an enormous splash of blood on the wet stones. The senator was on his back, arms stretched out as if on a cross. His eyes stared unblinkingly into the drizzle until a police lieutenant leaned down and stroked the lids closed. Paramedics who had been stationed at the corner of Forty-ninth Street were carrying equipment up the steps.

A television news team had eluded the quickly flung up barrier of police officers and was filming the scene from the base of the massive metal doors of Saint Patrick's. Other newsmen, held back by the barrier, were shouting with angry frustration.

The parade itself had become truncated. Those units that had passed the cathedral before the shots were still marching towards the Sixties. But, to the south, the formations had dissolved into confusion as word of the sniper had spread among spectators and marchers like a foul-smelling breeze.

Chairman Maguire, pulled out of the parade by policemen equipped with walkie-talkie radios, hurried up the steps with tears streaming down his cheeks. A police inspector took his arm and asked a question.

"Damn the parade," Maguire said. "Let me through, d'you hear me."

The inspector still held his arm and now he spoke urgently.

"Very well," Maguire said. He took out a big white handkerchief and blew his nose vigorously. He looked up toward the scarlet cloak that was darkening as rain water seeped into it, then turned and went to talk with a knot of officials standing in the middle of the avenue. They could hear the bugles and drums of the Saint Aloysius Cadet Corps Band as it approached Fifty-sixth Street.

Now the band was playing "Danny Boy." Punctuating his words with short chopping gestures, Maguire issued a stream of orders to the white-faced officials.

"All right, then," he concluded. "Get to it. The parade must continue."

By the time they had managed to restore some sort of order to the units and started them moving forward again, the rumor was passing through the crowds as swiftly as the earlier word of the shooting. There was a chance the cardinal might survive. Catholics in the throng crossed themselves. A group of nuns sank to their knees by the forecourt of the International Building and prayed. They prayed for a miracle.

As they stepped out of the elevator on the thirteenth floor, East said, "Just a moment, King." He waited until the door of the car had closed behind them and then he handed something to King. It was an automatic.

"You might need it," East said.

"I don't want it," King replied. "Guns aren't my thing."

"Don't be a fool. We have no time. Take it and come on."

King tried to hand it back, but Toby East was already walking swiftly along the corridor. King shrugged and went after him. His head was full of questions, but there had been no time to put them to East, no time to sort out his confused thoughts.

Turning a corner, they saw a man coming at a run toward them. He wore a black windcheater and something glinted gold on his chest. It seemed to King that he heard East sigh with satisfaction.

"O'Hara," East said. "Detective John O'Hara, by all that's wonderful."

Staring at them, the man slowed, came to a halt ten feet away. O'Hara.

For King, the picture was now complete. He could see his brother close to the front door of the cottage. He could see the narrow path and, standing on it, this tall, thin-faced killer raising his weapon, death in his cold eyes. He could see the bullets thudding into Martin, see the agonized expression, see Martin thrown back against the door, sinking then to the ground.

"Kill him, King," Toby East said. "You talked about justice. Now's the time for justice. Kill him and have done with it."

King couldn't move. He stared in fascinated repulsion at the man from the cottage path. Vengeance was in his right hand, but he couldn't move.

"Who are you?" the man demanded. His voice was puzzled, uncertain. There was a canvas bag in his hand.

"Ironic, isn't it?" Toby East said. "You'll never know, just as your victims in London and Ulster never knew who killed them. Do it, King. If ever a man deserved death it's him."

King brought up the automatic, but now it was as if he were the gunman on the cottage path, with murder in mind. He couldn't do it. He wasn't in the same league as O'Hara and Toby East, who saw killing as an essential part of their work. What was that quote from Brecht? *"Get down in the slime/Embrace the butcher..."* If he had been angry, as he had been angry when he stood on the path, he might have pulled the trigger and been glad to see the pain on his enemy's face. But now he just felt a weary disgust when he looked at the man with the canvas bag and the badge on his chest. He couldn't do it. He let the gun drop to the corridor floor.

O'Hara acted immediately. He flung away the bag and his hand went to his shoulder holster. It came out with the .38.

"Against the wall, both of you," he said harshly. "On your right, together. Arms against the wall, legs spread." Who the hell were these people? It didn't matter. He was still going to make it home to Ireland. Another minute and he would be in the elevator and moving down to freedom. He could still make it.

But then there were sounds along the corridor and he looked and there were people, blue uniforms and peaked caps, and Cahill was walking toward him, his hand stretched out to take his gun.

Cahill was the senior officer present and he took charge. Borrowing handcuffs from one of the patrolmen, he put them on O'Hara. King identified himself and Cahill stared at him with a curious expression.

"You stay here," he said. "I'll want to talk to you." He started to say more but then turned back to O'Hara and, blank-faced, read him his rights in a low monotone.

King, looking around, saw that Toby East had faded away. He thought he saw the man from London at the end of the corridor, but then a patrolman moved across his view, and when he could see more clearly, East, if it was East, had gone.

The patrolmen were making a lot of noise, all of them elated that they had been on the scene when the sniper was captured. They didn't realize yet that the badge on O'Hara's jacket belonged to him, that he was a member of the Department. They made jokes about who would get the collar, get instant promotion.

Watching the confused scene, moving with the mob into the Jobs for the Boys offices, King was close to Cahill when the handcuffed gunman said something to the inspector. It was only then that King remembered they were related.

Cahill commandeered the employment agency offices, ejected the employees, and began to make a series of telephone calls. When he finally put down the phone, he beckoned to two patrolmen.

"I'm going to talk to the perpetrator," he said. "Maintain a guard on this door and don't let anybody in until the crew from downtown arrives. The commissioner will be coming up."

He took O'Hara into Jiras's office and closed the door. King realized that nobody had been detailed to keep him on the scene. More patrolmen were coming into the office until it was crowded with blue uniforms. He moved to the door and slipped out. He had a story to write.

For a moment, the two men, uncle and nephew, servants of the Provos, believers in the movement, said nothing. Then Cahill walked to the partly open window and pulled it up to its full extent.

"This where you did it?" he asked.

O'Hara nodded. He felt numb with defeat.

"I'll help you as much as I can, John," Cahill said. "But McCloud's dead and the cardinal's close to it. There's no way you can get out of this one."

His voice was quiet, resigned. His lack of anger, of accusation, astonished O'Hara, who had expected overwhelming fury. From the avenue below came the sound of marching feet. A single drum beat a slow cadence, for the celebration had turned into a massive procession of mourning and prayer.

"They're going on with the parade," Cahill said. "Come and look."

His hands cuffed behind him, his shield still on his chest, O'Hara moved awkwardly forward until he was standing alongside his uncle.

They gazed down through the slanting rain at the foreshortened figures moving solemnly past the cathedral. The steps were deserted now, roped off and guarded by a square of uniformed patrolmen.

As he stooped to look out and down, O'Hara felt something touch his back and then an irresistible pressure thrust him forward. He couldn't save himself, not with his hands helpless behind him, and he plunged forward head first. He went out of the window and down to the base of the Atlas statue. He screamed all the way.

EIGHTEEN

King came into Aldergrove on the 10:00 A.M. shuttle from London. The night before, he had spent some time with Purgavie in the Stab in the Back, but he had drunk only moderately and now he felt clearheaded and alert. It occurred to him as the Trident banked over Logh Neagh that since the start of the hunt for O'Hara he'd been drinking less. At first there had been no time. But even after the detective's plunge from the window he had stayed away from the bars and the frenetic search for oblivion. He had other goals. He wondered if the dream of Ginny had been banished, too.

The airport looked different and for a moment King was puzzled. Then he realized it was because it looked like any other airport. The troop transports, helicopters, armored cars that had greeted him a few weeks earlier had gone. In the airport building he saw no soldiers, although two security men still studied the arriving passengers.

He went to the car-rental agency. It was a different clerk, too, an older woman.

"They say it's all over," she said. "No more bombs or shootings.

They say the Provos are finished. That's what they say. If you want to believe it, you can. Personally, I don't."

She picked up the telephone to order a car brought round from the parking lot. Looking toward the exit, King saw the walkway was still in place to keep vehicles away from the airport buildings. She put down the phone.

"We're out of the less expensive models," she said. "Will you take a bigger one at the same rate?" He agreed and went to pick it up.

It was a sleek, dark blue sedan, the result of a merger of Detroit minds and Italian bravura. Driving away from the airport, he saw it wasn't all over. Still set into the roadway were the bumps that forced him to slow while flak-jacketed soldiers examined him briefly before waving him on. He took the divided highway south toward Bessbrook. This time there was no angry sergeant blocking the road beyond Hillsborough, no soft-voiced soldier to search him. The scene was peaceful, pastoral, not a gun in sight.

He wondered if the events in New York had created a reaction in Ulster. Certainly, for the time being at least, they had destroyed Provo support in the United States. Although the cardinal had survived, the 30/30, deflected by the golden cross, had lodged in his spine and it wasn't expected that he would walk again. His wheelchair would be permanent testimony against the revolutionary violence he had deplored.

And Cahill. Cahill said O'Hara had committed suicide rather than spend the rest of his life in jail, but King didn't believe that. In those chaotic moments on the thirteenth floor, before the commissioner had arrived, he had sensed something between the two policemen, something more than their hidden relationship. Well, the public inquiry might turn up something.

King had been subpoenaed to appear. King would go back. He would tell them what he heard O'Hara say to Cahill before they went into Jiras's office: "I did it for you. For you and the movement and for lovely Ireland." Nobody else admitted hearing it, but King had.

He reached Bessbrook at noon. There were soldiers at the checkpoint down the road from the barracks, but his papers were examined by an unarmed, uniformed policeman. More evidence of the slackened tension.

"Is the major expecting you, sir?"

"He is. I telephoned him a couple of days ago."

"Please wait here, sir."

The policeman went to the telephone in the guardhouse. Through the window, King could see him talking, then nodding his understanding. He came back to the car.

"The major is coming down to see you, sir. If you'd be good enough to wait here." He was as deferential as a newly hired servant. King remembered the night scene outside the barracks at Crossmaglen—the spotlight, the rain drifting down on the bald head of the bomb-disposal man. What was his name? Curry, Creary? Jesus, the man had saved his life and now he couldn't even remember his name.

Loughton came on foot. He wore gray trousers and a sports jacket, the country gentleman at ease, but he looked as embarrassed and irritated as when they had helicoptered to the cottage outside Crossmaglen. He took the passenger seat and said, "Let's go for a drive. I've been cooped up in there for too long."

They didn't go far. Loughton directed King to a car park and there they sat listening to the tick of the cooling engine. It was April now, but there was still snow on the peak of the mountains to the south.

"Slieve Gullion," Loughton said, noticing King's gaze. "The border's on the other side." He hesitated, shifting uncomfortably in his seat.

"I used to meet your brother here. I liked him." He reminded King of a debtor at payment time. A grudging, ungraceful acceptance of the situation.

"I loved him," King said. "I didn't realize it until after he died."

Loughton's embarrassment deepened. King guessed he was uneasy with words like *love*.

"D'you have a wife?" King asked absurdly.

Loughton didn't seem to hear him. "Death makes you think things over," he said. "Sounds banal, but it's true."

There was nothing to say to that. King was silent.

"I've been thinking a lot about your brother. What they did to him."

"The Provos?"

"Oh, them as well." Loughton waved away the thought of the Provos as if they were of no consequence. "Then I got your phone call. Where were you?"

"New York."

"Thought so."

"I was with Toby East over there."

"He's coming here."

"To Bessbrook?"

"He wants you to stay here until he arrives. I told him you'd called, were coming down. I'm in the middle and I don't like it."

King had the feeling he was close to revelation. It came sometimes during interviews, this feeling, after confidence had been won. But something else was driving Loughton.

"I have certain standards," he said. "Most people have, I suppose." He sounded stiff and pompous, must have known he did, but he went doggedly on. For some reason, King remembered his father. Sometimes he had sounded pompous, too.

"I was brought up," Loughton said, "to believe in certain qualities. I think your brother was the same, the little I knew of him. Qualities like duty, courage, loyalty. Loyalty above all. You try to follow the rules, even if you fail."

"We all fail," King said uncomfortably. He had failed.

"Toby East and your brother, they came from the same backgrounds, had the same advantages in life, yet they were utterly different. Toby East has no understanding of those qualities, especially loyalty. Loyalty works both ways. You must be loyal to those who serve under your orders, otherwise there can be no trust. D'you believe that?"

King nodded. He was almost holding his breath for what was to come.

"East has no loyalty," Loughton said heavily, like a judge pronouncing sentence. "He manipulates people and he enjoys it. He used your brother as if he were a lump of bait to draw out some piranha. There was no dignity to it, no dignity."

"They knew he would be killed? They wanted it?"

"Of course. That's what I'm telling you."

Loughton looked at King as if he were thick-witted. "That was the whole point of it. They put him in that cottage like a sacrificial goat, tethered in front of a tiger. Funny how you use animals in similes when you're talking about ruthlessness, about killers. No animal would act the way these people act."

King stared at an enormous shadow thrown on Slieve Gullion by a gray mass of cloud. The car was now in full sunshine. He didn't know when he had begun to suspect the use they had made of Martin. It had seeped into his mind like a poisonous gas during the past few days. From Loughton he wanted no more than confirmation.

"You could have told him," he said.

"No, I couldn't. I was like him," Loughton said. "I believed them. Thought he was supposed to be gathering intelligence about stuff coming over the border. All I could tell him was, be careful. It was only afterward, when I heard more, that I knew."

"I guessed the same thing. That's why I came to see you."

"Yes, well, now we both know. You haven't got long. If I were you I'd head south over the border. Try for Dublin maybe."

"Dublin?"

"Toby East doesn't run things down there like he does here. You'd have a better chance. I'll tell him you said you'd drive back to Belfast."

"What does he want with me?"

"Well, he's not after your autograph, old boy. He wants you out of the way. You're a nuisance." King thought of the last time he had talked to East. It had been on the telephone the morning after Saint Patrick's Day when his story of the capture and death of O'Hara had been splashed on page 1 above a picture of the detective's broken body lying in the Rockefeller Center forecourt.

Toby East's obvious satisfaction with the resolution of the matter had infuriated King.

"I liked your story this morning," East had said. "Very deft."

"That's not the last word I'll write about it," King said. "I just have to check a couple of things out. The big story is still to come."

"What big story?"

"Why d'you do this kind of work, East?"

"What story are you talking about?"

"I'd think that obvious. The death of my brother, your coming over here, and then the dispatching of John O'Hara. The headline could be something like, 'The Anatomy of a Sacrifice.' "

"And you're going to write it?"

"I am."

"You signed the Official Secrets Act. If you mention my department—"

"Fuck your department. It's nothing more than an officially sanctified assassination team."

"You didn't listen to Redder. When he was talking about terrorism."

"I listened."

"You ever read Goethe? He said anarchy was worse than tyranny because it's random tyranny. King, the meek don't inherit the earth. We're defending the meek because they can't do it themselves."

"You didn't defend my brother, East. That's why I'm going to write the story. Everything goes in."

He had hung up then and put in a call to Loughton at Bessbrook.

Sitting there in the car with Loughton, King knew they'd be coming after him. Would keep coming unless he got the story into print first. Perhaps it had been a mistake coming back to Ulster.

Loughton said, "I can walk back from here. Your best bet is Newry and the A-1. It's a direct road south to Dublin. You can get a plane out from there. Good luck."

He opened the door and stepped out. Then, bending down to look at King through the open window, he thrust something into the car. It was a .38.

"We took it from the Provos," Loughton said. "They got it from the States. Untraceable. You may need it."

Everybody, King thought, was always pushing weapons into his hand. This time, though, he didn't argue. He took it and put it in his pocket.

"It's loaded," Loughton said. "Five rounds. Best I can do."

He stepped back, and looked at the hired car. "This big job's a mistake," he said. "Too conspicuous. Why didn't you get a smaller model?"

King didn't reply. He wanted to be on his way. He put the car in gear and swung around on to the road. In the driving mirror, he could see Loughton watching him, frowning as if he disapproved of the whole matter, including King and his big, powerful car. They had made a mistake with Loughton, King thought. Loughton and his standards.

He went through Newry fast. The border was two miles south of the town, invisible except for a military checkpoint. Cars were slowing to walking speed and then being waved on. On the other side of the road, he saw an officer sitting in a Land Rover talking on a radio telephone. A soldier carrying an Armalite over his shoulder glanced into the car and motioned King on. Just then, King heard a shout from the Land Rover. His foot was pressing down on the accelerator, the car drawing smoothly away.

The officer was running across the road and the soldier had the gun in his hands. Instinctively, King hunched down in the seat. He was going thirty, forty miles an hour now, faster every second, the powerful engine surging eagerly forward. He looked in his driving mirror. The soldier had his weapon up, but no shots came. He saw the officer running back to the Land Rover and then he was around a bend and the different lettering of the road signs told him he was in the Republic.

He didn't doubt they would have men in Eire and now they knew the road he was using. He wanted the west, the gridwork of country roads where he could lose himself in a green wilderness. Suddenly he thought of Cobh on the southern coast. Perhaps he could get a freighter there.

Years earlier, he had taken a freighter across the Atlantic and they had put in for a few hours at Cobh. He still remembered the soft evening sunshine on the unity of water, hills, and huddled buildings. It had seemed a peaceful place and now he began to think of it as a sanctuary. At Dundalk he found a road leading directly west and he took it. There were no soldiers, no checkpoints now, only fields and hedges and the sun beckoning him west.

*　　*　　*

In the room above the saloon bar of the pub in Dundalk, the brief argument was over. Cahill wanted it done, needed it to be done, and the movement owed him too much to look away. The commander of the First Battalion in south Armagh, a man who had done time in Long Kesh, was using the telephone.

"Yes," he said. "A dark blue, four-door job, license plate LHO 729. It went through Dundalk twenty minutes ago and now he's heading towards Carrickmacross. He's probably making for Shannon, but you'll catch him long before."

He listened for a moment and his face darkened.

"Tell McCarthy he can get back to that later. Right now he's to concentrate on this job. It's priority. What? . . . I don't care how it's done. Do it, that's all. Report to me here after you've taken care of it."

He put down the telephone. His intelligence officer said, "Did Cahill say what it's all about?"

"Something about an inquiry in New York. This fella was going to be a witness. You think he's going to Shannon?"

"Doesn't really matter, does it?" the intelligence man said. "He can't hide from us, whichever side of the border he's on."

King was ten miles from Cork, approaching from the northwest, when he pulled over onto the grass verge. He felt exhausted yet somehow exhilarated by the dash south. There had been no sign of pursuit. Probably they were hunting him in Dublin.

In the glow of a flashlight he had bought along with other items in Ballyporeen he looked at a map of the southern counties. Cobh looked to be about fifteen miles past Cork, but there was no point in getting there at this time of night. He thought of taking a hotel room in Cork but decided they would be looking for him in the towns. He'd be as safe here as anywhere. He could drive into Cobh at dawn and start looking for a ship. A ship to anywhere would do.

He made the dispositions in the car that he had pondered on the long drive. He was not defenseless, he thought. He had the gun and in the last few days he had received an education of sorts.

The lights of the approaching car could be seen nearly a mile away. They quivered in the blackness as the car went over a length of rough surface and, once, when they disappeared into a dip in the road, the reemerging beams pointed so high they touched the low, rain-fat clouds.

It was a battered old Humber, riding high on its big tires. It stopped immediately behind King's sedan. The doors opened and King could hear the low murmur of voices.

They came and stood, two at the driver's window, one on the passenger's side. The three of them fired, shattering the side windows of the hired car, pumping bullets into it from both sides. The noise of the explosions devastated the silence and the flare from the guns lighted their intent faces.

King, lying on his belly on the coarse grass fifty feet away, kept his sights trained on the man on the passenger's side. He could get one man, maybe two, before they could position him. Then it would be one against one. Fair enough odds, he thought. He couldn't shoot in the corridor of the International Building, but he could shoot now.

They opened the doors and broken glass fell from the side windows. King could hear their feet grinding the slivers. "Jesus," one of them breathed. Now they knew.

They stepped back and, with their guns coming up, they stared into the darkness, their bodies arched with tension. "He could be anywhere," one of them muttered. Far down the road, to the east where the rim of the horizon was beginning to lighten, the lights of an approaching vehicle showed briefly. It sounded like a truck.

They stood for a moment longer, rigid, listening, then at a muttered command they turned and walked back to the Humber.

King watched them go, his sights following the closest man. He had bought the bag of potatoes in Ballyporeen and half emptied it in a ditch ten miles back. He had put his raincoat around the sagging bag, tying it in place with a length of string, and leaned it against the steering wheel. The bullets from the killer team would be buried deep in new potatoes.

After the Humber had turned and gone back the way it came, King stood up and stretched. The wind felt good on his face. For a moment he wondered if they'd been Toby East's men or Provos. It didn't much matter. They all bore the same stigmata. He had other things to do.

NINETEEN

Toby East caught up with King in Cobh later the same day. When he had started looking for a freighter, King had thought it would be a simple matter of paying the captain, showing his passport and stepping on board. It might have been if there had been a freighter in port. There wasn't. There was nothing scheduled for at least a week, the harbormaster said, and even then it was chancy. Cobh, he said, was not on the regular transatlantic runs.

King was sitting on a pile of sacks on the deserted dock, gazing out to sea and contemplating a flight back to New York when he sensed somebody behind him. Twisting around, he saw it was East.

"Pondering your sins?" East said. "I'll join you in that, if I may." He was wearing sharply pressed cavalry twill trousers, a sports jacket, a polo-neck sweater and highly polished brogues. As he sat down and stretched out his legs, he looked relaxed, almost dreamy.

"Beautiful," he said. "Ireland can be such a heavenly place when the Irish stay out of sight."

"I've got a gun," King said. Blurting the words out, he felt gauche, out of sync. East always seemed to have that effect on him.

"My dear fellow," East said, "so have I. Nowadays, it seems that everybody has a gun. Personally, I hate the things. So noisy and they ruin all the efforts of a good tailor. Who gave it to you? Loughton?"

King said nothing and East sighed. "Such a stuffy fellow, Loughton," he said. "He probably thinks his heart is in the right place. That's probably what you think, too."

"He seems to amuse you."

"Lots of people do. It's unwise to take things too seriously."

"I'd just as soon you pissed off, East," King said. "I have nothing to say to you except that I'm convinced you helped arrange the death of my brother. There's very little difference between you and O'Hara."

"Except," East said softly, "that he's dead and I'm alive."

"Wherever you go, people seem to die. Somebody tried to kill me last night."

"Did they, indeed?" East didn't sound particularly surprised. "Where?"

"Back in the country. They shot up my car."

"And missed you. The Provos, no doubt. In general, a highly incompetent lot."

"Why the Provos? How would they know I was in Ireland?"

"Probably the same way I found out. You work for a fellow called Burr?"

King nodded, remembering again the sterility of the cable desk and its master. Burr had complained acidly about his absence from the desk during the hunt for O'Hara and had threatened him with dismissal when King said he wanted even more time. Had he told Burr where he was going? He couldn't remember.

"All it took was a telephone call to Burr," East said. "He was only too happy to oblige with information. I don't think you're one of his favorites, King. No doubt that's how the Provos discovered your whereabouts. Still, trying to kill you is really going too far."

"I wondered about you, East. I'd heard you were looking for me."

"I was. But not with a gun, I assure you. That's not my style at all. I just wanted to talk to you. More or less as we're talking now."

"I can't stop you."

"Can't I buy you a drink? They're open."

"You can talk here. I feel safer."

Toby East shrugged. "As you say. Perhaps it would be better if we talk away from the influence of strong waters. I have a confession to make."

"A confession?"

"Yes. Arising from our last meeting in New York. What a detestable town. You'll remember I gave you a gun there. Incidentally, what happened to it? It's not the one you're carrying now?"

King was silent. He felt no compulsion to tell East anything.

"Perhaps you wondered why I thrust that gun at you in such an unmannerly fashion?"

"You made it fairly clear. You wanted me to kill O'Hara. Do your work for you."

"Your first assumption is close to the truth. The second is not."

"Then why give me the gun?" King was watching an old man rowing a small boat across the harbor. There was a big black trunk in the stern, so heavy that the old man was lifted high and had to dig with his oars to reach the water.

"I was merely giving you a chance to achieve what you seemed to want so much. Justice." There was the word again. On Toby East's lips it sounded alien, bogus.

"I needn't have done it, shouldn't have done it. It was an unusual weakness on my part. A mistake. Still, I don't really regret it. It was up to you to make the final decision and you made it. The fact was, we had already achieved his destruction."

"You had achieved it?"

"Well, perhaps that is claiming a little too much credit. The truth is we knew he was about to do something horrendous. He was busy destroying himself, just as well as we could have done it."

King stared at the lazily smiling features. "You knew he was going to try to kill the cardinal and the senator? And you didn't try to stop him."

"What on earth could we do?" East asked. "We had no jurisdiction."

"You could have reported it to the authorities."

"Hmm. Yes, we could have. To Timothy Cahill, perhaps?" King said nothing. The old man in the rowboat was almost on the other

side of the harbor. Redder and his gang, he thought, could rational-
ize anything.

There was an answer to that.

"You know I'm going to testify at the public inquiry in New York
next month?" he said. "You've just given me additional material for
that, and for the story I plan to write. Remember?"

"Yes, that's why I'm here, actually. To persuade you it would be
a mistake."

"From your point of view, no doubt it would be."

"And from yours. From yours, and from your family's point of
view."

"What d'you mean?"

"I hate to bring up personal relationships," East said. "But have
you considered the effect of your allegations on your father?"

The old man in the row boat had reached the shore and a boy was
helping him carry the trunk across the beach to the harbor wall. King
watched them with something like wistfulness. It would be good, he
thought, to lead a simple, straightforward life, a life in which you
weren't constantly confronted with questions, the answers to which
would hurt other people.

He hadn't considered the general. Nothing new in that, he
thought. It was his mark, not thinking about other people.

East said, "Your father believes Captain King died as the result
of enemy action. Don't you think it would be best if he continued
to believe that? For everybody?"

"You bastard," King said. "You truly are a bastard." He knew he
was defeated. He sat listening to the lap of water at the base of the
dock. During the last few weeks he thought he had learned enough
to handle himself amidst the Toby Easts of the world. But he was
still an amateur trying to deal with professionals.

He had done enough to his father. Or not enough, he didn't know
which. He couldn't let the old man know that Martin had been
deliberately sacrificed by the country the general had served so long.
Sometimes, he thought, loyalty has to be protected.

King stood up and said, "I'm going to have a drink." Toby East
nodded. He knew better than to suggest accompanying a man who
wanted to lick the wounds he had inflicted.

"I'll wait here," East said. "I've got friends joining me."

I'll bet you have, King thought. More like you. Killers and corruptors and manipulators. He moved off in search of a pub. He didn't want to return to New York now. There was nothing for him in New York. He would go home to Gloucestershire and there he would decide what to do with himself. He walked away from the dock and into the town.

TWENTY

The old man was never aware of the disheveled and deadly background against which he appeared so briefly and if he had he wouldn't have understood it. He was a fisherman whose life in boats at sea hadn't included the notion of betrayal. He was no doubt the happier for it.

This day, the day the two Englishmen came to the town by the water, he was rowing his black trunk across the harbor with little more in mind than the hard work involved and the pains that assaulted shoulders that once would hardly have noticed the strain. The boat was almost as old as he and it moved reluctantly under its burden even though the water was without a ripple.

The trunk that he was taking to his daughter's house was full of the debris of his life—clothes, pictures, old tools, books. After living for years on his own he was moving in with his family. He had always been jealous of his independence. He didn't want to do it, but he was sensible enough to realize that he no longer could look after himself in the isolated cottage around the headland where he had lived since the day he married. That was nearly fifty years, he thought, with the shadows of regret that always accompanied him nowadays growing longer.

At the other side of the harbor, the boy was waiting and they brought the trunk ashore. He left the boy, who was his grandson, to guard it and went through the fitful sunshine to Finigan's Garage to get the trolley he needed to carry the trunk to the house.

From the water, he had noticed the two men sitting close to the edge of the dock, but now, as he walked slowly toward the garage, he saw that one of them had gone. The remaining man was slim and neat. He wore smart clothes, polished shoes. He didn't look right, sitting there in the sunshine on a pile of sacks. He looked as though he belonged in more sophisticated surroundings far from this lonely port on the rim of Europe. The old man stared at him and thought, a foreigner, maybe an Englishman. The stranger's expression was serene enough, as if he were just enjoying the pretty weather, but the old man thought to himself that there was something disturbing about him. Maybe it was the eyes. They were watchful, alert, in contradiction of his languid pose as he lolled back, careless of the danger to his trouser crease.

Standing at the curb behind him was a blue car with pock-marked sides, as if somebody had been driving nails into the doors. It was no way to treat such an expensive-looking machine.

Passing by, the old man said, "A grand day."

"Indeed," the stranger replied. "It's very pleasant. Hardly tropical, nonetheless." He was English all right. Superior and very conscious of it, the old man thought, moving on. What was he doing there on the dock?

Ten minutes later, the old man was in the greasy gloom of the garage. Finigan was talking to two men the old man had never seen before. For some reason he immediately made a connection between them and the Englishman. Perhaps because they were all strangers and the old man knew just about everybody who lived in Cobh.

Finigan saw him and nodded toward the far corner of the garage by the office. That was where he kept the trolley.

The old man heard the words "McLaughlin in Dundalk," or something like that, then "bloody Englishman."

Finigan, sounding impatient, said, "He's not been in here or anywhere else that I know of. If he had, I'd a told you."

Puzzled by it all, the old man went and put his hands on the trolley and began to roll it toward the daylight and the street. The two men seemed reluctant to move, as if they were unsure what to do. One of them kept rubbing his eyes, dislodging his steel-rimmed spectacles.

The old man was usually shy, even secretive, but something made him speak. "There's an Englishman down by the dock," he said.

At first, the two didn't seem to hear him. Their attention was still on Finigan. But then one of them turned and said, "What?"

"Well, now, I just said there's an Englishman down by the dock. If you're looking for one."

"Now?"

"A minute or so back. He's just sitting there. As if he's waiting for somebody. On some sacks on the dock."

"Show us." There was an urgency to the command that upset the old man. He wished now he had said nothing. He sensed there was something bad between the two men in the garage and the Englishman on the dock. Still, it was too late now. He pushed the trolley out of the garage and the two men followed him. He pointed. "Turn right down at the corner, then keep going until the water stops you," he said. They moved off swiftly, almost running. He watched them go. He would walk through the back streets, avoiding the dock. He didn't want any more to do with it.

Finigan came up behind him. "They're with the boyos," he said. "I don't give much for the Englishman's chances. They're hard, the both of them. Don't forget to bring that trolley back."

When the old man reached his boat, he glanced back at the dock. It was deserted except for Billy Dunne, who drove the doctor around, heading for his glass of beer in Paddy Duke's.

The car was still there, though, standing on the cobblestones with those funny holes in the side. He wondered what had happened. The two from the garage must have gone off with the Englishman. Maybe it was them he had been waiting for. The old man looked at the boy who was skimming stones across the water. He sighed. He wasn't looking forward to living with his daughter. He preferred his own company these days.

They marched East off as if he were a prisoner of war, making no attempt to hide their control of him. Both had guns and they pointed them at the Englishman for all to see, although it was lunchtime and there were few people about. To the west, the sky was darkening and the wind had picked up, the harbor water suddenly belonging to the ocean, not the land. Their car was parked near Finigan's garage and they put East in the back.

There was a brief argument between them. One wanted to wait for another man. The other was impatient to get on with whatever they planned.

"You're making a mistake," East said. His manner was easy, unconcerned. They ignored him. "You've got the wrong man," he said.

"Shut up," one of them said. His voice was harsh with tension.

"I could help pass the time with a story," East said. "A funny one. Loads of irony." There was genuine amusement in his words. They weren't listening, though. They were staring over their shoulders at a third man hurrying toward them.

"Part of it's about my superb judgment of organizations such as yours," East said. "I always said your lot was incompetent—in fact, I remarked on it less than an hour ago—and here you are proving me right once again."

The third man got into the driver's seat. "Where was he?" he said, starting the engine.

"Down by the dock. Just sitting there."

"All right. Let's get this over with." The driver let in the clutch and the car moved off, heading for the hills. Nobody saw it go. At least, nobody later admitted to seeing it go.

The three men weren't entirely incompetent. Redder put a dozen men into the area to look for East, but they could find nothing. They could only guess at what had happened, and death, of course, was part of the game that East and they played.

Two weeks later, the search was abandoned, partly because of developments in London. Redder suddenly retired and the department was disbanded. There were those who said that MI5 took over the secret war in Ulster because of whispers about the killing of Captain Martin King in Crossmaglen. That was not entirely true. The simple fact was that Redder lost the bureaucratic battle and, inevitably, with it his post.

The King affair was merely an embarrassment, a skirmish, which, like the death of Toby East, had little effect on the final result. On the day that Redder left his office for the last time, another soldier was shot in the back along the Falls Road in Belfast.